Just Outside of Hope

Sequel to

Road Without End

By Ron Kearse

ISBN 978 – 1-927848-34-0

Second Edition – Softcover

Filidh Publishing, Victoria, BC, Canada

filidhbooks.com

Second Edition cover design by cb eady design and Dan Weeds.

Other books by Ron Kearse:

Road Without End - Friesen Press, 2013; Second Edition: Filidh Publishing 2016

Lost History – Friesen Press, 2014; Second Edition: Filidh Publishing 2016

PART THREE

SEPTEMBER 1980 – JIM WHITELAW

I hear shuffling out in the hallway and the sound of the coffee machine as it gurgles. Sparky, my roommate, is awake. I reluctantly open one eye and close it again. The morning sun casts a muted light through the curtains over my bed. Mmmm, the smell of fresh coffee, tickles my nostrils, and I feel Bert's arm around my waist. Bert lives in Edmonton where he works for the provincial government, and it was funny how we met.

I was heading over to the southeast part of the city. We had arrived at a bus stop downtown at the same time and quietly exchanged glances. He was a really sexy guy, and I wanted to say something to him, but I didn't have the nerve. We got on the same bus, and he got off two stops before me. As he disembarked, he looked at me, smiled and nodded. I smiled back at him then cursed myself for missing out on an opportunity.

It was about a month later, and I was at a crosswalk downtown when I was aware of somebody standing next to me. I glanced to my left to see a handsome man smiling at me. I smiled, nodded and when we got the green light he walked quickly ahead of me. Then he stopped, did an about turn and approached me with a huge smile on his face.

"I promised myself that if I saw you again," he said, "I would talk to you."

It was then I recognized him as being that same guy from a month before. We chatted for a couple of minutes then exchanged phone numbers. We've seen each other quite a few weekends since.

He has a sister, Patty, who lives down here, and he stays with her and her boyfriend whenever he's in Calgary. The four of us have gone out together a couple of times during his visits. She's phoned me a few times while he's been up in Edmonton just to talk. I think she's starting to consider me some kind of brother-in-law.

I'm just drifting back to sleep when the din of a lawnmower from next door rattles the morning calm.

"Jim, tell that lawnmower to fuck off will ya," Bert moans.

"Why don't you?" I yawn.

"Because I asked you first," Bert smiles his eyes still closed.

I get out of bed, pick my underwear off the floor and slip it on. I go to the opened window. I look out to the sunny first morning of the Labour Day Weekend.

I watch Mr. Kwiatkowski next door as he pushes his lawnmower around the perimeter of his back lawn. He's done this most Saturday mornings I've lived here. He and his wife are very sweet. They emigrated from Poland after the war, and he retired about ten years ago.

His wife is always bringing over cabbage rolls, perogies or other tasty stuff for us. She believes Sparky and I are starving because we don't have wives or girlfriends.

"Two young single men," she'll say, "Tsk, tsk, tsk, you've got to eat. Women like nice big strong men."

When we chat, Mr. Kwiatkowski keeps me up to date on the latest rumblings over in Poland. The Solidarity Movement under union leader Lech Walesa has been slowly gaining strength all over the country especially in northern cities like Gdansk. He'll often say, "Lech Walesa," while giving the thumbs-up.

The smell of the freshly cut grass from the window reminds me of my boyhood days in northwestern Ontario. My grandfather used to cut the grass a couple of times a week. He always said it gave him a chance to be alone and think. I sometimes wonder if Mr. Kwiatkowski feels the same way. His lawn always looks like a golf course, it's so green, and well looked after.

He does a double take as he catches me watching him from my window. He smiles at me and waves. He idles the lawnmower motor and yells something to me. I open the window a little more.

"What's that?" I yell.

"I said you're not still in bed are you?" he yells back with his thick Polish accent.

I nod my head and smile, "Why? What time is it?"

"It's time to get up my young friend. Look at this beautiful morning." He takes a deep breath, pats his chest with both hands and says, "Don't stay in bed on beautiful mornings it's bad for your liver." Then he gives me the thumbs-up, "Lech Walesa!" he yells as he puts the mower back in gear and continues to cut the lawn. I chuckle, shut the window and get back into bed with Bert.

He puts his arm around my waist again. "Hey!" he says, "You're still wearing your panties! Does that mean I'm not getting any?"

"Fuck off!" I grin, "...panties..."

Bert reaches down, latches his index finger around the crotch of my underwear, and whips it down to my knees. I laugh as he tickles the side of my belly. Then his mouth meets mine. I run my tongue slowly across his upper lip, while he cradles the back of my head in his hand and kisses me deeply. Bert crawls on top of me when there's a sound at the bedroom door like somebody kicking it.

"Will you two stop sucking' face and open this door," says Sparky, "My hands are full!"

"Should I open the door?" Bert asks.

"C'mon," Sparky continues, "I know you're awake. I heard you talking to Mr. Kwiatkowski."

"Yeah," I whisper, "answer the door naked."

Bert jumps out of bed stark naked and opens the bedroom door.

"AHHH!" Sparky screams. "Here," he says handing Bert a couple of mugs. "Cream and sugar, both of them."

"Thanks, Sparky," smiles Bert, "that's really sweet of you."

"Next time, wear your nightie when you open the door," Sparky says. "Something that big shouldn't be staring a girl in the face first thing in the morning!" He runs back into the kitchen.

Bert shuts the door with his foot and comes back to the bed with the coffee mugs.

"He just wanted to see your cock," I say taking the coffee mug Bert passes to me. "I've been bragging about your big dick."

Bert and I laugh as he gets back into bed with me. He takes a sip of his coffee and asks, "How did you and Sparky meet anyway?"

"I got to know him really well while I was staying with David Tøllin."

"Was that the David we met briefly at the bar last night?"

"Yeah, if it weren't for him I don't know what I would have done that day I was kicked out of the military."

"That must have been a humiliating experience."

"When I was ordered to leave my quarters at the barracks, there were two guards placed outside my door the whole time I packed. Several of the guys on my floor silently stood and watched as I moved my stuff out of the barrack block. I felt like I was the bad guy and had to be removed."

"So David was allowed in to help you?"

"Yeah, I didn't know who else to call. Bryn wanted nothing to do with me, and the military wasn't allowing him near me anyway. So I got permission from the guards to call David at work, and they let him in to help me. They just wanted me off the base as soon as possible, and if David expedited my leaving, all the better."

"David sounds like he's an amazing friend."

"Since the tribunal, he's helped me get my life back together. I needed a place to stay, and he took me in. He let me sleep on the couch in his den. He was there when I needed someone to talk to, and he listened when I needed someone to understand. Best of all, I needed a job, and he's pulled some strings with some of his business colleagues."

"So just like that," says Bert snapping his fingers, "you got work."

"Something like that, yes," I chuckle.

Music begins from the living room. Sparky's turned on the radio, and Steely Dan's new single, *Hey Nineteen* is playing. I'm silent as I stare into my coffee cup again.

Bert waves his hand in front of my face.

"Sorry," I say, "Steely Dan was Bryn's favourite group."

"You still miss Bryn and Marcel?" he asks as he puts his arm around my shoulder.

"Yeah, it's been three months, and I still miss them a lot. If it weren't for me, they would still be here in Calgary, but because of my stupidity, they've gone to make a new life for themselves in Halifax. You know, Bert, looking back I can't believe I was that careless with those Polaroids. Especially after Bryn asked me to be careful with any photos I had in my possession. Not only did I get myself in a lot of trouble, but Bryn as well. No wonder he wanted nothing more to do with me before he left."

"How Bryn reacted to everything was his choice. As for your naiveté, welcome to life's school of hard-knocks. All of us take our turns at learning something the hard way."

"Yeah, but I regret what happened so damn much."

"Well," Bert says, "The way I see it *you* have a choice. You can wallow in the past and blame yourself forever, or you can be in the present with me right now."

I look over to his bright smile and say, "I'd rather live in the present."

Bert puts his cup aside, leans over and kisses me. He takes my cup from me and puts it aside as well. He wraps his arms around me, leans me back on the bed, and his mouth meets mine once more.

∞

I stare out of the kitchen window as Bert, and I clean up the breakfast dishes.

"I notice the sun is casting longer shadows these days," I say.

"Yep," Bert answers, "before we know it the leaves will be gone from the trees and winter will be settling in."

"My life has been going through so many changes this year that I didn't even notice the summer slipping by. And now it's gone."

"Yeah, it's amazing how fast time moves on," Bert says as he moves behind me and puts his arms around my waist. "Just remember to stay in the present with me," he whispers in my ear. Then he rubs his crotch against my ass.

"Hey, no fair!" I protest, "I've got both hands in the dishwater!"

"Just the way I like it," he laughs as he licks the back of my neck. I turn my face to his, and our mouths meet again.

"Will you two quit sucking face!" Sparky yells as he enters the kitchen. "It's disgusting!"

"Did you hear something?" Bert says to me as we continue kissing.

"Nope," I say.

The phone rings and Sparky retrieves the receiver from the wall.

"Hello. Yeah, just a minute. It's for you Asshole," he says pointing the phone in my direction.

I dry my hands and take the phone from Sparky as he goes into his bedroom.

"Hello."

"Hi, Jimmy."

"Glenn? Is that you?"

"The same. So now you're known as Asshole since I saw you last?

"Pay no attention to my neurotic roommate. How's it going?"

"Where do I begin? I'm still at the same radio station in Brandon, but I'm now Station Manager."

"Really? Congratulations. When did that happen?"

"Last year Jimmy."

I Pause. "It *has* been six years since we last spoke hasn't it?" I say.

"Yep."

"How are Marny and the kids?"

"Doing great. Marny is back teaching, Mikey is in grade three and Tiffany is in grade one."

"Oh my God! Last time I saw Tiffany she was just a baby!"

"Like you said, it has been six years. Hey, Dad told me what happened with you. How are you feeling these days?"

"Well, life goes on and so do I."

I look over to Bert who smiles at me and winks.

"I was worried about you because nobody's heard anything from you all this time."

"Yeah, and I'm sorry about that. I just needed some time to lick my wounds so to speak. It's already been a few months since it happened. I was just saying to a friend of mine here that I can't believe how quickly the time has flown."

"Oh, you've got company there?"

"Yeah, but that's okay."

"No, I won't keep you. Listen, I'm coming out to Calgary to see you."

"That would be great."

"Do you have room at your new digs for me?"

"Sure do. When are you thinking of coming?"

"Well, I want to take a few days off before the end of this month…"

"Will Marny and the kids be coming with you?"

"No," says Glenn, "I want to spend some time with you alone, brother to brother."

"Glenn I would love that. C'mon out and let's have some fun together."

"I'll phone you by next weekend to let you know the exact dates and time of arrival."

"Great."

I can hear a child's voice whining on the other end of the phone, "Daddy."

"What is it Peanut?"

"Mikey keeps pointing and laughing at me."

"Well, point and laugh at him."

"Is that Tiffany?" I ask.

"Yeah." Then he addresses Tiffany, "Do you want to say hello to your Uncle Jim?"

"Okay," then the sound of a phone being passed to someone else, "Hi."

"Hi Tiffany, how are you?"

"Mikey keeps pointing and laughing at me."

"Well do like your daddy says and go point and laugh at him to show him how it feels."

"Okay." Then there's silence.

"Hello?" I say.

"She just handed the phone back to me and went into the living room," says Glenn.

"Oh. Ok. Anyway, I guess I'll hear from you by next weekend."

I can hear Tiffany's voice in the background going, "A-ha-ha, A-ha-ha!"

"Yep," Glenn laughs at Tiffany's mock laughter, "I'm looking forward to it."

"By the way," I quickly interject before the conversation ends, "how's dad?"

Glenn is momentarily silent, "He's okay Jimmy. Nothing ever changes with him. He still has his daily routine. He still gets up at 5:30 in the morning, has his tea, putters around the house, and he still has his buddies that he sees regularly at the Legion."

"Have you told him you're coming out to see me?"

"I'll be seeing him today. I'll tell him then."

There is silence between us. "And how are things generally in Lefler?" I ask.

"If you came back here tomorrow you would say that absolutely nothing has changed at all," says Glenn. "Hey look we'll have all kinds of time to catch up when I see you. I'll tell you about everything then."

"Yeah," I smile, "It'll be fun."

"We'll talk in a few days then."

"You bet."

"See ya."

"Yeah Glenn, see ya."

I hang up the phone and quietly go back to the dishes. "That was my brother Glenn," I say to Bert, "he's coming out to see me later this month."

"Where does he live?" Bert asks.

"Lefler."

"Where the hell is Lefler?"

"Manitoba. It's over near Brandon. It's where I grew up."

"I thought you were raised in Thunder Bay."

"I was born there, and my family lived there until I was five years old. Then my father got a really great job opportunity in Lefler, so away we went."

I finish the last of the dishes and drain the water from the sink.

"So you and Glenn are pretty close then?" says Bert.

"Yeah, he and my mother both knew I was gay before I did. In fact, he's the one in the family that told me that I'm gay."

"*He* told *you* that you were gay?"

"Well, not in so many words, but it was like he was just waiting for me to say something to him. Ever since we were kids, he's always been protective of me, and he's gotten himself into a lot of trouble because of it as well."

"Really?"

"Yeah, I remember once he was suspended from high school for a couple of weeks during his senior year. He got into a fight because he heard some guy call me a faggot in the hall during lunch hour."

"They suspended him for fighting?"

"Well that, but more because he refused to apologize to the guy. He gave the Principal his standard answer whenever this type of thing would happen, 'Nobody hurts my brother.'"

"Wow. I'd like to meet him while he's out here visiting."

"That's easily enough arranged."

"What does he do in Lefler?"

"He and his family live there, but he works in Brandon. He's a disc jockey at one of the local radio stations, at least he was. He just told me he's now Station Manager."

"Did I hear you guys say you're going to Chinook Mall today?" asks Sparky as he comes into the kitchen from his bedroom carrying last night's newspaper.

Bert looks at me and asks, "Did we say that?"

I look back at him and smile, "No. But I guess we're going now whether we want to or not."

Sparky smiles and says, "Asshole. I mean if you're going I wouldn't mind coming along. They're having a big Labour Day sale on today, and I want to get some jeans."

"We were going to go to some of the Alberta 75th Anniversary celebrations," says Bert, "but I suppose we can work in a trip to Chinook Mall while we're at it."

A knock comes to the front door. "I'll get that," Sparky says as he flits into the living room.

"I suppose I should have a shower if we're going to go out," Bert says.

Sparky appears back in the kitchen and comes over to where I'm standing. He has a puzzled look on his face.

"There's a woman at the door that wants to talk to you," he quietly says.

"Who is it?"

"I don't know, but she asked for you."

I go to the front door to see a grandmotherly-type woman waiting patiently on the doorstep.

"Can I help you?" I say.

Both her eyes and her mouth are wide open as she looks at me in disbelief.

"Can I help you?" I repeat.

Her mouth moves a bit and then she says, "I wanted to speak to the lady of the house."

∞

Entry #163-Saturday September 20, 1980: Sparky and I have been sharing a house for a few months now. The opportunity to move in with him was serendipitous, as I wanted to move out of David's place anyway. It's not that I got tired of David always wanting sex from me, but I know that I was cramping his style. Unless I or the guys he brought home were willing to get in a three-way, four-way or whatever. This didn't always work out…

I write this in my journal while the passing scenery slows down as the Airporter Bus pulls up in front of another hotel. Since I don't have a car, this is the way I'm going out to meet Glenn at the airport. Then we'll grab a cab back to my place. He'll be staying with me for a week, which will give us a chance to get caught up. After all, the last time I saw him was the night before I left for Kingston and Royal Military College.

I watch the handful of people in front of the hotel's main entrance waiting to board and notice a rugged looking middle-aged man in the crowd. He has a stocky build, appears to be about 6 foot tall, he has salt and pepper hair, blue eyes and a beautiful moustache. It's almost like he senses that I'm looking at him because he turns from the person he's talking to and looks directly at me. I avert my stare and pretend I'm still writing.

I secretly keep my eye on him as he boards and takes the seat just across the aisle from me. He smiles and nods at me. I do the same with him. Man, he sure keeps himself in good shape. I look out the window once more as the bus pulls away. I go back to writing my meandering introspections.

I was walking aimlessly through the Eaton's Centre downtown one Friday after work. I took an escalator down from one level of shops to another, when I saw Sparky. He looked like he was in deep thought. He glanced toward the escalator, and I waved at him. His face lit up. When I approached him, I asked him why he had looked so down.

He said that his roommate had just told him that morning that he was moving out at the end of the month, and Sparky couldn't afford the rent by himself. He didn't want to give up the house he was renting because it was such a great deal...

I pause from my writing and glance out the window again. In the time it's taken for me to write this passage, the downtown core has turned to a light industrial area as the bus heads to the airport. Then I turn to look at the sexy man across the aisle from me. It looks like he's reading some kind of a manual.

I had seen the house he was renting and expressed interest in sharing the place. I moved in with him at the end of the month. The one thing that made me feel a bit uncomfortable about moving into the house was its close proximity to the military base. But after a couple of weeks, I got used to it, although I still get a chill whenever I pass by Currie Barracks.

I stop writing and look across the aisle once more to that ruggedly handsome guy, only to find I'm looking right into his eyes. He smiles and nods his head to me again. I smile back and return the nod.

"You writing the next great Canadian novel?" he smiles.

"No, just some random notes."

He laughs. "Where are you flying?"

"I'm going to meet my brother," I reply. "He's flying in from Winnipeg. How about you?"

"I'm going back home to Vancouver later this afternoon."

"Were you here on business?"

"Yeah, just for a couple of days."

"I've never been to Vancouver, but I've always wanted to go. I understand it's a beautiful city."

"At the height of the summer, it's one of the best looking cities in the world."

"How long have you lived there?"

"I was posted there in 1978."

"Posted? Are you in the military?"

He reaches into his jacket pocket and takes out his wallet. He opens it, takes out a card and hands it to me. It reads *Sgt. Michael Bader, Royal Canadian Mounted Police, Burnaby Detachment.*

I laugh, and he gives me a quizzical look.

"Sorry," I say. "Up until a few months ago, I was an officer in the Canadian Military."

A huge smile lights his face, "What's your name?"

"Jim, Jim Whitelaw."

"Pleased to meet you, Jim."

We reach across the aisle and shake hands.

"Likewise Michael," I say.

"Just call me Mike. So you're not in the military anymore?"

"No. I decided the time was right to move on."

"You seem kind of young to make that decision," he observes. "Usually a guy doesn't do that until he's been in the service for a number of years. So what was it that made you decide to move on from the military?"

I'm lost for an explanation. "Oh…I don't know…the timing was just right to move on I guess."

"I hear you. It can really get to be a pressure cooker," Mike smiles.

I don't know whether he accepts what I've said as any kind of answer or not, but at this point in my life, I would rather not think about any of that. The airport is coming into view.

"Are you meeting your brother right away?"

"I'm a bit early. His plane won't be arriving for another hour."

"I'm going for a drink. Why don't you have one with me while you're waiting?"

"Sure."

While there's excited chatter starting to happen among the other passengers, Mike and I are silent as we approach the airport. I put my pen inside of my writing pad, and put them into an inside pocket of the jacket I'm wearing on this cloudy, slightly windy day. The bus pulls up in front of the airport, the driver opens the door, and people line up to grab their luggage from the front racks and file out of the vehicle. I notice that Mike doesn't take any luggage.

"You didn't bring any luggage with you?"

"Yeah," says Mike, "It's up in my room." He points to the Airport Hotel across the road from us. "C'mon up," he says, "I have to get something before we go for a drink anyway."

I follow him up to the fifth floor.

"Just one moment," he says, "I've got to piss like a racehorse."

The first thing I see is his R.C.M.P. *Red Serge*. The beautiful red coat hung neatly on a hanger from the top of a door with the brass buttons fastened down the front; the Stetson neatly hangs by its string from the neck of the hanger. His riding boots are carefully spit-shined and sit at the foot of a chair in the corner. His breeches are folded and placed on the seat of the chair.

I'm automatically drawn to the uniform. I caress the jacket and Stetson. I can feel myself being sexually aroused merely by touching everything. I barely notice the sound of the flushing toilet and am slightly startled as Mike comes up behind me. He puts his arms around my waist and rests his hands on my crotch.

"I had a hunch you'd like that," he whispers in my ear.

"Yeah? How did you know that?"

"I'm a Mountie. I'm trained to observe. Especially when I caught you looking at me from the bus window."

"So there must have been something formal going on for you to be wearing your Serge."

"Some big-wigs from Ottawa in town."

"There weren't enough Mounties from here for duty?"

"The bureaucrats in Ottawa wanted R.C.M.P. representation from Vancouver and Edmonton as well. So they sent me."

I look back to his Red Serge and say, "I'll bet you look hot in this."

"I'll bet you look hot with no clothes on." He kisses me and unbuttons my shirt.

∞

Our clothes lay in two heaps on the floor, and the bed that was neatly made when we entered the room is now a complete mess. Blankets and sheets are strewn all over the bed, and Mike and I lay in the middle of all this holding each other.

"So where in Vancouver do you live?" I ask him.

15

"Right down in the Cookie Jar."

"The Cookie Jar?"

"The West End," he says, "where all the other gay guys live."

"I hear Vancouver is a lot like San Francisco that way."

"That's why I wanted a posting there. You should come out to visit me." He grabs a pen and notepad from the side table. "Give me your address and phone number."

I dictate my address and phone number to him. He looks at what he's written and says, "I'm going to keep phoning and writing you until you come to see me."

"Okay," I laugh having heard this from other guys, "do that."

"You've been warned." Then he has a serious look on his face. "Level with me," he says, "You got into trouble in the military, didn't you?

I'm stunned by that remark. "How did you know that?"

"I'm trained to know. Besides, it was your hesitant answer to my question on the bus that clued me in."

"You're right," I sigh, "I was dismissed from duty."

Mike holds me close to him. "What could a nice young guy like you have done to warrant that?"

"The military doesn't like gays in their ranks, especially if they're officers."

"I hear you. The Mounties are the same way, even though there *are* a lot of us there. So obviously you were found out somehow."

"It's a long story, suffice it to say The Special Investigations Unit raided my quarters and found some damning polaroids."

"You got a little careless, huh?" Mike says.

"Yeah, and it cost me."

"Don't tell me," he says, "You were charged with *"Conduct Unbecoming an Officer?"*

"Scandalous Behaviour by an Officer."

"Oh shit."

"Yep. I lost everything I've worked for over the last few years."

"That's a really shitty thing to happen to a nice guy like you."

"Thanks, although at the time I didn't feel like a nice guy."

"Oh," says Mike with a start, "What time were you supposed to meet your brother?"

"3:30."

"Yikes," he says looking at his watch, "it's ten to four. Let's get a quick shower and get you across the road."

Out of bed, we get, into the shower and, in a matter of what seems like merely minutes, I've bid my goodbyes to Mike, who promises he'll keep in touch.

I cross the road at the airport terminal and walk into the Arrivals section. I check the monitor and see that Glenn's flight was indeed on time. That was three-quarters of an hour ago by now. Shit, I hope he didn't get impatient waiting and catch a cab back to my place. I begin cursing myself at that possibility, *God Jim, the things you get yourself into at the slightest hint of sex.*

I slowly turn away from the monitor while considering whether I should look for him or not when there he is. His weekend bag slung over his tall, well-built frame, a suitcase by his side. His warm, friendly smile, sparkling brown eyes and his arms opened wide to me. I notice his hairline is receding a bit.

"Jimmy Boy, late as usual," he says.

"Glennster!" I laugh and walk toward him stumbling over my feet in the process. We laugh at my clumsiness and wrap our arms around each other. Glenn, is the one person in the world, after my mother, who was always my best friend. He was never embarrassed to tell me out loud that he loved me, regardless of what others thought, or regardless how awkward it would make me feel.

"Let me have a look at you," he says while holding me arms-length from him. He looks me up and down, and then places his hand under my chin. "You look like you've been taking care of yourself."

"I've had a lot of help from some great people," I respond. We embrace again.

"It's so good to see you again Jimmy."

"Words can't describe what it means to me to have you here right now," I say to Glenn. "Let's get a cab back to my place."

"You still don't have a car?" he smiles.

"Don't start," I say to him knowing he's going to rib me about that, "a car isn't necessary in the city."

He laughs out loud, "Okay, if you say so."

I take his suitcase, and he follows me out of the terminal. We get into the first car of a line of cabs, I tell the cabbie where we're headed, and we get on our way.

The trip back to my place is peppered with stories of his wife Marny, his kids Tiffany and Mikey, and the folks back in Lefler. I'm almost in a state of disbelief as he tells me what's been happening. In just a matter of six years nothing appears to have changed, and yet so much has changed. The babies and toddlers have become school-aged children, the school-aged children have now become teenagers, many singles are now married with babies on the way, and one or two of our friends are no longer with us. But the town itself, sleepy little Lefler remains the same as it ever did.

The cab pulls up in front of my place. Glenn and I get out, and while I pay the cabbie, he collects his suitcase from the trunk of the car. As the cab pulls away, Glenn has a look at the house.

"You know," he says, "your little white bungalow looks like it should be in Lefler rather than in Calgary. All that's missing is the picket fence."

"Spare me," I joke as I lead the way up the sidewalk to the front door.

I unlock the door, and we enter. "Sparky!" I yell. Silence. "I guess he's not home yet," I say: "I'll put your luggage in my room for now," I say as we take off our shoes.

"Sit down. Do you want a beer?"

"Sure."

I put his luggage in my room and then go into the kitchen. That's when I see the note Sparky's left taped to the fridge door.

Dickhead,
Gone to my sister's place. Thought you and your brother would like some time alone together. Back later this evening.

I grab two beers from the fridge, take them into the living room, and I tell Glenn about Sparky's note.

"That's really sweet of him," Glenn says.

"Yeah," I agree, "he's thoughtful that way."

"Um-uh," Glenn says, "you don't still have any of that amazing hooch do you?"

"Sure do, want to smoke some?"

18

"Yeah, I haven't smoked any since the last time we got together."

"Ok, I'll roll a jay."

"You mind if I put on an album," Glenn asks.

"Go ahead, have a look through the ones we have," I say pointing to the row of records by the stereo as I go into the kitchen. I take the hooch box out of one of the drawers and look out the kitchen window to see Mrs. Kwiatkowski in her garden picking some veggies. I hear the radio go on in the living room, which is quickly silenced as Glenn turns the switch on the receiver from *FM* to *Phono*. Then the opening chords to *Broken English* by *Marianne Faithfull* slice through the air.

I roll a joint, and head back into the living room, hand it over to Glenn who sparks it, has a toke and passes it to me. After a couple of tokes, I get up the nerve to say to Glenn, "You haven't told me how Dad is."

He has a solemn look on his face, "He's okay, Jimmy."

"What did he have to say when you told him you were coming out here to see me?"

Glenn shakes his head, "Nothing."

I look down at the hardwood floor. Glenn butts out the half-smoked jay, and then he sits closer to me on the couch.

"Jimmy," he says putting his arm around me, "You were absolutely right in telling him what happened to you. It was the right decision that he heard about the tribunal and what happened coming from you, rather than from other places. I'm sorry he had such a bad reaction to it all."

"Do you know what it feels like when your own father tells you that he hates you?"

"He doesn't hate you. And you'll see, he'll come around. You know Dad; he always shoots first then asks questions later."

I stare into space while my elbows are resting on my knees and my hands are folded in front of my mouth. "It still hurts, Glenn." I can feel a knot forming in my gut, and it's starting to work its way up into my chest.

I make an excuse to leave the room to compose myself for a moment. "I'm…uh… going to…uh…clean up the mess, I made in the kitchen. I'll be right back." I go into the kitchen to the counter where I left the remnants of rolling the joint. My hands shake uncontrollably as my emotions start getting the better of me. I try to

19

clean the remnants when my elbow accidentally hits the hooch box, and it falls to the floor.

"FUCK!" I yell.

"What's happening in there?" Glenn calls from the living room. I'm silent.

He comes into the kitchen, sees the mess on the floor and me leaning over the sink my head bent forward.

"Hey, what's up?"

"Glenn," I sigh, "I'm a fuck-up."

"Who told you that and why did you believe them?" he says.

"Look how I've fucked everything up," I say turning to him. "I messed up my military career. I dragged a guy I cared for a lot into the middle of the whole damn thing, and he's gone. Now I have a father who doesn't care if I live or die."

Glenn puts his arms on my shoulders. "Hey, you know that's not true. He loves you, Jimmy."

"I wish I could believe that right now."

"Don't let his old-school beliefs fool you. He comes from another generation where attitudes were different, that's all. You'll probably find that he's struggling with this as much as you are."

I'm silent again.

"Hey," he says turning me around to face him, "do you remember that night we spent together before you left for Royal Military College?"

"Yeah," I quietly answer. "You and Marny had that big going-away barbeque for me, and you and I stayed up long after everyone had left or gone to bed."

Glenn laughs, "Yeah then we went for that walk at 3:30 in the morning and smoked some of that hooch of yours."

"God we must have walked and walked," I say as it all comes back to me.

"We ended up at our favourite spot as kids," says Glenn, "that little hillside just out of town."

"I remember lying on that hillside that night looking up at the stars," I say. "I don't think I've ever talked with anyone so much in my life. We talked, we laughed...remember those shooting stars we saw?"

"Yeah," he laughs, "One for me and one for you."

We both laugh. Then Glenn gets serious.

"You're not a fuck-up Jimmy. What happened with the tribunal and all that shit, is just that - shit. It's history, and you don't need to be bothered by it ever again. Look where you are right now. Your life is getting back on track, you've got a whole new set of friends, and you've still got a family that loves you…"

"Even Dad?"

"Even Dad. So why are you tearing yourself down? What good is it doing you?"

I feel a smile draw across my face.

"That's more like it," Glenn says. "Now c'mon, we have a whole week together. Let's have some fun."

∞

Entry #164 - Thursday, September 25, 1980 - Glenn's been here for five days already, and we've been having a great time. I've been a tourist in my own city, wandering around downtown like I'm seeing it for the first time. Glenn's been especially interested in going to the record stores because he doesn't get much of a chance to buy new music in Lefler. He's a real audiophile and has a separate room in his home that has nothing but his stereo equipment, and every wall is filled with shelves of records of all kinds. He's been collecting records for years and, since he's been here, he's already spent a small fortune on buying albums

On Sunday, he met Mr. Kwiatkowski from next door, and the two of them hit it off right away. They joke and talk politics (one of Glenn's favourite subjects), and he invited the two of us over to his place the other night for a glass of his homemade wine, that stuff is not a drink, it's a drug. I drink two glasses of it, and I get that giddy semi-drunk feeling. When Mrs. Kwiatkowski drinks it, she fills half of the glass with 7-Up just so it isn't as strong. But it is tasty none-the-less.

Yesterday we rented a car because Glenn got tired of taking the bus everywhere. So we went to the zoo and spent a great day. Today we were going to go to Heritage Park. However, we discovered that it's only open on weekends from Labour Day until the end of October when it closes for the season. So we'll go on Saturday before he heads back to Manitoba. In the meantime, he's rolled a joint, and we're sitting on the couch smoking it just before we head out for something to eat.

Glenn passes the jay to me, "I've got something on my mind."

"What's that," I answer while having a toke.

"Why have I hardly heard a thing from you in six years?"

That question strikes me dumb. I quickly search for an answer. "My silence hasn't been intentional Glenn."

"Then why?"

I look at Glenn not quite knowing how to answer that. "I...I guess I just got busy at R.M.C. and..."

"Horse shit," Glenn says, "too busy to pick up a phone for a few minutes or write a few lines on a piece of paper?"

"Glenn I wrote letters."

"Oh that's true," he says sarcastically, "occasionally we'd get a letter. But c'mon Jimmy, I got promoted two years ago, and you didn't know about it. You haven't seen Tiffany since she was a baby and now she's in school. The last I heard from you, I got a short note saying you had been posted from Suffield to Calgary. You said you'd write back with a forwarding address, but we heard nothing."

I wrap my arms around my legs in a fetal position on the couch and rest my chin on my knees. "You're right Glenn," I sigh feeling ashamed, "I haven't been very communicative."

"What have I done to deserve the silent treatment?"

"Nothing, Glenn. It was nothing you did. It was nothing anybody did. I'm really sorry about not keeping in touch with you or anybody else. Up until the tribunal I was having a lot of fun. I was meeting new people, seeing places like Europe and the Middle East, going here, doing this, and having a three-way love affair; I guess I forgot."

I feel Glenn's hand on my shoulder as he sits closer to me. I look into the hurt in his eyes. "Am I hearing you right?" he asks, "You forgot about me?"

"Glenn, I'm sorry. It wasn't intentional. Please understand. The experiences I was having during these past years I could never have dreamt of getting in Lefler."

He lays back and rests his hands behind his head and quietly stares at the wall.

"I was into every new experience and I...I just got swept away by it all. The people I was meeting and all the places I was seeing. I remember my six-month tour with the United Nations troops over in Cypress. You should see a sunset on the surface of

22

the Mediterranean, and the Northern Lights up in the North West Territories. Not to mention all of these new sexual things I was trying...and liking. Then when the tribunal happened, I felt so ashamed of myself I just wanted to hide somewhere."

"Too busy having fun to think about the Glennster," he says.

I look back to him, "I have no excuses, Glenn. I just didn't think."

"I've been really hurt by your silence," he says, "don't you ever forget about me again. Your lovers will come and go, and your experiences in life will begin and end, but your blood are the ones who'll always be here."

It's been many years since my brother has lectured me and this only makes me feel like a bad little schoolboy. "I'm sorry Glenn," I repeat bowing my head, "It won't happen again."

He's silent for a few moments more. Then he places his hand under my chin and lifts my head to meet his eyes once again. "In spite of all that Jimmy, I love you, and I'm proud to call you my brother."

"Seriously?"

"Do I usually say what I mean?"

"Yeah," I smile.

"That's right. But now you and I have a couple of more days together so tell me about some of your adventures."

"Where would I begin?"

"Wherever you want," he smiles. "But in the meantime, I'm starving."

"I'm ready to go any time you are," I say.

"Let's go," Glenn replies.

∞

My favourite Italian restaurant is a tacky little place located in a small shopping plaza on Crowchild Trail. The walls are festooned with plastic climbing vines, and large Styrofoam disks are painted grey and cut to look like ancient Roman stone carvings. The décor is tacky, but the food is great. Diana Ross sings *Upside Down* on the speakers from the radio station the management constantly plays. We sit on the chrome and red vinyl chairs which surround each table. Red and white checkered tablecloths adorn each table in the room. A Mateus bottle sits on our table with a lit red candle plugged in its opening. Glenn surveys the place as we wait for our steaks. The hooch we smoked has really taken its toll with us because we both have a really bad case of the munchies. We've devoured the breadsticks put in front of us in record time, then asked for more, which disappeared seemingly within seconds of being placed on the table.

"Now *this* place reminds me of Lefler," Glenn grins.

I chuckle knowing exactly what he means.

"Look at the plastic plants," he chuckles, "and those Styrofoam carvings."

"Yeah," I add, "in Lefler, this would be considered fine dining."

That's when we both snigger uncontrollably. I giggle so hard I nearly spill my beer. Our steaks are brought to us, and we settle down to eat.

"You know," says Glenn, "I would really like you to come back to Lefler for Christmas this year."

"Will Dad be there?"

"Of course he will."

"I don't know, Glenn."

"You can't avoid Dad forever, Jimmy. If Dad is upset with you, he'll have to get over it, and like I've said…he will."

"It could get tense Glenn, and I don't know if I could handle him verbally spitting at me, or worse yet, totally ignoring me."

Glenn puts down his knife and fork. "Jimmy, do it for me. Marny would love to see you again; Mikey barely remembers you and Tiffany has never met her Uncle Jim. It *has* been six years."

"I know Glenn." Then I draw a deep breath, "I suppose by now the whole town knows about me."

"I'm not going to lie to you Jimmy; you know what life can be like in a small rural town. Most people have heard that you got into some kind of trouble in the military, but they don't know exactly what. Marny, Dad and I are the only ones who know, and we're not saying anything."

"I suppose I'm going to be like another Bob Duke," I say with a tinge of fear.

"Bob Duke was different. He ripped off a lot of people, and he fucked a lot of other people around. You know that. That's why he was driven out. But people have always liked you. You're not out to double-cross or do anybody any harm. In fact, when people heard that you were in trouble, they all hoped that you were ok."

I silently look out the window to the passing traffic on Crowchild Trail.

"Has anyone seen Bob since he was driven out of town?"

"He was last seen in a bar in Winnipeg. He was a mess, a hopeless alcoholic. But he brought that on himself."

"So did I," I interject.

"Be that as it may, c'mon back for a few days Jimmy and say hi to everybody. People would love to see you again. Maybe you and Dad can start on a new footing."

"Fat chance. He won't listen to me; you know what he's like."

"You're selling Dad short, Jimmy. You're his son, he does love you, and everything came as a shock to him that's all. He had no idea that you were gay, to begin with until you told him about the tribunal. Well, maybe he always suspected."

I silently look out the window once more.

"You did the right thing by telling him what happened. Yes, you've been through hell over these past few months, and it probably does feel like you've lost everything. But give people a chance. Especially people in your own hometown, the people who watched you grow up, and the people who know you the best."

"What will I do if they start asking questions about what happened? I don't want to talk about that part of my life anymore."

"I'm sure most folks would understand that. So why don't you just cross that bridge when you get to it? Maybe they won't ask."

I silently cut into my baked potato. "Ok, Glenn," I sigh, "I'll come back to Lefler for Christmas, but I can only go for a couple of days."

"Great, you can stay with us. Let's make arrangements before I leave."

I look at him momentarily, "So I don't change my mind?" I grin.

"I know you too well," Glenn smiles as he gives me a gentle rap on my upper arm.

"Ok, I know somebody who works at a travel agency. We'll pop in to see him before you leave."

"I knew you'd see it my way," he grins.

∞

Back at my place Glenn, Sparky and I sit in the front room listening to one of Glenn's new records. *Kate Bush* is singing *Babooshka* so loudly that we barely notice the knocking on the front door. I turn down the volume and answer it to find Mr. Kwiatkowski standing on our doorstep with a huge grin on his face. In his one arm, he carries two magnum-sized bottles of his red wine, while he holds a plastic shopping bag in his other hand.

I invite him in. Glenn has a huge smile on his face, "Hi André," he grins.

"I hope I'm not troubling you," Mr. Kwiatkowski says with his thick Polish accent. He gets Glenn to take one of the bottles.

"That's for you to take back to Manitoba," he says to Glenn, "and this is for us to drink tonight if you don't have any other plans."

"We have no plans," Glenn says.

"I didn't think so," Mr. Kwiatkowski says handing the other bag to Sparky, "This is for my young friends," he smiles. "My wife made some more perogies for you."

"Oh yum!" Sparky exclaims as he takes the bag into the kitchen. "I'll get some wine glasses," he says as he goes.

Mr. Kwiatkowski, who I suspect has already had a couple of glasses of wine, wobbles over and sets the bottle he brought on the coffee table beside Glenn's. He cocks an ear toward the stereo like he's listening. "A-ha-ha," he laughs, "Babooshka," he says quietly. Then he picks up Glenn's bottle, "Glenn, put your wine away," he says, "We don't want to drink it on you."

Glenn laughs and takes his bottle into the bedroom just as Sparky comes back out to the living room with four wine glasses.

"I'll have to thank Mrs. Kwiatkowski for the perogies," I say. "Is she coming over too?"

André slowly lowers himself onto one of the chairs and says, "You know her, she always has something going on at her church. But that's okay, she likes it, she wanted me to go tonight, but I said no, I was coming over with a bottle of wine to see our young friends. She didn't like that. She told me, 'You stupid!' I say to her, 'I no stupid, you stupid!'" Then he gives a short, sharp nod of his head and winks his eye at me as if to say, *I told her.*

"So what's been happening with André?" Glenn says as he settles back onto the couch.

"I was bringing the last of the vegetables in from the garden today."

The phone rings in the kitchen and Sparky goes into the kitchen to answer it, "Hello…oh hi Terry! What's the poop de jour?"

"It's his friend Terry," I say to André, "so he's going to be awhile on the phone."

André chuckles.

"So you were saying that you got all of the vegetables in from the garden today André," says Glenn.

"Oh yes, it was a good year for the garden. My wife is already starting to get her winter canning done."

There's a shriek of laughter from the kitchen. Mr. Kwiatkowski turns his head in that direction.

"Oh, Mary! You're kidding! Smell that one!" shrieks Sparky on the phone, "Ain't she one big bad bitch!"

I feel embarrassed by Sparky's outburst.

Mr. Kwiatkowski listens to Sparky for a few moments, and then he turns to me and says, "Please don't be offended by what I am about to ask, but I've never seen either of you entertaining any young ladies. Why do two nice young men like you and Sparky not have any girlfriends?"

Damn it! I knew this would happen. I don't know what to say. I look over to Glenn who is smiling at me. He nods his head and winks to say, "It's ok."

"Well André," I say slowly, "um…because we both like other men."

Mr. Kwiatkowski smiles and says, "I thought so," he says as he reaches over and gives my arm a gentle shake. "That's ok," he adds. Then he leans over to me and quietly asks, "Are you and Sparky, you know, together?"

"No André, he'd drive me crazy." Glenn and André laugh. "Even though we get along well, we're very different people," I say.

André looks toward the kitchen then chuckles. He takes a sip of his wine. "I thought this was the case as well," he says. "But, my young friend, please be very careful," André warns, "my wife and I, we like the two of you. But many other people wouldn't like you because of this."

I nod my head in agreement knowing all too well how true that is.

"I remember during the war," he continues, "back in Poland. It was during the Nazi occupation. My wife and I were living in Krakow. We had a neighbour, a good-looking, quiet young man; he was a banker I think. Anyway, we all knew that he only ever entertained other men at his flat. One young man, in particular, used to come around a lot."

"Oh, really!" Sparky continues from the kitchen, "You're kidding! I just knew she was one of us!"

André glances toward the kitchen a smile draws across his face, "Anyway," he continues, "I heard a commotion out on the street early one morning. I got out of bed and looked out the window to see six Nazis standing in a small circle pushing this young man and his regular guest back and forth between them. The young men were naked, and their hands were tied behind their backs. The Nazis were laughing at them. I forget what month it was, but I do remember there was snow on the ground and it was cold. The Nazis were making fun of them calling them *schmutzig*. They kept pushing them back and forth between them…until the one young man who was noticeably angry spat at one of them."

Mr. Kwiatkowski is silent.

"What happened then?" I ask.

He takes another sip of his wine. "Three of the Nazis pushed the guy to his knees and held him while The Nazi he spit at slapped him then urinated in his face. They all laughed and called him 'Swine!' That's when they pushed the two of them face down to the ground, and they all kicked them. They yelled, '*Schmutzig!* and "*Faggots!*" and kept kicking and beating the two of them until the snow around them was red. Then two of the Nazis held their rifles to the back of the heads of these young men and fired. They walked away laughing and left the two of them dead. I looked to all of the surrounding buildings. Everywhere there were people looking silently staring in horror out at what happened. None of us did anything."

"Why?" I ask.

"In those days, my young friend, the Nazis could do whatever they wanted to do. If you tried to stop them, you would simply be shot right there and then."

I have a picture in my mind of what it must have been like to witness that scene. The three of us are silent.

André says to me, "Please be careful my young friend. There are still many Nazis around to this day. Many don't wear uniforms anymore, but they are still out there. My wife and I would really hate to see something horrible happen to you or Sparky just because of who you are."

"Thank you, André," I say solemnly, "thank you."

Glenn grins and puts his arm around me, "Don't worry André as long as I'm around, I'll make sure nothing like that ever happens to him."

André smiles, "That's nice, a close family." He takes another sip of wine, "But this is not a time for sad stories. " He raises his glass and says, "Lech Welesa!" We all raise our glasses to Lech and drink.

"André?" Glenn asks, "Didn't the Nazis order the removal of all the men in Poland to concentration camps?"

"Yes," says André, "the idea was to empty Poland of her people and re-populate it with Germans."

"Were you sent away," I ask.

"No, I was lucky, the Nazis missed me."

"How did they miss you?" Glenn asks.

"I was in the basement of our building one afternoon when I heard a loud noise upstairs. I realized the building's main door was being kicked open. I heard the sound of several heavy boots on the floor above me. I knew right away they were Nazis, so I hid behind the coal bin and prayed really hard for safety for my wife and I. For some reason they never came down to the basement. But I had to remain in hiding within the building during the final few months of the war. But by that time, what I knew of Krakow was gone. Most of the city was in ruin."

I can't help but think of that young banker in André's story. What must that have felt like to be dragged naked from your bed with your lover, publicly humiliated, pissed on then shot in front of your neighbours? I feel a cold rush, and Glenn looks at me.

"Are you okay," Glenn asks.

"Yeah," I say, "I guess I just have to put on a sweater. Excuse me a moment." I go into my bedroom where I fumble through my chest of drawers looking for a sweatshirt that I really don't need to wear anyway. The cold rush I felt was more a moment of fear than chill. André's story of that young banker swirls in my mind. I find a sweatshirt, put it on and go back into the living room.

Over the next two hours, the four of us get drunk on André's wine. Then André looks at his watch and tells us he'd better get back home. We all thank him for the wine and the perogies as he leaves, then we shut down the house for the evening before retiring.

∞

December. It always makes me introspective, and this year I'm more introspective than usual. Christmas is less than three weeks away, and it seems like a lifetime ago that Bryn, Marcel and I were still together and still happy. This year has been for me; proof that an individual's world can change radically, and forever, in what seems like an instant.

It's a starry and clear Monday night, but Bert took an extra couple of days off, so he isn't heading back to Edmonton until the day after tomorrow. The snow crunches on the sidewalk as Bert, and I walk along with our hands in our pockets.

Whenever he visits, we've gotten into the habit of taking a long walk after dinner, no matter what the weather is like. I'm sorry I didn't bring my gloves because it's colder than I had anticipated tonight. Our breath condenses as we walk and it quickly vapourizes into the evening air. The cold fresh smell of winter is all around. I love that smell and the feel of the cool crispness this time of year. We stop at a *Don't Walk* signal at a corner and wait as a handful of cars continue on their journeys.

The daylight fades early; it was dark by 3:30 this afternoon but now brightly coloured Christmas lights twinkle at us from every hand. Some of the homes in my quiet, neighbourhood have gone all out and created huge Christmas displays. We just walked by a brightly lit, life-sized display of the Manger, Mary, Jesus and Joseph, and a host of Angels. I remember as a boy I would always get excited about this time of year, and I always enjoyed being at home. We cross the street as the signal turns to *Walk*.

"You're quiet tonight," Bert says as we head back to my place.

"I'm thinking about my going back to Lefler for Christmas. I don't know how things are going to go between my father and me."

"I don't know what to say, Jim," Bert says. "I wish I had some brilliant answer for you or some humourous comment to cheer you up a little."

"I appreciate that Bert but there is nothing that can be said."

"Your brother might be right, with a little time between what happened at the tribunal and now, maybe your father has had a change of heart."

"I can only hope so. I just remember hearing his words so clearly the day I told him what happened.

"Did he really tell you that he hates you?"

"Well, no. But his message was clear to me."

"What did he say?"

"He said, *I don't even know who you are anymore! But I do know one thing; you are not my son!*"

"Hmph," Bert responds.

"I tried to talk to him, but that's when he hung up the phone on me. So you see, I don't know how Christmas is going to turn out. I'll try my best with my father, but I don't know if he'll have any of it. He's a very stubborn man, anyway, sorry to be so heavy duty. Enough of my problems."

Two women bundled up against the cold pass us on the sidewalk as they walk in the opposite direction.

"That *is* fantastic news," the one woman says excitedly to the other.

"Yes," answers the second woman, her voice muffled by the scarf around her face, "we'll be opening the shop in April."

"What part of town is it going to be in?" asks the first woman. But their conversation becomes muted as they pass us and carry on walking.

"That reminds me," I say, "you told me earlier that you have some news."

"That's right, I've put in a transfer with my job, and it looks like I'm going to move down here."

"Really? When?"

"Looks like it will be the spring."

"How long has this been in the works?"

"Quite a while. I've been thinking that it's time for a major change in my life."

"Well, that is good news. When will you have an ETA?"

"It could be anytime now. You'll be one of the first to know when I hear anything."

"When did you put in for a transfer?"

"Back in August."

"Why didn't you say anything about it?"

"I didn't want to say anything until I knew for certain what was going to happen," Bert smiles, "Hopefully by Easter."

"I guess your sister knows."

"Oh yeah. Patty and Keith have known all along."

"Where will you be living once you get down here?"

"Well at Patty and Keith's of course, at least for the first while. They have that extra bedroom in their basement."

"It'll be fun having you living down here."

"Not to mention the travel costs we'll both save," he adds.

"True," I respond. We silently walk a little further.

"You know what?" Bert says.

"What."

"I really like you, Jim. I like spending time with you, I like hearing your voice, and I especially like lying beside you in bed at nights."

I feel a smile draw across my face.

"The thing that's really great," he continues, "is Patty and Keith like you too."

"Bert I like you too, and don't get me wrong, I'm flattered by what you're saying. But there's still a lot in my life I have to work through right now, and I don't want to rush into anything. I couldn't take any more heavy emotion now."

"I understand," Bert says solemnly.

We walk a little way further when we arrive at the front of my place.

"Jim," I hear Bert say.

"Yeah," I answer as I turn to face him only to be met with his mouth planted firmly on mine. The ice crystals in his moustache are cold and wet against my clean-shaven face.

"To hell with this *like* bullshit," he says as he breaks his kiss momentarily, "I *love* you. I don't care if the whole world is watching right now." He kisses me again.

I'm taken aback by this sudden public display of affection. I gently pull back from him, "Bert, I really have strong feelings for you as well, and I appreciate what you're telling me. But I've got too much going on in my life right now to jump into a serious relationship. Please try to understand; I need time and space."

"I understand, Jim, I do. But I want you to know how I feel."

"And I'm letting you know what's going on inside of me because I care a lot about you. The only thing I'm going to commit to now is getting my life together."

We look silently at each other for a moment. "Let's at least go inside out of the cold," I say.

"What cold?" he smiles as we break our embrace, "I don't feel cold at all anymore." I smile as the two of us go up the front walk, and I open the door.

We come in, and Sparky is in the living room watching one of his favourite TV shows, *That's Incredible*.

Bert looks at the TV screen. "That's Incredible?" he says, "You honestly like that show?"

Without turning his attention from the television, Sparky says, "Don't give me stress girl."

"He watches Magnum P.I. too," I say.

"Who doesn't?" Sparky answers, "Tom Selleck's a hunk, and I just know he's a sister."

"You mean you *wish* he was a sister," I say.

"Never mind, **Sl**eazette," Sparky says, "By the way you got a call from Vancouver while you were out."

Bert and I momentarily look at each other. "Vancouver?" I say, "Who was it?"

"He said to tell you it was Sgt. Michael Bader from the R.C.M.P."

Bert smiles at me, "What kind of trouble are you in now?"

"Oh he's ahhh, somebody I met that's all," I smile.

"Isn't he that trick you had at the airport while you were waiting for your brother to arrive ya slut?" Sparky interjects while he turns and smiles at us.

Bert laughs. "Really? You had a Mountie while you were waiting for Glenn to arrive?"

"He wasn't wearing his uniform," I reply. "I had no idea until I was in his hotel room."

"You *are* busy aren't you?" Bert laughs as he takes off his snow boots.

"Thanks, Sparky," I sardonically quip to him as I remove my parka and hang it up.

Bert is still laughing as he takes off his coat and puts his arms around me.

"Now I'm jealous as hell," he says, "I've always wanted a Mountie, and you get one without even trying. Was he fun?"

"Well, yeah he was…"

"Is he cute?" Sparky asks.

"I thought he was very…"

"Did you play cocks and robbers with him?" Bert quips.

"Well it happened really fast and I…"

"Did he have a big dick?" Sparky interjects.

"Well yeah, I guess he…"

"Did he wear his uniform while you were fucking?" Bert asks.

"No, he was totally out of his uni…"

"Did you guys get kinky?" Sparky asks.

"Well no we just played a little and…"

"Did you get him to arrest you?" Bert smiles.

"Like I said everything happened so…"

"Are you going to see him again?" Sparky asks.

"I guess that's why he call…"

"Well, what the fuck are you waiting for?" Sparky demands.

"Yeah," Bert agrees, "Phone him back right now."

"Get him out here Dickhead," Sparky says, "don't keep him all to yourself."

"Yeah I have to meet this man," Bert agrees.

"That's right!" Sparky continues, "A Mountie with a big dick, and you're keeping him to yourself ya selfish bitch. Hell, *I'll* phone him!"

I almost stagger into my bedroom from the barrage of questioning. I get my phone book, I find Mike's card and take it to the phone in the kitchen. I sit at the kitchen table and dial the number he's written on the back of the card. After two rings he picks up the phone.

"Hello."

"Hi, Mike."

"Jim! Didn't I warn you that I would call?"

"Well yeah, I guess I didn't think that you actually would."

"Never doubt a police officer," Mike replies. "I got thinking of that cute man I met in Calgary a couple of months back, so I gave him a call."

"And how is he?" I ask.

"I was about to ask him that."

"I'm okay."

"You don't sound very sure of yourself."

"Some personal problems I'll hopefully work out over Christmas."

"I don't suppose it's anything you want to talk about."

"No, it's family."

"Ah, I hear you."

"So how are things?" I ask as Sparky appears in front of me with a big stupid grin on his face.

"Good, really good. The big news is I've been seeing a guy on a regular basis."

"Ah, so that's what's taken you so long to call. How long has this been going on?"

"Just a couple of months."

What's his name?"

"Robert."

"How did you guys meet?"

"Through work. We needed some information regarding a case we were working on, so I went to his office and got the information I needed from him."

"What does he do for a living?"

"He's a Constable in the Vancouver Police Force."

"You mean you're having an affair with another policeman?"

"Two cops fucking each other AAAHHHH!" Sparky screams as he heads out of the kitchen.

There's a pause on the other end of the line, "What the hell was *that?*" asks Mike.

"Just my neurotic roommate, pay no attention to him. Well, I'm interested, how did you guys establish that each other was gay? I would think that would be risky to talk about things like that openly."

"Jim's Mountie friend is dinkin' another cop!" Sparky exclaims to Bert in the living room.

There's another pregnant pause on the other end of the line. "I guess you have a little problem with confidentiality in that household," Mike observes.

"Well...I..."

"I mean your roommate appears to like making public announcements."

"That's too true," I agree.

"Okay, whatever I tell you on this line is for your ears only okay?"

"Okay."

"You've been through the mill, so I trust you know what it feels like to have other people prying into your personal life."

"Again, too true."

"So I'm trusting you with some of my general personal information."

"Understood."

There's another pregnant pause on the other end of the line.

"Are you still there?" I ask.

"Oh my God," Mike says, "I'm sorry I just got distracted by something that was flashed along the bottom of the television screen."

"What's going on?"

"It says that John Lennon's just been shot in New York City.

"What? You're kidding?"

"They've taken him to the hospital; he's in critical condition."

"I hope that he's okay," I say.

"He's my favourite Beatle," says Mike. There's more silence.

"I guess we'll have to wait to see what happens with him," I add.

"I suppose you're right," Mike answers. "Anyway, where were we?"

"You were about to tell me how you and Robert established the two of you are gay."

"I thought he was a good-looking guy so I would make any excuse to get over to Vancouver Police headquarters to see him. So it turned out I had to go to see Robert a few times for several bits of information regarding this case, even though I could have collected those bits of info over the phone."

"...and Robert never suspected you had ulterior motives for showing up so many times right?" I add.

Mike laughs and says, "He told me later that he did."

"By 'later,' you mean...?"

"I mean, when I went to a house party of a friend of mine in Burnaby, and he was there."

"This didn't happen to be a gay house party did it?"

"Well of course."

"So you guys talked and..."

Mike laughs again, "and at the end of the evening, he came back to my place. We've spent as much time together as we can since then."

"Well, that's great news. I'm happy for you Mike."

"Sooo, when are you coming out to see Robert and me?"

"I'm not sure at the moment Mike. I'm off to see my family in Manitoba for Christmas in a couple of weeks, and I probably won't get any time off from work again until late spring or summer."

"Well, whenever you can make it would be great, even for a weekend, it's just over an hour plane ride to get here."

"Well, I suppose I could manage to fly out for a weekend sometime after Christmas."

"Just remember," says Mike, "we have cherry blossoms in February out here."

"Oh come on," I say, "That can't be true."

"Hop on a plane and find out for yourself."

"Ok, I'll do that."

"Don't forget," he adds, "this is the San Francisco of Can..." There's another long silence from Mike's end.

"Are you still there Mike?"

"Damn, I had a feeling that would happen," he says quietly.

37

"What?"

"They just flashed another announcement on TV; John Lennon's dead."

∞

The streets are unusually dry as we drive along 33rd Avenue S.W. in Bert's 1979 Camaro.

"I know that you always speak highly of David," he says looking at me and trying to drive at the same time. "Were you and he ever lovers?"

"We talked about it, but you know with everything that went on at the tribunal I wasn't in the headspace to be with anybody at the time, and he seemed to understand that. Besides, deep down I don't think he wanted me as a lover."

"Why do you do that?" Bert asks.

"Do What?"

"For some reason, you keep putting yourself down, and I don't know why. You're not going to change what happened with the tribunal and everything..."

"But what happened at the tribunal was my fault," I answer defensively, "and somebody I loved was humiliated through no fault of his own. Now my father wants nothing to do with me."

"There you go again. You've totally imprisoned yourself." Bert's momentarily silent. "Answer me this," he continues, "what are you going to doing to do about this situation?"

I think about that for a moment.

"I'll tell you what you're going to do," Bert says, "nothing..."

"What do you mean?"

"What can you do about the past?"

"Bert, you don't understand..."

"You're right, Jim, I don't understand. For some reason, you've got it in your head that you're a bad person. And I'm not the first one to say this to you either, because didn't you tell me your brother said these things to you back in September? Do you honestly believe you don't deserve to be happy?"

I'm silent. I've never thought of it that way before. "Well, what do you suggest I do?"

"Stop carrying around all that guilt," he says as we turn north onto 14th St. S.W.

"You're wearing it like a life sentence and all it's doing is keeping you down."

"I guess you're right," I say meekly.

"I know I'm right. Take it from me, the more you dwell on your past, the more you can't see what's going on right now. It becomes a rut of self-pity."

I'm silent once more.

"Jim, I know what happened was a major upheaval in your life, and this ongoing thing with your dad must be really hurtful. But why do you crucify yourself?" He looks at me then watches the road again. "Like I've said before, there's nothing you can do about your father's reactions. And as for what happened with you and Bryn, well, didn't he and Marcel take off together? Didn't you tell me he didn't want to see you at all after the tribunal?"

"Do you blame them after all the trouble I caused?"

Bert sighs like he's exasperated. "Yes, I do blame him. In fact, I blame them both. They're a pair of first class pricks as far as I'm concerned."

"Bert, what happened wasn't their fault."

He impatiently drums his fingers on the steering wheel. "Jim, do you know what I feel like doing right now?"

"What?"

"Getting out of this car, dragging you out on the sidewalk and giving you a good shake."

"Why?"

"You told me Bryn and Marcel gave their consent for those pictures of the three of you to be taken, and when the going got tough, they both left you to hang alone. That's hardly what I call love." As he speaks, he raises his voice to me. "Don't you think it's time you've forgotten about them, period? I'll bet they've forgotten about you. But you've let your guilt nail you to the wood, and now, just like you've told me, it's all somehow your fault. Aren't you tired of that?"

"You're pissed off at me?"

"I'm not pissed off at you. I'm pissed off about how you've let yourself be beaten the way you have. The more you allow that to happen, the more it *will* happen. Where's all of that training you got at Royal Military College? As an officer, aren't you supposed to be on the front lines making life and death decisions? What about *your* life? Where did all of *that* training go? What happened to that bright and self-assured guy who I pursued last summer? Was all of that real?"

"Of course it was real."

"Show me then. Better yet, show yourself how real you are!"

We crest the 14th Street S.W. hill as *The Rolling Stones* make fun of the *Bee Gees* over the radio, *"I'll be your Saviour steadfast and true, I'll come to your emotional rescue...."* We descend to the intersection at the bottom of the hill where 14th Street meets 17th Avenue S.W. The entire downtown core spreads briefly before us to our right, like a carpet of multicoloured lights. Then the passing trees and small apartment buildings quickly hide it once more.

"I'm sorry, Jim, I didn't mean to raise my voice to you," Bert apologizes, "I'm only saying these things because I hate to see you hurt yourself all the time."

I quietly look out of the passenger window as we wind our way eastward through the side streets of the Beltline. *Bert's right*, I think, I *am* tired of holding myself back. As we pass the building that Marcel, Bryn and I used to spend our weekends, I look up to the old apartment. What Bert has just said to me goes through my mind.

It's true, the three of us were in this together, and they took off without me. At least Marcel came over to David's place to say goodbye to me, but Bryn, he didn't want to see me at all. He didn't even have the courage to face me to tell me why. I loved him but was he more interested in his career than he was in seeing how I was doing? Those questions really bothered me. I feel my brow furrow as I cross my arms.

"Are you okay, Jim?"

"No!"

"I'm sorry if I pissed you off but…"

"Bert, I've just realized you're absolutely right about everything you've said. Why have I been carrying a cross for those two?"

Bert looks at me and raises his eyebrows in agreement as he nods his head. We continue to drive through the Beltline, finally parking beside one of the many imposing high-rise apartment buildings downtown.

We approach the front entrance and buzz the intercom.

"Hello."

"It's Bert and Jim," I say.

"C'mon up," answers David.

A short buzz is heard coming from the door, then a click. Bert opens the door, and we go through to the elevator. On the way up I say to Bert, "Dammit it *is* my life. Why *have* I been holding myself back for them? They really didn't give a damn about me did they?"

Bert shrugs his shoulders and shakes his head. The guy on the elevator with us smiles at me as if to say, "I hope you don't expect an answer from me." We stop at the seventh floor, and the guy silently casts one last glance my way as he exits. The elevator door closes then Bert bursts into laughter. I chuckle along.

"That poor guy didn't know what to do," I say. Bert nods his head. Up to the 14th floor and out of the elevator, down the hall, and a knock on #1406.

David opens the door, looking as sexy as ever, dressed in a pair of 501 jeans, and a peach coloured Lacoste shirt. A tuft of chest hair peaks from the opening of his shirt and his eyes sparkle with mischievous vigour.

"Hey c'mon in," he says with a grin.

We enter to the smell of something savoury baking in the oven, and the music on the turntable.

"How are you doing little honey," he says as he wraps his arms around me and gives me a kiss.

"Great," I respond. "David this is Bert Gilhius."

They shake hands, then David says, "Gilhius. Do you know a Jan Gilhius from Red Deer?"

Bert looks at David surprised, "Yes, he's my cousin."

"I've done some contracts supplying office furniture with him up in the Red Deer/Edmonton area."

Bert's face lights up, "So *you're* David from Vastervik Imports! Jan has talked about you…"

"In a good way, I hope," David smiles.

"Definitely in a good way. I'll have to tell him I've met you now."

"Say hello to him for me."

"I sure will."

"This guy knows everybody," I say as I pat David's shoulder.

"I get out a lot," David smiles. "Well give me your coats," he says. He takes our coats and hangs them in the hall closet while Bert and I move into the living room. A Christmas tree in the far corner of the room is draped with small, blue blinking lights, tinsel and a couple of strings of small Swedish Flags, those, of course, being a tip of the hat to his Swedish heritage. Christmas cards are hung neatly from strings of red ribbon on opposite sides of the room. As usual, everything is in its place as if we are in a show suite. Tasteful and business-like, that's David.

"Does everyone want a drink?" I ask immediately taking over bartending duties.

"Bert, what would you like?"

"Rye and water."

I go into the kitchen to get the drinks ready and am quickly joined by David.

"It's so good to see you again little honey," he says as he puts his arms around me from behind and his bearded chin tickles my ear. "Bert's quite handsome," he whispers in my ear.

"I thought you would approve."

"I do indeed. How's everything going?"

"Good," I say feeling energized by the conversation in the car.

"How's work?"

"Really good, I like working there."

"Always something new to do?" David smiles.

"Always," I say, "thanks for pulling some strings like you did to get me that job."

"That's okay," David says, "I'll take it out in trade," he winks. "But on another subject," he continues with a serious tone, "I've been wondering how you think Christmas in Lefler is going to be?"

"I'll get through it. Bert and I had a talk on the way over here, and he's right, I have been crucifying myself this whole time over what happened at the tribunal."

Bert appears in the kitchen, "My ears are burning," he says.

David smiles as he motions Bert into the kitchen and turns his attention back to me. "That's true," he says, "but you've told me you're concerned about how you and your dad are going to get along."

"Yeah," I say, "he's old school. He sees things like being dismissed from the military as bringing shame on the family."

David puts his arms around my waist once more, "When you were living here with me what did I always tell you?"

I shrug forgetting already.

He smiles and says, "Experience is the only thing that matters. It's the only thing you take with you. You may not feel it now, but one day you'll see that whole tribunal episode was pivotal in making you a stronger person. Maybe going back to Lefler and seeing your dad is going to be the first test of this."

"Maybe," I say.

"By the way," David says, "did you bring some of that wild pot of yours?"

"Always."

"Are you into smoking some?" he asks Bert.

"Always," Bert answers.

"Good, let's have some while everyone has a drink. Do you want the grand tour?" he asks Bert.

"Sure," Bert smiles.

"I'll roll a joint while you guys are doing that," I say as I hand Bert his drink.

"That'll be great. You know where the rolling papers are," David answers while Bert follows him down the hall. "Jim tells me you live in Edmonton."

"Yeah, I've lived up there for several years."

"How long are you in town for?"

"I go back tomorrow morning."

David's voice and the music on the turntable meld together as Bert and David walk down to the end of the hall and into David's home office. I sit on the couch in the living room, reach over for the small pottery jar in the middle of the coffee table, lift the lid and take out the package of Zig Zag Blues. Their voices are mere rumblings with an occasional outburst of laughter.

As I roll the jay, I think about the conversation Bert, and I had on the way over here. Why did I never see how Bryn and Marcel abandoned me, and Bryn wouldn't even come over to David's to see how I was doing? Especially, when I think about it, neither one of those guys were in any of the photos the S.I.U. had. I roll the joint as the two of them move from one room to another. "Damn!" I say getting flustered as the rolling paper splits and I have to start another one.

How could you so easily torture yourself for all of this? I think. Bert's right, what's happened to all of that training at R.M.C.? What about *my* life? More importantly, what am I going to *do* about it? I twist the ends of the joint and take out the book of matches from the small jar as they appear back in the living room.

"The joint is ready to smoke," I announce. "Bert should see the view from the balcony," I suggest.

"Good idea," says David, "we can smoke the jay out there."

I go over and pull the balcony door back. The three of us file on to the balcony and take in the sight that greets us. The entire downtown core spreads out in front of us, and the eastern end of the city beyond that. The neon signs, the high-rise apartments and office buildings all sparkle together in the winter darkness. The white noise of the city night surrounds us, and the Christmas lights make the city look more alive than ever. The cold winter air causes our breath to steam from our mouths.

"Brrr," I shudder as we step into the December chill.

"But a fantastic view," Bert adds.

I pass the joint to David who sparks it up, has a toke and passes it on to Bert.

"Yeah, I really like it. You should see it in the summertime. Isn't that right Little Honey?"

"Yeah," I agree as Bert has a toke and gives the joint to me. "David gets the morning sun in the summer and from this vantage point the city is spectacular."

"So Bert," says David, "When are you moving from Edmonton?"

"Soon, I hope."

"Do you find the gay life is better down here?"

"It's not so much that, but a change of scenery is the main thing. I've lived in Edmonton for a lot of years, and I have a sister who lives down here, and she's been after me for a couple of years to get a transfer down here."

"So a transfer came up, and you went for it," states David.

"That's right."

"Edmonton's a real blue-collar-party town," says David, "I think you'll find life here a little different in that this is more of a head-office-cocktail-hour town."

"Hmmm," considers Bert, "sounds a little on the stodgy side."

"Don't believe that," I interject, "we've got our share of parties down here."

"No doubt," says Bert.

"True, we may not have many bars," David says, "but there is always a big house party to attend somewhere in the city..."

"Most of which end with an orgy," I add.

"If Jim here has anything to do with it," David smiles.

"Look who's talking," I say.

David laughs out loud and continues to pass the joint. We quickly toke until David snuffs the roach into a small ashtray he's brought onto the balcony with us.

"I'm cold," he says, "let's go inside."

We go back inside while I close the patio door and the curtains. Bert and I sit on the couch while David disappears briefly into the kitchen.

Bert notices a hardbound book of male nudes on the coffee table and begins to look through it.

"Jim French," he says while looking at the photos, "I've always liked his photography."

I lean over and look at the photos with him as he slowly thumbs through the book.

"You know what?" I say.

"What?"

"Toking makes me horny."

Bert laughs.

"I heard that," says David who comes out of the kitchen and joins us on the couch.

"Did you notice how quickly he came out of that kitchen?" I say.

Bert laughs again.

David looks through the book with us and says, "They are good photos," as he puts his hand on Bert's knee.

Bert smiles at David and says, "I was told this might happen," indicating David's hand.

"I don't hear any objections from you," David smiles and gives Bert a really deep kiss. He unbuttons the top of Bert's shirt and kisses his chest while I play with his nipples. I kiss and lick down Bert's neck while Bert lays his head back with a big smile on his face.

David looks up at him and says, "I think we should take this into the bedroom. What say you?"

"Great idea," I agree. We look at Bert who says, "Let's go."

The three of us take our drinks and quietly walk into the bedroom.

∞

I'm lying in a field of tall prairie grass looking up to a cloudless blue sky. A multicoloured kite floats lazily way above, and a gentle breeze rushes by me. All is peaceful.

"There you are," I can hear a voice say.

"Mom? Is that you?"

"I've been looking for you all afternoon. What are you doing out here?"

"It was such a nice day and…"

"Just don't forget that you have chores to finish today young man."

"Where are you, I don't see you."

"I'm here, right beside you."

"Where?"

I can hear her laugh. "Stand up," she says.

I do and find myself looking out over the expanse of a rolling southwestern Manitoba prairie. I turn around and there she is, just as I've always remembered her. Her shoulder-length brown hair being tousled by the prairie breeze, her soft brown eyes, and that multicoloured sundress she liked to wear during the summer. The little gold cross she always wore around her neck glistens in the afternoon sun.

I run to her and put my arms around her like a little boy.

Holding her close to me feels so real. I start to cry.

She holds me close to her like she always did.

"I miss you, Mom."

"Jimmy, how can you miss someone who's never left you? Now stop talking silliness. Your father will be home from work soon, and you don't want to have to answer to him for not finishing your chores do you?"

"No Mom I don't," I smile.

"Ok, well gather your stuff up…oh no," she points, "There goes your kite."

I turn around just in time to see my kite string wiggle itself from the rock that secured it and rise higher in the sky. I run to retrieve it, but it's too late. My kite gently sails away like a bird taking my childhood with it. I turn back toward my mother but she's gone, and I'm left standing alone in the wind-blown waves of prairie grass.

It's then I'm awakened by the sounds of giggling and shuffling feet that appear to be coming closer to me. Then one of the living room lamps flips on.

"Santa's been here!" yells Mikey as I hear *chink-chink-chink* of dog tags and Rufus their clumsy old Bloodhound leaps onto the couch where I'm lying. He lands squarely on my chest and belly with tail wagging wildly and snorting, he licks and slobbers all over my face. He's always loved me for some reason.

"Merry Christmas, Uncle Jim!" shouts a delighted Mikey.

Still disoriented from my sudden wake-up call I'm barely audible as I try to get Rufus off of me. "Rufus get down please," I weakly plead, to which Rufus releases one of his usually smelly dog farts, and continues to lick and slobber all over my face.

"Rufus peeee…yeeewwww!" I yell.

Tiffany and Mikey laugh.

"Come here Rufus," Mikey calls.

Rufus jumps from the couch, and the *chink-chink-chink* of his dog tags is what I hear as he goes over to Mikey leaving me to bask in the vortex of dog flatulence. I slowly rise and check my watch while doing so. 6:00 AM.

"Oh wow!" shouts Mikey his voice reverberating in my ears, "The Dukes of Hazzard!" He puts on a white Stetson with a Confederate flag across its front.

Tiffany remains glued to the spot she was when she realized I was laying on the couch. She has a shy smile on her face as she clutches a Raggedy Ann-type doll with a huge pink bonnet, red yarn for hair, a short red dress and green-striped legs.

"Hi Tiffany," I smile labouriously.

"Hi," she says barely audibly.

"Do you know who I am?"

She shyly nods her head and says, "You're Uncle Jim."

"That's right." Then I point to the doll she clutches and ask, "What's your friend's name?"

"Strawberry Shortcake," she shyly smiles.

"Oh isn't she cute," I slowly say through blurred eyes, trying to sound as sincere as I can with four hours sleep and a bit of a hangover from drinking the homemade wine that André had me bring to Glenn.

"Why don't you go see what Santa brought you," I smile. She nods her head and slowly moves toward the tree while not taking her eyes from me.

"You kids excuse Uncle Jim a moment while I go to the washroom." I get up from the couch and stumble to the bathroom. I run some water in the sink to wash my face, and I catch a glimpse of myself in the mirror. I feel like a bag of dirt and look twice as bad.

My plane had arrived late into Winnipeg from Calgary the night before. Then there was the two-hour car trip to Lefler, and then sitting up until two in the morning drinking and getting caught up with Glenn and Marny. I have no idea where the kids are getting their energy this morning. It would be wonderful to be that innocent again. I wash my face and go back out to the living room feeling a little more alive.

Marny appears in the living room doorway, her hands on her hips and a broad smile on her face. "Merry Christmas," she says.

I manage a smile and wave at her.

"Hey mom," Mikey laughs, "Rufus did a stink-a-rama on Uncle Jim!"

"And you survived?" Marny asks with a bit of a chuckle in her voice. "How are you feeling this morning?"

"I'll be fine after a coffee," I reply.

"Glenn will get some ready in a couple of minutes," she says.

She no sooner mentions his name than he appears in the living room with a huge grin on his face. He's fully dressed and has his jacket on, "Tied one on a bit last night?" he grins.

"Spare me," I mumble.

Glenn laughs and says, "C'mon Rufus let's go!"

Rufus immediately bounds over to Glenn his dog tags *chink-chink-chinking*. Glenn puts the leash on him, and they head out the door.

Marny comes into in the living room, crouches beside the Christmas tree and plugs in the lights. Instantly that corner of the room is spectacularly lit by tiny multicoloured twinkles of lights that reflect off the tinsel and bulbs hanging from the tree.

In what seems like a very few short moments, Glenn has come back inside with Rufus. The dog runs excitedly into the living room with the leash dragging behind him. His tail flails wildly, and he snorts, grunts and sniffs everywhere he possibly can.

"Rufus get back here!" barks Glenn.

Head down the dog appears to tiptoe back into the front hall, then moments later both Glenn and Rufus appear in the living room. "I'll get coffee happening now," he announces while he disappears into the kitchen followed by Rufus.

"Oh look, Tiffany," Marny says pointing to a large wrapped gift, "I think there's another one from Santa."

Tiffany darts over to the package and savagely tears the wrapping off of it to reveal a dollhouse.

"Hey," Marny says to Mikey, "it looks like you've got another one as well." Mikey goes under the tree to retrieve the large brightly wrapped package. He tears into it to reveal a complete set of Star Wars action figures.

"Oh wow!" Mikey shouts just as Glenn comes back into the living room. I hold my head to keep it from falling off my shoulders. It's then I hear the welcomed sound of the coffee percolating in the kitchen.

"Daddy is Uncle Jim feeling well?" asks a concerned Tiffany to him.

"Oh I think Uncle Jim celebrated a little too much last night," he smiles.

"You mean he has a hangover?" asks Tiffany.

Glenn and Marny laugh, and I smile. Glenn disappears into the kitchen and emerges with two cups of coffee, one he gives to Marny, and the second he hands to me. The taste of coffee is touching my tongue and makes me feel a little better.

"Here's one for you Uncle Jim," Mikey says as he approaches me with a small wrapped package in his hand.

I smile as I put my coffee cup aside. I take the small gift from him and read the tag, "To: Uncle Jim, From: Mike."

I slowly undo the wrapping while Mikey looks on. "Oh thank you, Mikey," I say. In my hands is a sports cap with the Winnipeg Jets hockey logo emblazoned on the front. "You like the Jets?"

"Who doesn't? They're everyone's favourite team."

"Yeah, I guess here in Manitoba they would be," I agree as I put the hat on my head. "Didn't they just get a new head coach?"

"Yeah," says Mikey, "Bill Sutherland's the new guy."

"Do I look like a true blue fan Mikey?"

"All that's missing is a beer can in your hand Uncle Jim."

I pick up my coffee cup once more and take another sip. "Will this do?"

"Yeah, I guess," Mikey shrugs.

"Thank you, Mikey, I really like this. I'll wear this all the time."

He has a big grin on his face like he's really pleased with himself.

"Here Tiffany," Marny says as she hands Tiffany a small package, "Go give this to Uncle Jim!" Tiffany takes the small crudely wrapped gift, looks at me and shyly smiles.

"Go ahead," Marny coaxes

Tiffany brings the gift over to me, and I read the tag, "To: Uncle Jim From: Tiffany."

I open it to find a pair of black socks. "Thank you Tiffany," I say, "I always need more socks." I pull her close and give her a quick thank you kiss on the cheek. She rushes back to Marny giggling then stares at me smiling. Rufus jumps up on the couch beside me and licks my face as if to say, "Don't forget about me."

∞

I feel a lot better having just finished my shower. Now feeling more human and fully dressed, I open the door of the bathroom and step into the hall. The house is full of the intoxicating smell of turkey slowly roasting in the oven, and all is silent except for the song *Happy Xmas, War is Over* by John Lennon.

I follow the sound as it echoes down the hall to Glenn's stereo room to see him alone and silently staring out the window. I enter the room and look around.

All four walls are obscured by floor to ceiling shelving units full of records, reel-to-reel and cassette tapes, all still filed in alphabetical order no doubt. In the centre of the far wall is the stereo system and the way it's set out reminds me of an altar in a church. Two spotlights are focused on the area where the instruments of worship sit: a Revox reel-to-reel recorder, a Technics turntable, a Harmon-Cardin receiver, a NAD tuner, a brand new Sony cassette tape machine, and a small mixing board with two brightly lit volume control meters and slide pots with small red lights on each one. It's a veritable home recording studio where all that's missing are the microphone, and I'm sure Glenn's still got a couple of those somewhere.

Above this alter is a framed poster of John Lennon. With his beard, wire-rimmed glasses and shoulder-length hair he almost looks the picture of Christ himself. And now with his recent murder, that poster is more poignant than ever.

Glenn is unaware of my having entered his temple. "Hey," I say walking up behind him, "what are you looking at?"

Glenn turns from the window and smiles, "anything and everything Jimmy." He looks back out of the window to the yard. He has a pensive, almost worried look on his face.

The snowy yard is empty. Just beyond it, the neighbour's kids are playing hockey on a small ice rink in their yard. Like all local backyard rinks it was probably shovelled out and made by the family, now all the neighbourhood kids congregate there. Only a few blocks away the two Lefler grain elevators tower over the entire town like prairie sentries. Some things just don't change. This is a scene exactly as I remember from my childhood. I look at Glenn.

"You're deep in thought," I say.

"It's the end of an era, Jimmy," Glenn sighs, "John Lennon's gone, Ronnie's gonna be in the Whitehouse soon, and God knows what's gonna happen next." He shakes his head, "The world is about to become a more serious place."

"Sure seems that way," I solemnly agree.

"I wonder sometimes what kind of a world Marny and I are bringing our kids into Jimmy. The Soviets have invaded Afghanistan, American hostages in Iran, trouble in the Polish shipyards..."

"Not to mention millions of TV viewers wondering 'Who Shot J.R.," I quip.

Glenn chuckles, and the two of us silently stare out to the neighbours' kids while the final notes of the song fade.

"Was the world really a better place when we were kids? Or does it only seem like it was, Jimmy?"

"What's brought on this blue funk, Glenn?"

"I don't like the news I'm hearing on the radio Jimmy. This big ol' World is changing again and who knows what's going to happen next. At times like this, I worry."

"I'm sure Mom and Dad probably had the same worries during things like the Cuban missile crisis," I say. "As far as I can see that old saying about things changing yet remaining the same is true."

Glenn smiles, puts his hand on my shoulder and says, "Please don't ever change, Jimmy. Promise me you'll always be that same little brother I've always known."

This unusual sentimentality coming from my no-bullshit brother takes me aback. "I can't promise you anything like that. Especially after what I've been through this year, I can never go back to being the person that I was."

Glenn sighs again, and then he silently gazes back out the window. I've never seen this side of him. Glenn, who is usually so confident about everything, is now so unsure of himself and vulnerable. Feeling like I should add something I say, "I know something that will never change."

"And what's that?"

"I love you, Marny and the kids."

Glenn smiles gently pulls me away from the window and holds me close to him. I rest my head against Glenn's chest, and we stand silently locked in this embrace.

"We all love you too Jimmy," Glenn says to me quietly. I can see Rufus in the doorway of the room. His head is cocked to one side as if to say, "What are you guys doing?"

"Are Marny and the kids still at church?" I ask.

"They're at Dad's place. They'll come back here with him soon."

He no sooner says those words then we can hear the muffled sounds of Marny and the kids outside and the front door opens.

Glenn and I break our embrace, and I'm nervous at hearing the sound of my father's voice talking with the kids. Glenn turns his attention back to his stereo and puts on a new record. I muster my courage to see my father.

I stand in the doorway of Glenn's stereo room and look toward the front door where I watch Dad help Tiffany take off her coat, boots and scarf. Every nerve in my body feels like they're standing on end. My hands are shaking a little, so I put them in my pants pockets to hide them from view. Mikey is first to come darting in front of the doorway.

"Hey Uncle Jim," he greets. Dad looks up to see me standing in the doorway. His face is emotionless, and he returns to helping Tiffany put her coat on a hook on the wall.

"Mike, how many times have I told you not to run in the house?" scolds Marny as she comes past the room next. She smiles at me as she passes by.

Then Dad and Tiffany come past where I'm standing.

"Hi Dad," I smile.

His face still emotionless he says nothing. He doesn't even look at me as he moves on to the kitchen. I sink back into the stereo room. I knew this would happen. I feel a hand on my shoulder, "I saw that" Glenn says in a low voice, "I'm gonna have a talk with him."

He heads toward the door of the room with fierce determination. Knowing that his "talks" with Dad usually turn into shouting matches, I pull him back and say, "No don't do that, Glenn. You know it's only going to make things worse."

"How much worse can it get, Jimmy? He deliberately walked right by you like you weren't even there."

"It's Christmas Day Glenn. Let it go for now."

"You're right. It is Christmas Day which makes what Dad just did even worse." He starts out the door again.

"No Glenn."

Glenn pauses. "Then what do you suggest?"

"Just don't, not today."

"Jimmy, I'm not gonna let this go. I don't care how he feels about what happened to you in the military; that gives him no right to treat you like this."

I'm momentarily silent. "Then maybe it's best I leave for a couple of hours. I'm going to go for a walk."

"That's bullshit, Jimmy! You don't have to leave the house because of Dad. He's the one with the problem here…not you."

"I'm not leaving because of Dad."

Glenn looks at me incredulously.

"Well, ok, maybe I am. But it's clear to me that if I stick around the house all day, there's only going to be tension between Dad and I, and that would make everyone else feel uncomfortable. Think of the kids. It's their day as much as anybody else's."

Glenn looks at me then casts a furrowed glance back to the direction Dad went. I go to the front door and put my boots on. "Since I'm only in Lefler for a couple of days, I might as well look in on some old friends anyway."

"Where's Uncle Jim going?" asks Tiffany who appears in the front hall hanging on to Glenn.

Glenn looks at her and smiles, "He's going to visit some of his old friends, Peanut."

"Will he be gone for long?"

"Don't worry," I smile at her, "I'll only be gone for a couple of hours. I'll be back in time for dinner."

She looks at me, smiles shyly and partially hides behind Glenn.

"Why don't you go and see Mom," Glenn says to her. Tiffany goes back into the other room. Glenn and I look silently at each other. I pause and try to prevent myself from being emotional about it, but this hurts.

Glenn comes over, puts his hands on my shoulders and says, "I'll make sure that he knows exactly how I feel about this."

"Glenn, I just don't see how that's going to endear me to him."

"I don't care how he feels right now, Jimmy. I can see how hurt *you* are. You're his son too, and I'm not going to stand by and watch him treat you like this."

I know what scrappers Glenn and Dad can be. Although they will have their shouting match behind closed doors, everybody's going to hear it anyway, and there will be cold

54

remnants of it when I return in a few hours. Hopefully, I'll be able to handle that. I'm silent as I finish buttoning my jacket, and put on my gloves. "I'd better tell everyone I'm leaving for a while," I say.

"I'll do that," Glenn smiles, "see you at dinner." I pause, and we look at each other. "I'm in your corner," he says, "as long as I'm around *nobody* hurts you."

I put on the Winnipeg Jets cap that Mikey gave me this morning, smile and nod to Glenn, and walk outside into the crisp Manitoba air.

∞

I've been walking around town for about half an hour and, to my surprise, nothing has changed. I find that incredible when I think of how much my life has changed in six years. It's like I've had a lifetime of experiences, but somehow it's all been an illusion. I walk aimlessly. My mind wandering, drifting like the Marie Celeste going with the current with nobody at the helm to guide the ghost ship.

Then I'm startled to find myself at the entrance to the small cemetery where Mom is buried. The gate is open, so I go in. I approach my mother's headstone. A bunch of frozen flowers lean against it. That would be Dad still making his weekly visits here to bring her flowers and talk to her.

A long silence hangs between the headstone and me. I miss my family. What happened to us? What was the salvo that blew us apart? Was it Mom dying of cancer? Was it me being dismissed from the military for being gay? Is it Dad and Glenn both being headstrong and stubborn? Was it all of the above? We used to be so happy and close, now I feel like a remnant of the past twisting in the breeze.

"Mom," I say, "I wish you were here right now. I wish there was something I could do to get Dad to talk to me again. If you were here, I'd ask you to say something, anything to him that would get him to treat me like a son again rather than an unwelcome stranger."

That's when I hear the snow crunch near me. I look to where the sound came from, but there's nobody there, and I get the feeling I'm not alone. Every hair on the back of my neck feels like it's standing on end. I look back to the headstone, and that feeling is getting stronger like there's somebody now standing beside me. I try to ignore this feeling, but the more I do, the stronger it gets.

I turn and leave. But before I go back out the gate, I take one last look back to my mother's headstone. That's when I see a second trail of footprints in the snow going up to the place where I was standing, a trail of footprints that was not there when I arrived. At least, I can't remember it being there. I get spooked and continue on my way.

I walk directly across the street from the Mennonite Church, and there are a handful of people standing outside in the cold after the service has finished. They're probably on their way home after the usual Christmas Day get-together in the church hall after the service. Out of the corner of my eye, I can see one of the men do a double take in my direction. Oh no, it's Mr. Burton. I can see him tap his wife on the shoulder and point at me. Mrs. Burton starts waving and yelling, "James!"

Oh great, the Burtons have spotted me. Mr. and Mrs. Pissy Pants we used to call them because of the way they've looked down their noses at other people. They've always had delusions of being the blue bloods in a town of country bumpkins. But they liked me because, at my parents' insistence, I've always been polite to them. Mr. Burton waves me over.

"James," he smiles as I cross the road to meet them, I've never liked being called James. "We thought that was you."

"My goodness, let me have a look at you, James," says Mrs. Burton as she looks me up and down. "How long has it been since we've seen you?"

I'm about to answer when Mr. Burton says, "We saw Marny with your father and the children not three-quarters of an hour ago, and she said you were in town for a couple of days."

"So how are you, James?" Mrs. Burton asks.

"I'm fine, Mrs. Burton."

"You've certainly grown into one handsome young man," she continues.

"Thank you," I smile.

"So are you married yet, James," asks Mr. Burton.

Here we go already. Here in Lefler if you're not married and have kids by the time you're thirty, then there's something wrong with you. "Not yet," I reply.

56

"Ohhh nooo," says Mrs. Burton as she sympathetically touches my hand, "You're not still a bachelor are you?"

Bachelor. Now that's always been a magic word here in town. Because when the term bachelor is used to describe a guy, a steady stream of local mothers with single daughters in tow, magically appear everywhere he goes.

"Yes, Mrs. Burton, I'm afraid that's the case," my smile now pasted on my lips.

"We wondered," she says, "after the things we heard…"

"Ahem, Mother," Mr. Burton warns as she covers her mouth like some secret has been let loose.

"What you heard?" I ask.

Mr. Burton jumps in, "It's just that there were some rumours about you circulating around town that were, shall we say, of an unbecoming nature."

"Oh?" I ask.

"Some people were saying you were discharged from duty in the military for reasons that were most unsavoury."

"Of course," Mrs. Burton hastily adds, "we didn't believe any of them."

"We know the breeding you come from," Mr. Burton continues, "and with you being a military officer, well, we knew those things could only be said by those who are jealous of their betters."

They haven't changed at all. "I am aware that my name was being passed around town because Glenn told me. I can only say that I left the military because I needed a change and now I continue my life as a civilian," I lie. The expectant looks on their faces tell me they want more information, but I'm silent.

"Well," Mrs. Burton continues, "We knew those nasty rumours couldn't be true. So, tell us, what are you up to these days, James?"

"I've started what could be a promising career with an oil company."

"An oil company?" Mr. Burton says, "So there could be a lucrative future for you?"

"That is what I'm working toward, Sir."

Their eyes widen as if they've landed a huge trout in a small boat.

"Debra!" shouts Mrs. Burton excitedly, "come here for a moment."

A young woman in her late teens comes over to us. She has long dark hair with hazel eyes, her complexion is flawless, and she has a bright, sweet smile.

"James," says Mrs. Burton, "you remember our daughter, Debra."

"Why, yes I do," I answer and shake her hand. She smiles sweetly back to me. Debra, the Burton's spoilt bratty little girl, has grown into a beautiful young woman.

"Debra has been accepted to the University of Calgary this September," Mr. Burton says proudly.

"Wouldn't it be grand," adds Mrs. Burton, "If you could be her escort while she's there..."

Something catches my eye in the distance. The next block over I see a red truck turn off a side street and clatter down the road toward us. It approaches from behind the Burtons and slows as it comes closer to the spot where we stand.

"You know," Mrs. Burton continues, "someone such as yourself who could show her only the proper places to go in Calgary and the decent people to meet..."

As the truck draws nearer, I notice the engine hood is being held down with a bungee cord that's attached to the bumper. That can only be one person in the world. The truck crawls to a stop, the driver's window rolls down, and a voice yells, "Jimbo! Is that you?"

My buddy, Cliff Beaudry, leans out of the window of his 1972 Ford half ton. He's had it for what seems like forever, and after all these years it still belches blue smoke from the exhaust. *Tequila Sunrise* by *The Eagles* flows from the open window like a sweet river, and he's still wearing that damn black trucker's cap with the Ford logo on it.

The Burtons are startled by Cliff's intrusion on this tasteful little scene.

"Aren't you supposed to be in Calgary making a fortune in oil wells?" Cliff yells.

"Is that what they're saying?" I yell to him.

"It's what I heard, " he smiles as he jumps out of the truck, runs across the road, slaps the side of my shoulder and shakes my hand. "Look at you, Mr. Big Shot," he grins, "he lives in the big city now! He's too high and mighty to come visit his friends in Lefler."

Then he turns his attention to the Burtons who seem offended at his presence. "Hey Mr. B, Mrs. B.," he smiles. "Hi Debra," he winks.

"Clifford," Mr. Burton stiffly acknowledges.

"Hello Clifford," Mrs. Burton quietly says as she wrinkles her nose.

Debra furrows her brow at him and says nothing.

"I heard tell that you were coming for Christmas," he says to me.

"Well, I'm glad the grapevine is still in good working order," I answer.

"Yeah, your brother told me."

"I was going to come by to see you anyway," I tell him.

"Good thing you didn't 'cus I'm not home right now."

"Well dear," Mrs. Burton addresses her husband, "we really should be going now. It was so nice seeing you again, James."

"Likewise, Mrs. Burton."

"Yes, James," smiles Mr. Burton as he shakes my hand, "we should like to see more of you in future."

"You probably will Mr. Burton," I reply.

"See ya, Mr. B., see ya Mrs. B," Cliff says.

Mr. Burton looks at Cliff. "Clifford," he says stiffly once more as the three of them turn and walk to their car. We're momentarily silent as we watch them go.

"Stuck-up Arseholes," Cliff mumbles under his breath.

I chuckle then quietly say to him. "I was about to get roped into being Debra's escort when she goes to school in Calgary."

"Pfff, little Miss Snooty-Bitch," he says as he watches them walk further down the street. He nudges me, "It's a good thing I came along then, eh?"

"I see the Burtons still don't like you." I smile.

"Mr. and Mrs. Pissy-Pants have never liked half-breeds," he answers. "So whenever I see them I always say hi to them," he laughs. "I love watchin' 'em squirm. Anyway, I'm going out to see my sister for a couple of hours."

"Flo! How is she?"

"Why don't you hop in the truck and come out with me to find out?"

"Yeah!" I say, and we both get in the truck while The Eagles croon *Best of My Love*.

I look around the truck's cab, and things haven't changed here either. Cliff still keeps it in a mess; old gum wrappers and a couple of potato chip bags, a small pad of writing paper is discarded on the passenger side of the floor with a big muddy boot print on it. One lone speaker with no casing sits on the dashboard makes the music playing sound tinny. As we get underway, I can hear a bottle rolling back and forth behind and underneath my side of the seat.

Cliff is the guy that I chummed around with throughout school. *Mr. Cool* everyone would call him because he was a handsome, laid-back guy, He never was a jock, but he was outgoing, gregarious and popular, especially with the girls. He was the guy that I always admired. To be truthful, I had a crush on him. When we had girlfriends in high school, I secretly wished that he and I were together. But as we got to high school, everyone started calling him Mickey because he'd win most **of** the drinking contests at our parties. He could suck back a mickey of vodka in seconds and be ready for more.

All these years later he is one ruggedly handsome man with his copper skin and his unkempt dark hair. His generally dishevelled appearance and his constant thick five o'clock shadow makes him look like a young version of the Marlboro Man. Then there are his eyes; his bright blue eyes, which, as I look at him, still capture me.

"I see you're still driving the Ford Fiasco," I say.

"Yep, until the day she drops."

I smile while I point at the eight-track player he's had forever, "The Eagles on Christmas Day?"

He gives me a serious look and says, "I still feel the same about Christmas as I always have."

"Still? After all these years?"

He nods his head.

Christmas obviously still holds some terrible memories for him. Cliff and I were about ten years old, and his brothers, Flo and their mother went over to a neighbour's place that Christmas afternoon. Their father was to join later, but he stayed at home and got drunk. For some unknown reason, he had lit a couple of candles in the living room and had knocked one of them over as he passed out on the couch. By the time his mother got a call at the neighbour's place, their whole house was engulfed in flames. They lost everything including their dad.

Unlike Cliff, who's a lover, not a fighter, his dad was always a scrapper. "Frenchy" everyone would call him, which he always hated. On the nights he would go out drinking he'd usually exchange words with somebody, the next thing you would know everybody would be out in the parking lot. They'd circle the cars and turn their headlights on to watch Frenchy and somebody else duke it out. Until one of the combatants lost and then they would both go back inside the Legion and buy each other drinks the rest of the night.

"So how have you been?" I ask changing the subject.

"What can I say," he shrugs, "things don't change in this town."

"That's true," I say, "I've been having a look around town, and it seems like I've never left. Are you still working at the Co-op?"

"Still there. I guess I'm a lifer in Lefler, and Flo's still there too."

"Is she still the Shipper/Receiver?"

"Yep. She loves that job, and it suits her too. She's the only woman I know who fits right in with the guys." Then he pauses, "I guess you know that Karen and me called it quits a couple of years back."

"Glenn mentioned that when he was in Calgary in September. I'm sorry to hear that."

"It's ok, it was my fault. I guess we realized that the relationship wasn't strong."

"Must have been a tough realization."

"Yeah, and my drinkin' didn't help."

"It finally got the better of you, eh?"

"Yeah, it was a problem, so I quit just after Karen and me packed it in. I guess you remember the trouble I used to get into whenever I'd hit the bottle."

"Yep, I recall the many nights you spent in the company of the local R.C.M.P."

"Yeah," he adds, "usually for being an asshole drunk." Then he chuckles and says, "Like the time I was drinking all afternoon, and then I wanted you to go to the Legion with me."

"Yeah," I add, "I remember as we sat at a table the server wouldn't serve us because you were drunk."

"Do you remember what I said then?"

"How could I forget? You stood up and said, 'You can't serve us because I'm drunk, you can't serve us because we're not properly dressed!' Then you dropped your pants in front of everyone."

"Yeah," he laughs, "that was another night in the drunk tank for me."

"Or remember the time that you were hung over and went into work with a cowboy boot on one foot and a work boot on the other?"

"Those were good times, eh?" he says.

"I never thought I'd see the day when Mickey Beaudry would stop drinking."

"I go by Cliff these days."

"Hmm, that will be difficult for me to get used to."

"That's ok," he says glancing at me, "I'll make an exception for you."

"Thanks. Do you ever get tempted to start drinking again?"

"Yeah, but I go to the AA meetings at the Mennonite church every week, and it helps."

We head south on Highway 10 toward Turtle Mountain Provincial Park, which is right on the US/Canada border.

"Is Karen still around?" I ask.

"No she moved to Brandon, and last I heard she's living with her new guy."

"Have you had any girlfriends since?"

"No. Single and free for now."

"How are your brothers?"

"Bill and Larry are doing good. Larry and Paula are living in St.Paul, Minnesota. He's been gunnin' for a promotion at the company he's workin' for. It would mean a lot more money for him, but it would also mean he'd have to move to their office in Alaska."

"Alaska? He really wants to move to Alaska?"

Cliff shrugs.

"How do prospects look for him getting the promotion?"

"He doesn't really know because there's a few people who are going for it, and they're all as qualified as he is, so everyone's keeping their fingers crossed."

"And how's Bill?"

"Him and Ruth are living with Mom looking after her."

"Has she not been well?"

"Mom's gettin' old and a little senile, she'll do weird things like go out to the store and forget where she is or she'll start walkin' and just keep goin'. It's like she gets confused sometimes and thinks she's heading back to her place when really she's going in the opposite direction. So Bill and Ruth decided to move in with her about a year ago to look after her."

"Was your mom getting lost, or something?"

"No, lucky for us somebody would usually spot her and bring her back home. But it's got us worried, she's not gettin' any better. We're thinkin' if things get worse we might have to put her in a home or somethin'."

"I'm sorry to hear that."

"We'll see what happens."

We're silent for a moment as I glance out the window to the passing southwestern Manitoba scenery. The thick woods that line the two-lane highway give way to open expanses of rolling snow-covered countryside, then back to thick woods.

"So how long has it been since you've been back here, Jimbo?"

"Six Years."

"Six years," Cliff repeats, "It seems like forever since I last saw you. By the way, is it true what I heard?"

"What did you hear?"

"That you were kicked out of the service for bein' a fruit."

Clearly, this thing is going to stick to me.

"Yeah Mickey," I sigh, "It's true."

"I hate to say it old buddy, but I could have told you that would happen."

"How could you have known that would've happened?"

"You're an honest guy, Jimbo. You would have trusted someone enough to tell them about yourself. The bad news is that people just can't keep their fuckin' mouths shut and word gets out. Am I right?"

"Well, yeah," I answer, "that's what happened. I trusted somebody," is all I say.

"See, I knew that would happen," he says shaking his head. "You're too nice, Jimbo. You're too nice to people who really need a good kick in the balls."

I watch his profile while he's driving. Cliff and Glenn were two of the few people who I came out to while I still lived here. I remember the night I told Cliff that I'm gay. We had been drinking, and we were alone in the basement rec room at my folks' place. He looked at me silently for a few moments after I told him. His face showed no emotion.

"A fag, eh?" was his response. "Well, it's not like I didn't know."

"How did you know?"

"I seen the way you look at other guys."

"What does that mean?"

"You look at other guys the way other guys look at women."

"I didn't know it was that obvious," I said taking another swig of my beer.

"It's been obvious to me," he smiled drunkenly. "So," he continued, "why do you like guys?"

"I just do, Mickey."

"So like, are you the woman or what?" he asked.

"What do you mean?"

"Well, like, do you fuck other guys or do they fuck you?"

"Both."

He shook his head and said, "So what's that all about anyway?"

"What are you talking about?"

"Well, you know, that ass-fuckin' thing you fags do."

"Why do you want to know?" I smiled at him.

"Well, I'm just curious," he answered.

There was a long silence between us. Then I noticed him looking at me with a weird smile on his face.

"Hey, ya know somethin'?" he asked.

"What?" I responded.

"I'm thinkin' about when we were kids, and we'd play together," he drunkenly grinned.

"Play together?"

"Yeah, you remember?"

I knew he what he was talking about, the sexual experimentation we did together as boys.

There was another long silence then he playfully brushed my knee, "Ya feel like doin' somethin'?"

There it was, the chance I had dreamed about. That moment I still regret. To this day I don't know why I refused his advances that night, but that's what happened. Mickey went home about twenty minutes later. Neither of us has ever mentioned that evening again. I stare at his profile while he drives and all of those old feelings are being stirred inside of me again. I wish I had done things differently that night.

I'm jolted back to the present as Mickey says, "Ya know I never understood why you're a fag. Ever since I've known you, the women have always liked you, and you never had any problems getting girlfriends."

"It's like I've said to you before, Mickey. I just like guys."

He shakes his head, "I guess that's up to you." Then he turns to me and says, "You'll always be my old buddy no matter what."

"Thanks, Mickey," I smile with a warm feeling inside of me, "you know I'll always feel the same about you."

"You bet," he grins. He continues to watch the road in silence then says, "Think you'll ever settle down, Jimbo?"

"If I find the right guy, Mickey."

He glances to me again and then turns his attention back to the road. "Ya know what?"

"What Mickey?"

"Whoever gets you will sure be one lucky guy."

"Well, Jeez, thanks, Mickey."

He looks back at me, gives me a wink and makes a click sound with the corner of his mouth.

Now, what do you suppose I should make of that? I think to myself. If I remember correctly, that's the gesture he's always reserved for the women he's liked. We drive on and say nothing more.

We turn off the two-lane highway and drive down a thickly wooded dirt road in what seems like no time at all. The truck bounces from side to side as we follow the tracks in the snow left by Flo's vehicle. We round a bend in the road and come into that familiar clearing on a hillside. There it is, exactly as I remember it. The small house that Flo' built with our help ten or eleven years ago. The clearing is surrounded by tall bare forest that opens to rolling prairie around the front of the house. We face the back entrance to her place. Smoke wisps out of the chimney and a Malamute barks in the yard as the truck rolls up and stops.

"That's not George is it?" I ask pointing at the dog.

Cliff smiles and nods his head turns off the engine and hops out of the cab. "Hey Big fella!" he yells, and George immediately bounds over to Cliff with his tongue hanging out and tail wagging furiously. The two of them play together.

I get out of the cab. The crisp, quiet Manitoba air and the smell of wood smoke greet me. Even though Cliff doesn't like or celebrate Christmas, I'm glad to see Flo has strung a line of green and red Christmas lights around the perimeter of the roof.

"Go and see Jim," he says to George, who looks at me and hesitates momentarily, then comes bounding over and jumps up on me almost knocking me backward. Cliff laughs and then calls George back to him. He glances around the yard and says, "I don't know where Flo got to, her truck ain't here." Then he looks around again and says, "Ya wanna see somethin' new?"

"Something new? What's that?"

"We put a new addition on the house a couple of summers ago, it's Flo's new bathroom."

I follow him around to the side of the house where the small addition juts from the wall like an afterthought.

"How long did this take you guys to build?" I ask as I put my hand against the side of the new addition.

"He stops and thinks about it briefly, "We started in late spring, and we were done by the time first frost was here. It's the inside that took us longer to do. By the time that was done we were into the new year."

"I guess Flo's happy to get this done."

'Well I sure am," Mickey answers, "'cus when I'm visitin' her, I don't have to walk down the path to have a dump anymore."

My attention is drawn to the front of the house, and I wander over in that direction. Cliff joins me, and we walk over to the front of the place. I quietly gaze out to the rolling prairie that spreads in front of us. It's funny, here in Manitoba these are called the Turtle Mountains, while in Alberta these would be called foothills. I take a deep breath and watch as everything slumbers, and the snow covers this scene like a flannelette sheet. Every sound is muffled. The bare trees on either side of the clearing lead down the hillside where I can see a narrow road run diagonally across my line of sight. A couple of farms lay on either side of the road. I watch as a small speck moves from one of the farmhouses out to a barn. I'll bet that's Hans. He moved here from Holland after the Second World War, and he and his family have lived on that farm since. He's always going out to his barn for something because he's a real pack rat and his barn is his favourite storage area.

This stillness is spiritual. It stirs something inside of me, and I'm reminded of what I've missed since I've been away from here. This is all a part of the man I am, the subtle changes over time and the things that don't change. This was my beginning, and no matter how hard I've tried over the years, I realize it's in my blood and always will be a part of me.

I look down at George who sits beside me with his tongue hanging out and is also looking out to the valley. He too appears to be taken by the same scene. "I've always liked this view," I say to Mickey as I turn to him to see him quickly look away from me.

Hmm, interesting, I think to myself.

"Ummm, we might as well go inside and wait for Flo," Mickey quickly suggests, "I could use a hot coffee."

We return to the back door and Mickey pushes it open.

"Doesn't Flo lock her door when she goes out?" I ask.

Cliff grins at me. "You've been livin' in the city for too long, Old Buddy." I follow him inside, and George follows us.

I see a big, orange tabby cat as I enter. It rouses itself from its curled up position near the stove and stretches.

"That can't be Bennie is it?" I ask.

"Yep," says Cliff, "that's the Old Gal."

"She must be ancient by now," I say as she comes toward me.

"I think she's 15 or 16 years old and probably has a good few years left in her yet."

I reach down to pet Bennie's head, and I look around the kitchen.

"I see Flo's painted the walls white since I was last here," I observe taking off my coat and boots.

"Yeah,' Mickey responds as he follows suit, "at least the inside ain't that snot green colour anymore."

Mickey grabs the poker resting beside the white enamelled McCleary wood stove, opens the door, shuffles the contents around inside, then adds a couple of more logs and shuts the door.

"There," he says, "the place will be really warm in a couple of minutes. "C'mon through and have a look around," Mickey says as he saunters into the living room. I follow him, and the first thing my eyes fall upon is a prairie buffalo scene that's been burned into a piece of framed raw plywood by a soldering iron. Flo's name appears in its bottom right corner. The next thing I see is her hunting rifle hanging just beside it.

"Is Flo still a member of the Rod and Gun club in Brandon?" I ask pointing to it.

"As far as I know," Mickey says, "but she hasn't used that rifle in a while."

There's a window beside the rifle covered in white lace and below that a small antique table, which is also covered in white lace with an old oil lamp standing on top.

She's put up a few Christmas decorations. Not many, but enough to indicate that the season is here. There are lights around the windows, and a string with cards suspended along one of the walls. Her portable stereo stands on a small table in one corner. I move in closer to see an Anne Murray record sitting waiting on the turntable.

A small Christmas tree stands in another corner adorned with strands of popcorn and cranberries alternately strung together.

"I guess Bennie still likes popcorn," I say indicating a few gaps along the strings on the tree.

"Yeah, I don't know why Flo does that every year because she gets pissed off when Bennie eats the popcorn off the tree."

Then I see a small framed photo of Flo', Cliff, Larry, Bill and me taken when Cliff and I were still teenagers. I go over and pick it up to have a closer look at it.

"You remember when this picture was taken?"

"Yeah," he smiles, "That was around the time we graduated from high school," I look at the photo. My eyes slowly scan all of our smiling faces that are ready to take anything the world can throw at us. Then I remember what the old Mennonites around here always used to say, we get too soon old and too late smart. These last few months have given me a taste of what they meant by that.

"Come'n see the bathroom," Mickey directs me to a nondescript door just off the kitchen. He pulls the door open, and we enter.

"You guys did a great job," I say as I look around.

The walls are painted a pale pink with a white and pink striped curtain strung across the small window above the tub.

"Where did you guys find this?" I ask resting my hand on an old claw-and-ball foot bathtub.

"Flo found it in Winnipeg. She knew about an old house that was being torn down and managed to rescue this tub. Bill and me helped her load it on the truck and brought it back here."

"Do ya want a coffee?" Cliff asks.

"Sure." I follow him back into the kitchen.

"As Flo' would say, 'make yourself ta' home that's where ya oughta be,'" he says to me pointing to a chair at the small table in the kitchen. He grabs two coffee mugs from the dish drying rack beside the sink.

"It's only that instant shit," he says, "but it's better than nothin' for now."

"That's okay."

I look back into the living room to see Flo's old guitar. "Mickey, do you still play?" I ask pointing at it.

Cliff glances at me, smiles and says, "I never stopped." He finishes preparing coffee for the two of us and places a mug in front of me. He goes into the other room and takes the instrument from its resting place. He comes back, sits on the chair across the table from me, and strums a few chords.

"Anything you wanna hear?"

"How about a Christmas song?"

He thinks for a moment and says, "This is just for you." He picks the opening chords to The Eagles' Desperado. He's always liked The Eagles, I watch and listen to him play.

Desperado, why don't you come to your senses,

You've been out ridin' fences for so long now,

I watch him as his eyes travel back and forth from forming the chords on the guitar neck to looking at me, then back to the guitar neck,

Oh and you're a hard one, but I know you've got your reasons,

The things that are pleasin' you can hurt you somehow.

Then, for a moment, our eyes lock onto each other's with serious intensity. I'm taken aback by the moment, and he falters in his singing. We both look away quickly. He loses his concentration.

George starts barking at the door, then we can hear the sound of a truck pull up outside.

Cliff stops, smiles at me and says, "Let's surprise her," pointing to a wooden chair just behind the outside door. Cliff puts the guitar aside as we hear the truck engine shut off and a cab door slam shut.

"She won't notice you right away if you sit there." I quickly move to the chair, just as the front door opens and in she bounds. She sees Cliff.

"Merry Christmas, Cliff," she smiles. He doesn't answer. "Be with ya in a sec," she continues as she disappears into the bathroom. Mickey chuckles to himself then looks at me and puts his index finger to his lips.

In a moment, we can hear the toilet flush followed by the sound of running water in the sink. Then the bathroom door opens, and Flo' comes lumbering out like a great momma bear.

"Sorry 'bout that Cliff," she says, "had my water pill today and I've had ta' squat ta' pee wherever I've gone." Then she stops suddenly when she sees me. A huge grin draws across her face, and she says in her booming voice, "Well look what the cat dragged in and the dog left behind!"

"Thanks a lot," I smile as I give her a hug. She gives me a bear hug that makes my eyes feel like they'll bulge out of their sockets. She hasn't lost her grip after all these years. She's a strapping woman with short dark hair and thick plastic rimmed glasses. She's always been like a big friendly bear with a smile on her face. She still wears that faded plaid jacket and that same trucker's cap, (which she calls her sex hat – because that's what the truckers call theirs). That hat of hers is probably ten years old, and many times she's been mistaken for a man when she wears it. She doesn't seem to mind.

"Look at you Mr. Big City Guy," she says, "You're lookin' good. I heard tell you were gonna be around this Christmas."

"You're looking good yourself, Flo."

"I keep myself busy and out of trouble," she smiles, "just like Cliff here's learnin' ta' do, ain't that right, Cliff?"

"Yeah, I guess it's about time," Cliff responds, "and where have you been?"

"Over ta' Shirley and Bob's place in Boissevain." Then she looks at me and says "Well make yourself ta' home that's where ya oughta' be."

Mickey and I smile at each other. She hasn't changed a bit.

"I like what you've done to the place, Flo."

"Well, it's about time I did something with it. Right, Cliff?"

"Yep!" is his reply, "It was about time to join the 20th Century."

Flo has always done things herself, even if that means building her own house, heating it with firewood, and living out here on her own. "Have ya seen the new bathroom?" she asks.

"Cliff showed me a few minutes ago. You three did a fantastic job on it."

"Ah, it weren't nothin'. So how long are ya stickin' around?"

"Not long. I'm flying back to Calgary the day after tomorrow."

"That's too bad, after all these years it would have been nice to see you a little longer. But I'm glad you're here now. It's about time that you came back to see everyone."

"Yeah, you're right. I've been away too long. So, any men in your life?"

"No," she says, "still single damn it."

"That's because some people still think you're butch," Cliff smiles kiddingly.

Flo sighs, "Yeah, I guess some people still think I'm a lezbeen."

"Although she's always liked you," Cliff points at me with a smile.

"What?" I chuckle, "really?"

"Well," she says, "I always used to say 'if that Jim Whitelaw's pendulum swung the other way I'd go for him.' But that was a long time ago."

I look at Cliff and shrug.

"I guess for now," Flo continues, "I have to be happy to be single. Can't go around bein' miserable 'cus you got nobody, ain't that right, Cliff?"

"Yeah, I guess so," he answers with another shrug.

"Besides," Flo continues, "nothin' much goin' on as far as single men around here now. Most everyone is married. Not too many eligible bachelors, except for Cliff here of course, and he doesn't count."

"Thanks a hell of a lot," he grins. "But there's no eligible women either," he continues, "it's not like back in high school when everyone was still single, and there were parties all over the place, and you could meet different women. Now it's just the same people all of the time and nothin' ever changes."

"Unfortunately," Flo continues, "that's too true. What about you Jimmy?" You got yourself a man?"

"I did. Until I was discharged from the military."

"You're not seeing him anymore?" Cliff asks.

"No. He was an officer like me, and he was the guy I got into trouble with. The military posted him to Halifax, and the other guy we were seeing went with him."

The two of them stare at me silently.

"The other guy you were seeing went with him?" asks Flo.

"Yes," I answer realizing I have to explain myself. "The three of us were having a relationship together."

They stare at me, look to each other, then back to me.

"How the hell does that work?" Cliff asks.

"Admittedly it sounds a little weird…"

"A little?" says Cliff.

"Okay," I say, "it's not for everybody, but everything kind of clicked between the three of us."

"You mean like, the three of you were goin' with each other?" Cliff asks.

"Yes."

"…And like, you guys had sex with each other all the time?" Cliff continues.

"Not all of the time, but yeah often enough."

He sits back in his chair looking stunned. "What the hell kind of a weirdo sexo thing is that?"

Flo and I laugh. Cliff doesn't like it. He folds his arms across his chest, slumps in his chair and pouts. He's never liked being laughed at. It has always made him defensive, especially when he's serious about something.

"Sorry Cliff," I say, "it's just the way you said it, that's all."

"Hmph," he snorts snatching his mug and taking a swig.

"Well I never heard tell of such a thing either," says Flo, "but whatever gets you through the night. So I guess you're going to Glenn's for dinner tonight?"

"Yes, I'm going to try to get my father to speak to me again."

"He's not talkin' to ya?"

I shake my head sadly.

"Well, I knew he wasn't too happy with ya, but I didn't know he wasn't talkin' to ya."

"No, he hasn't spoken to me since it happened."

Flo shakes her head and says, "We felt bad for ya when we heard about you bein' thrown out of the military,"

I chuckle to myself.

"What's so funny?" she asks.

"That has to be the worst kept secret I've ever had. Since I've been back, it seems like the whole town knows."

"That's something' I do hate about living here," Cliff pipes up as he gets out of the chair, "everyone knows everything about everybody."

"Yeah, ain't no secrets in Lefler," Flo agrees.

"That's why I sometimes think about leavin' this shit hole," Cliff says.

"Hey Bucko," Flo says, "What's with this sudden mood change?"

"Well, it's true I sometimes hate it around here."

She looks at me and says, "Must be Christmas Day."

"I thought you were happy here Mickey," I say to him.

"Well, yeah, I guess," he answers.

"Hey, how come he can still call ya Mickey," Flo says pointing at me.

Cliff casts a wry glance at her and says, "'cus I said he could."

"Uh, Cliff tells me you're still working at the Co-Op Flo," I say changing the subject.

"Yeah, I like it there. In fact, next month I'll be there thirteen years."

"Congratulations."

"Thanks, and Cliff's been workin' there almost as long. Ain't that right, Cliff?"

"Yeah, eight years workin' for nothin' in this go-nowhere town," he bristles.

Flo shakes her head, looks at me and says, "He's in a mood again. Have you got room in your luggage for him back to Calgary?"

He casts her a dirty look.

"Are you serious, Mickey? Do you really hate it here that much?"

He's silent for a moment and says, "I don't know. Sometimes I'd rather live in a place like Calgary, but other times, well...."

"Calgary is booming right now," I say, "I know of people at work who get better positions at other companies for more pay and better benefits on their lunch hours."

"No kiddin'," Flo says.

"It's true, you'd have no problem getting a job there."

"Are you listening to this?" Flo asks Mickey.

"I hear him."

"You'd have a place to stay while you were out lookin' for a job too," she says, "Ain't that right, Jimmy Boy."

"That's true."

"Well," he says like he's thinking about it...

"Well if you didn't lay around in the fart sack till all hours on your days off," Flo grins, "then maybe you'd do something about it, and you'd be living in Calgary by now!" She gets up, throws off his hat and grabs him in a headlock.

"Fuck off Flo," Cliff responds as she gives him a head rub.

"Ain't that right Cliff, you just like lyin' in bed all day don't ya," she continues to playfully chide him.

"Fuck off Flo," he retorts as he struggles to break free of her headlock.

"Call your arse Flo, and you'll have it with ya all the time," she grins.

"FUCK OFF FLO!" Cliff repeats breaking Flo's grip. He pushes himself back from her, and his face is red. His brow is furrowed as he grabs his hat, plunks it back on his head, then plops himself in his chair once more and pouts again. This is just like the old days when Flo' would wrestle him all of the time, and he'd respond in the same way.

"So are you going to Mom's for turkey tonight?" she asks him.

He sits in brooding silence.

"Well?" She asks waiting for an answer. He's still silent. She smiles at me then looks back to him and says, "C'mon, Cliff, it was just a joke."

"I always go," he snorts.

"Well ain't ya gonna dress up or nothin'?"

"Hmmph," is his cool response.

She rolls her eyes and shakes her head, then does a double take.

"Bennie, get away from there!" she yells at the cat as it jumps away from eating yet another kernel of popcorn off of the tree. "God that cat," she mumbles. "Anyway I hate to cut this visit short, Jimmy Boy, but we gotta get over ta' dinner at Mom's in just about an hour, and I still have ta' get ready then drive into town."

"Okay, I should be getting back to Glenn's anyway."

"So I'll meet you over at Mom's place," she says to Cliff.

"Yeah Okay," Mickey says.

"Before you guys leave though," she says, "here's something for ya, Jimmy." Flo' goes to the Christmas tree, retrieves a package and hands it to me. It's beautifully wrapped in shiny silver paper with dark blue ribbon. I recognize by its shape it's a record album.

"Flo, you didn't have to do that."

"You know me; I always get extra presents in case of unexpected company. Go ahead and open it," she says.

I do.

"Ohhh," I say feigning excitement, "Anne Murray."

"Well I know you like music," she says, "Enjoy it. I've got the record, and I really like it."

"Ah…thank you Flo'," I say as we give each other bear hugs. She looks at Cliff and says, "You'll get yours over at Mom's."

"I don't know why you buy me things every year Flo," Cliff says. "I don't buy things for anyone."

"Yeah, I noticed that Ebeneezer," she answers. "And I don't know why I buy you things every year either. Now the two of you get out of here because I gotta have another whizz."

∞

It's five-thirty in the afternoon, and December darkness has fallen as we travel back to Lefler. The silence of the surrounding countryside is disturbed only by the sound of the truck. And as we pass the occasional farmhouse, I glimpse small crowds of Christmas celebrants inside each home through their opened living room curtains. Mickey and I have been driving while his eight-track plays Kenny Rogers. I've noticed him glancing at me.

"Do you know something, Old Buddy?" he says turning the music down.

"What's that?"

"I've always admired you."

"You've admired me? Why?"

"Ever since you left six years ago I've thought there's a guy who did it, he had the balls to do what not very many people in this town do. He left. I'd hear Glenn and your Dad talking about when they would hear from you. You would be meeting all kinds of people, and you'd be working in other countries…"

His voice trails off. Then he says, "Most of the people we went to school with still live around here. They're gonna be here till the day they die. I always wanted something more than that, just like you have."

"Careful, Mickey. You know the old saying about the grass being greener…"

"Yeah, but sometimes there's only so much of Lefler I can take. I feel like time's goin' by and there's still so much for me to see and do."

"Why do you stay if you want to leave?"

"My job is here, Mom, Flo and Bill are here…"

"If you keep thinking that way you'll never leave."

"I guess you're right."

We drive on with the sound of that damn bottle rattling back and forth underneath the seat. I can see the lights of Lefler on the horizon as the lonely county-side gives way to more buildings as we approach town.

"Jimbo?"

"Yeah?"

"Do you like bein' a fag?"

"I guess so Mickey," I answer surprised at this question from out-of-nowhere. "It's part of who I am."

He furrows his brow, "I guess I don't understand."

"What do you mean?"

"Well, I mean, why be somethin' that so many people don't like?"

"I guess a lot of people still don't like fags and lots of us still get beaten and even killed for being who we are."

"Have you ever been beat up for bein' a fag?"

I think about that for a moment. "I guess the military gave me a good beating..."

"Then how can you like bein' a fag after all of that?"

"Sometimes I don't. All I'm saying is that once I admitted that I'm gay, there was no turning back..."

"Like you got no choice or nothin'? You're a fag, that's it?"

"Some people say you've got no choice about it, others say you do. I say it's all up to each person whether they're gay or not."

He silently keeps his eyes on the road.

"Jimbo?"

"Yeah?"

"If it's all up to each person, how come you're not straight? Why would you want to be something that people hate and beat up?"

"Okay Mickey, what's with these questions?"

He looks surprised like I've hit him. "I'm just curious man, that's all."

"In spite of everything that's happened to me over this last little while, it's hard for me to explain why I feel the way I do. I guess it's all about accepting who you are and following wherever it might lead you. Yes, sometimes I encounter people who hate me. But other times some incredible doors open for me that would not have done so if I had been afraid of who I am. And I guess that's my point. I've learned it takes an awful lot of courage to be the person you are. There are a lot of people who will hate and despise me for it. I don't know why, but that's true if you're gay, straight, whatever. What I went through with the military, and what I'm going through with my father hurts me a lot. But it's like a friend in Calgary told me, it's other people who have the problem, not me."

Mickey quietly watches the road.

"I suppose I always could have married and started a family, but somehow, somewhere I know these feelings I have for other guys would have kept coming back to me. Then what do I do about them? Do I sneak around on my wife? Then I'm left with nothing but feeling guilty, and possibly a broken home and marriage. All because I was too afraid of what other people would think of me. What good does that do anybody?"

Mickey pulls the truck over to the side of the road and stops. He silently stares straight ahead. I put my hand on his shoulder.

"Are you okay?"

He turns to me. He looks defeated.

I keep my hand on his shoulder, "It's Jimbo. Talk to me."

He bows his head, "I'm a loser, Jimbo," he says quietly.

"Why do you think you're a loser?"

He hesitates, and then says, "I'm that guy you're talking about, and I'm that guy who cheated. I'm that guy who didn't tell anyone, especially Karen. I'm that guy who lost her, my marriage…"

"Hold it," I say, "start from the beginning."

Mickey folds his arms across his chest and looks out the driver window. He's silent like he's thinking about what to say.

"There was this guy…" he falls silent again. He looks at me and bows his head once more.

"Yeah?"

"Back when I was still goin' to the Legion, there was this guy that started comin' in. Frank was his name. I'd never seen him before, but he'd show up once in a while with Bob Ward…you remember Bob, eh?"

"I remember Bob. Was Frank a friend of his?"

"He was a guy Bob did some contracting jobs with." Mickey's silent again.

"Was he from around here?"

"He lived in Portage."

"Well, what happened?"

"Frank was coming into the Legion with Bob, and I got to hangin' out with the two of them whenever I'd see them. We were just hangin' out at first, and then…"

Silence.

"And then what Mickey?"

"Well, we really hit it off, Frank and me. He was funny; he always had me in stitches. He started comin' down to the **Legion** quite a bit. And when he would leave, I'd think about him a lot. Like, I mean I was thinkin' about him all the time."

Silence once more.

"It was like...it was more than just two guys getting' together. I can't explain it. I mean I really wanted to see him all the time. I really wanted to be with him all the time. Fuck I was even jackin' off thinkin' about him. But I couldn't let him know, I didn't want him to think I was some kind of freak..." Startled, he looks at me realizing what he's said, "Oh shit man, sorry."

"That's okay," I assure him, "continue."

"Well, everything was just like that, until the day I started callin' him. I wanted to go up to Portage all the time. I had it really bad for him."

"Did he mind you going over to Portage?"

"No, he always seemed to be glad to see me. And then that night happened."

"That night?"

He takes another deep breath then continues.

"One night I was up there, and he got this new porno video, and we started watching it, I don't know, I guess I was drunk enough that I wanted to see how far I could take whatever this was I was feelin'. I needed to know if he felt the same way about me that I felt about him. I came on to him."

"And what happened?"

"We were watchin' that porno, and I could see him glancin' over to me every once in a while. He was rubbin' his crotch, so I took that as a sign he was interested in doin' somethin'."

"So what did you do?"

"We were both sittin' on the couch, so I ran my hand up and down his leg. I guess I read him all wrong. He got pissed off and threw me out of the house. He told me never to come back. That's when Karen found out."

"That you came on to Frank?"

"No. I mean, I don't know if she ever knew about that. All I know is that was the same night she phoned the Legion for me. Of course, they told her I wasn't there like I said I'd be. And they told her they hadn't seen me in a while. I guess she knew I was having an affair."

"Hold it. How can you say you were having an affair? You just said you weren't doing anything with Frank."

"I wanted to have something with him, Jimbo, that's the point. I was chasing him like I was doing something with him. I sure felt like we were doing something together."

"Do you think maybe you're just feeling guilty for having those feelings in the first place?"

Mickey sighs, "Maybe."

"So did Frank tell Bob or anyone else that you came on to him?"

"I don't know. He never came back to Lefler. But I seen Bob a lot since then and he's never said anything and I ain't heard any talk around town."

"Did you ever tell Karen?"

"No," he sighs, "I lied to her."

"What did you tell her?"

"It doesn't matter. I lied to her and I lost her, and that's why I'm a loser."

We're silent as Mickey slumps into the truck seat. He sighs once more, "I guess I need to know if I really am a fag, Jimbo. If I'm not a fag, then why did I come on to a guy when I was drunk?" Then he slowly turns to me, and our eyes meet. We're silent.

"I really like bein' with women, but I really liked bein' with Frank too. And I really like bein'…"

He withdraws and immediately looks away from me.

"And you really like being what Mickey?"

He sits up and securely wraps his arms around the steering wheel then looks over to me. Our gaze does not shift from each other. I look into his sleepy blue eyes, as he looks deeply into mine.

"I really like bein' with you, Jimbo. I have the same feelin's about you that I did with Frank. I always have."

We silently stare at each other again.

"So if you really want to know if you are a fag, here's a question for you to think about Mickey."

"What's that?"

"Have you ever kissed a guy?"

He looks at me like I've asked him if he's ever had sex with a goat.

80

"No!"

"Have you ever wanted to kiss a guy?"

"Well...I...I," he responds.

Our eyes don't move from each other, and I can feel something inside me building, something drawing me closer to him.

"I mean it, Mickey. Have you ever wanted to kiss a guy right on the lips?" I ask as I move toward him, "...deeply...kiss him like you would a woman. Kiss him with everything you have." I move closer to him still. His eyes grow wide as if asking what the hell are you doing? "...Kiss him like you really mean it, kiss him like he's the most important person in the world to you...kiss him until you think your cock's going to explode because it's so hard?" He slowly lets go of the steering wheel, and I move even closer to him. "...Kiss him like your life depends on it. Kiss him like there's nothing you won't do for him, kiss him like the two of you are going to melt right into each other..."

Our faces are so close together that our noses almost touch, and our eyes don't move from each other. Silent tension. He runs his tongue nervously over his lips. Then, as if a dam has suddenly burst, Mickey presses his lips to mine. I watch him as he closes his eyes and I feel the electricity of his lips, the warmth of his body as he wraps his arms around me, and my cock's instant arousal as our tongues meet. I press my face closer to his. Our mouths and our faces are wet as we lick and kiss each other. A wall has crumbled. I want to climb on top of him and rip his clothes off right here, right now.

Then the cab is flooded with light through the back window as a pair of headlights pulls up behind the truck. The two of us quickly break our embrace and straighten ourselves up as the car door slams, and someone approaches the truck. A tap comes on Mickey's window, and he rolls it down to an R.C.M.P. constable shining a flashlight in the cab.

"You folks all right?" he enquires.

"Ah yeah," Mickey answers awkwardly. "I was just driving my buddy here back home when we got talkin' about some family problems."

"Can I see your driver's license?"

"Sure," Mickey answers fumbling nervously for his wallet. He takes his license from his wallet and hands it to the Constable who shines the flashlight on it.

"Sorry about this guys," the constable apologizes, "but we've had a couple of reports of break-ins around here today. So we have to investigate anything that looks a little out of the ordinary."

"No problem sir," Mickey mumbles stiffly.

"Mind if I have a quick look in the back of your truck?"

Mickey shakes his head no. The constable moves to the back of the truck where I can see his flashlight scan the emptiness of the truck's cargo bed. Mickey watches him through the rearview mirror. Then he glances out of my side of the truck.

"Shit," he mumbles.

I look around out the passenger window. Mickey and I were so into each other we failed to see two houses nearby. I can see silhouettes in the widows of both houses looking in our direction.

"Shit," he mumbles again.

The constable returns to the driver's window.

"Sorry, again guys but I do have to check everything. You haven't had anything to drink today have you?"

"I don't drink no more sir," Mickey answers quietly.

"Good stuff," answers the cop handing Mickey's license back to him. "OK, you two have a Merry Christmas."

"Same to you sir," Mickey responds.

The constable returns to his patrol car, and we can see him pick up the microphone on his car radio and say something into it. He puts it back to its resting place, puts the car in gear and drives away.

Mickey quietly puts the truck in gear and says, "I guess I should be getting' you back to Glenn's place."

I nod my head. He's very quiet as we drive, nervously checking his rear view mirror every once in a while like we're being followed.

"Mickey, is something wrong?"

He's quiet for a moment, "I sure hope that cop didn't see what we were doing," he says. "And those people that were watchin' us in them houses near where we were parked…," his voice trails off again.

I am acutely aware of what he's fretting about. Being back in Lefler for this short period of time has reminded me of what it's like to live here. People around here still don't take kindly to gays. We drive down the quiet streets until we stop outside of Glenn's house.

"Well, it was great seeing you again Mickey."

"Yeah," he says with a self-conscious smile.

"It was great seeing Flo as well," I continue. He nods his head in agreement.

"Thanks for the lift back," I say as I open the cab door to get out.

"Jimbo," he says as he grabs the sleeve of my coat.

"Yeah?"

"I really liked what happened before that cop came, I really did. I'm, I'm just not sure…"

"I understand, Mickey."

His brow furrows, and he still looks around as if searching for something else to say, but nothing is coming.

"I guess I'd better let you get inside," he says.

I get out, "I'll keep in touch then," I say.

"Yeah," he smiles, "do that."

I shut the door and watch as he drives down the street.

∞

There is excited chatter around the Christmas dinner table as Glenn's best friend Matthew, his wife Bonnie and their three kids join us. Matthew and I have always gotten along well. But when I was younger, I had to cover my ears sometimes when he was around because he had no volume control. And after all this time nothing has changed.

It would take a novel to describe Matthew; he's always loved arguments, panics, rows, chaos, and bullshitting. He's like his father that way. According to local legend when his father was much younger, he stood on a hill outside of town, shouted and could be heard three miles away. Knowing Matthew's family for all these years, there's no doubt in my mind that actually happened.

Matthew's always been sports-minded, especially watching it on television. He is also a terrible hypochondriac. From a runny nose, he can instantly develop a full blown case of pneumonia, and he has this peculiar way of referring to himself in the third person. Even while sitting around the table right now, I notice his kids look at him while he's talking and roll their eyes. Mikey ignores him, and Tiffany covers her ears.

"Mommy, my ears hurt," she says to Marny.

"Okay Matthew, enough," Bonnie admonishes. He is immediately quiet. Bonnie's the one who keeps everything in that family together and Matthew would be lost without her.

She's gotten into computers since I left. She says she wants to get in on the ground floor of what will be incredible for business.

"Just you wait," she says continuing her conversation with me, "Twenty years from now there are going to be computers in every home."

"Not at the prices they're charging you for that stuff," Matthew says. "You're paying a fortune for this crap…"

"It's not crap Matthew…"

"It is crap Bonnie. How the hell is something like that going to be useful to people?"

"Matthew, it's going to revolutionize the business world, the entertainment industry, the way things are taught in schools and life as we know it in general."

"Ahh Bullshit! It's just an expensive toy, nothing's ever gonna come of it."

"Matthew. That expensive little toy might one day put you right out of work."

"How's it gonna do that?"

"Your customers might find they can order their supplies directly from the manufacturers instead of going through you."

"That'll never happen," Matthew laughs."

"Well we'll see," smiles Bonnie knowingly.

I've learned to trust that knowing smile of Bonnie's, because whenever it brightens her face you just know that she's going to be proved right about what she's saying.

Except the addition of their five-year-old son Danny who, of course wasn't even born when I left town, I remember their twin daughters Patty and Rhiann as small toddlers and I marvel at how they've grown so quickly since I've been away. I also marvel at how quiet they are. But Matthew's volume probably has more to do with that, than anything else.

My father says nothing to me, but glances at me every once in a while from across the table. I notice something different. He doesn't seem angry. Rather, he seems like he's studying me, at least that's the impression I get. Our eyes meet a couple of times and we both quickly look away. I look over to Matthew so I can **be** distracted from what is happening, and he is prattling on about something to Glenn.

"Did you see Cliff today?" My father calmly asks. I look back at him to see him looking at his plate of food, and then he looks at me.

I'm startled by his sudden interest in what happened to me today. I look over to Glenn who smiles, winks and nods his head as if to say, It's alright.

"Um-eh, yeah," I answer.

"How's he doin'?"

"He's fine. He's fine, Dad," I say as a little reassurance draws a smile across my face.

"I don't know what to make of him since he and Karen split up," he says.

"What do you mean?"

"He's quit drinkin' and that's good. He keeps out of trouble now. But he keeps more to himself. I think he's a pretty lonely guy these days."

"That's what he told me," I answer. I'm amazed. He's talking to me just like he used to before the tribunal. I quickly add, "But in spite of that it seems to me that he's doing okay."

"That boy needs a new life now," Dad continues, "he needs to do somethin' different and it isn't gonna happen here in Lefler."

"Are you suggesting he move away or something, Dad?"

"I don't know, maybe. All I know is he really needs a major change in his life."

"He told me that he sometimes thinks about moving away," I add.

"Why doesn't he just leave then?" asks Bonnie.

"He says his family and job are here."

"Well Lefler's all he's known," Dad says, "he's scared to make any kind of move, that's all. Any bigger place would feel like it's too much."

The phone rings in Glenn's audio room and he goes to answer it. Matthew is once again nattering away as Glenn appears in the doorway of his room and motions me inside. I excuse myself and join him.

"Sparky's on the phone from Calgary," he says leaving the room and handing me the receiver.

"Hello, Sparky?"

"Jim," (he's never called me Jim), "something awful happened," he says with a seriousness I've never heard from him before.

"What's the matter?"

He breathes a sigh, "David Tøllin's dead."

"What!" I'm stunned. "When did this happen?"

"This morning. They found him at his place."

"What happened?"

"Nobody had heard from him in a couple of days. He was supposed to show up for Christmas Eve at his parents place but didn't. I guess he hadn't shown up for work either."

"Really? That's not like David."

"Yeah. So his family and the people at work were trying to phone him, but because there was no answer his brother went around to his place to see what was up. He found him on the living room floor."

"What was the cause of death?"

"He had a brain aneurysm. He collapsed and died. His sister said they had been told he'd been lying there for about twenty four hours."

"When were you talking to his sister?"

"I got a call from her just now, she was asking for you. The family is going through his stuff and she found his address book. They've been calling all of the people he knew to tell them what's happened. I told her I'd let you know right away."

I'm silent. My head is spinning with this news.

"Are you still there?"

"Yeah, sorry Sparky. I…I don't know what to say."

"I understand. Are you still coming back to Calgary the day after tomorrow?"

"Ah…yeah…I guess nobody knows when the funeral will be yet."

"No. His sister left me her phone number and wants you to call her when you get back to town. I'm sorry to have to tell you news like this on Christmas Day."

My shock at this news silences me.

"Are you still there Jim," Sparky asks.

"Oh, yeah, sorry Sparky," I answer.

86

"Are you gonna be okay? I know you guys were best friends."

My head is still spinning as I hear something drop behind me. I turn to see Dad picking up his pack of cigarettes he's dropped on the floor. He looks at me, points at the pack to tell me this is why he entered the room, and starts walking out when he does a double take at me. He furrows his brow in confusion as he looks at me. I guess I look as shocked as the news I'm getting.

"Well, sorry again for telling you this," Sparky continues, "but I thought you would have wanted to know right away."

"Yeah," I answer, "thanks Sparky I'm glad you've called."

"I'll see you the day after tomorrow."

"Yeah. See you then."

I slowly hang up the phone. I'm numb. I slowly turn and look at Dad again who looks at me sympathetically.

"It's bad news isn't it," Dad says quietly.

I quietly nod my head, "One of my best friends has been found dead."

He comes over to me and puts his arms around my shoulders. Feeling him holding me like this causes a tidal wave of emotion to well from within and I'm like a small boy again. The only word that manages to escape my mouth is, "Dad."

∞

It's after 11 PM as I walk with my father through Lefler's silent streets. All around us the Christmas celebrations are winding down. Lights are turned off on the occasional Christmas display, as the inhabitants of Lefler are getting ready to go to bed. The prairie cold seems especially stinging tonight. David is on my mind.

"Thinking about your friend?" Dad asks taking his cigarette pack from his coat pocket.

"Yeah. I don't think it's sunk in yet that he's dead," I say sorrowfully. "It doesn't seem real. I was at his place for dinner last week and he was fine…he was the same old David that I've always known, and now…"

Dad shakes his head, "It always is a shock when someone you care for dies so suddenly." He takes a cigarette out of the pack and offers me one.

"No thanks, Dad, I've quit again."

He shrugs his shoulders, puts the pack back in his pocket then takes out a book of matches and lights up.

"He was a great guy," I continue, "if it weren't for him rescuing me when I needed it I don't know what I would have done."

"You know," Dad says exhaling smoke, "Death is a funny thing. I don't know if I've ever believed in ghosts or not. But when you're mother died, for a long time afterward I thought I saw her everywhere. I know it was all in my head, but it seemed real at the time."

"I guess that's how I feel, Dad. It's like David's all around me, and yet nowhere near me at the same time. But I guess it's like Glenn said earlier, at least I found a true friend in David while he was alive." I'm momentarily silent, "And that's what I'm really going to miss."

Just then a car rounds a nearby corner and slowly comes down the street toward us careful not to slide on the icy road.

"Merry Christmas!" yells a jovial Keith Desjarlais from out of his rolled-down window. Dad and I glance back to the car. Keith has his wife and kids piled into his '67 Olds Cutless, the same one he bought brand new years ago. It slowly passes us like a mini-Sherman tank on their way back home.

"Merry Christmas," we both reply.

We watch the tail lights of the car disappear around a corner and hear the low rumble of the engine fade in the distance.

"Well, speaking of your brother," Dad says taking a deep breath, "he got me aside and gave me supreme shit this afternoon."

"I was afraid that would happen," I say.

He pauses and takes another deep breath, "I, uh, guess I haven't been much of a father to you when you've needed one."

There's a knot in my gut that works its way to my throat. I try to keep it down.

"Dad, I can understand you're being upset over what happened with the tribunal, but what I don't understand was you're not talking to me all this time. Why, Dad? Why did you do that?"

"I don't know. I don't know. That afternoon you told me what happened with your hearing, something snapped. I can't explain it."

"I'd like you to try."

He looks like he's considering his words carefully. "I don't understand these kinds of things. I'm a small town boy, I always have been. Your grandparents took me to church every Sunday, and I was taught that all this…gay stuff…was just plain wrong. In my day it was a shameful thing to be. People like that were to be avoided."

"But, Dad…"

"Let me finish." He pauses, "I guess I always knew you were that way but I always had some hope for you. All the women have always liked you, and you seemed to like them too. I was really proud of you when you graduated from Royal Military College. I knew then you had a chance be a real man. But then we hardly heard from you in six years; and the next thing I know you're gettin' kicked out of the military because you're caught with pictures of you and other guys cornholin' each other, that was too much for me."

"Dad, that was a stupid thing I did and…"

"Just listen," he interrupts, "if you want to do that with other guys in your own private place that's up to you. But havin' someone else there takin' pictures of it, and you keepin' them pictures…where the hell was your head at, boy? What the hell was you thinkin'? What would it have done to your poor Mother? God rest her soul."

"Don't bring Mom into this."

"And why not? Don't you have any respect for her memory?"

"Yes I do Dad, but this is between you and me. Mom has nothing to do with it…"

"She has everything to do with it because we both raised you kids to do right! This…stuff you've gotten yourself into is…is…"

"Is what, Dad?"

"Like I said, it's wrong!"

"Don't I have a right to make up my own mind about my own life?"

"Yes you do as long as it's the right decision."

"And what's the right decision?"

"To get married, to have kids…"

"As far as I'm concerned the decision I made about my life is the best one for me."

89

"Yeah, and look where the hell it got ya", he grunts disapproval as we both continue to walk.

"That had nothing to do with my being gay, Dad. That was a stupid decision I made…"

"Your whole life's been a stupid decision," he snaps.

I stop cold. "Is that how you really feel?" I say angrily. "Because if it is I'll leave Lefler and be out of your life for good."

"Don't you talk to your Father like that," he growls.

"Don't you treat your son like that," I say while my voice cracks with emotion. He looks at me like I've slapped him back. We glare at each other.

"Don't you think I've asked myself where my head was at a million times since it happened? Don't you think I've cursed myself over and over again? Because of what I did I lost everything I'd been working for these past years. Do you know what it feels like to be left alone, Dad?"

"How do you think I felt when your Mother died?"

I'm taken aback. "Do you know what it feels like when you discover all the people you thought you knew suddenly want nothing more to do with you?"

"I know what it feels like to discover that you don't know your own son like you thought you did."

"What do you mean?"

"You know what I'm talking about. All of this business that's gone on with you and the military…that type of stuff only happens to…perverts and misfits…not my son!"

There's a long silence between us. Anger courses through my veins, I feel it pounding in my ears.

"When you told me that you were found guilty on those kinds of charges," Dad continues, "that wasn't the Jim that your mother and I had raised. It's like you've become a stranger to me. I don't know who are you are anymore."

"I'm still your son…"

"You are like hell! No son of mine would be doing these types of things. No son of mine would be parading bare-ass nekkid in front of a camera. And no son of mine would be thrown out of the military for it!"

I feel my hands shake with fury. I want to say something, yell something at him, but I'm afraid of what might **come out of** my mouth. I don't want to blurt out anything that everyone will regret, especially me.

"I see all of that high and mighty education hasn't taught you a damn thing," Dad yells. "You were goin' places in the military boy…"

"Nobody knows that better than me."

"Then why did you screw yourself out of a promising life? You could have learned to be a real man not some pervert!"

That hurt.

"Listen", he says pointing his finger right in my face, "You've had your fun now just you grow up and quit playin' these stupid games! They've gotten you into enough trouble and brought enough shame to this family!"

My anger raises again, "Games? What do you mean games?" I raise my voice to him once more. "I am not playing games and furthermore I am not a shame to the family!"

"You're not doin' this family any favours are ya?" he yells back. "The whole God-Damned town knows about your perverted goin's on! What the hell kind of example are you for your niece and nephew? You've made this family a laughing stock!"

"Dad," I say through gritted teeth, "whether you like it or not I'm gay, and furthermore I like it."

He glares like he's ready to shoot me if he had a gun in his hand.

"Why did you come here?" he growls.

I'm trying to keep my anger in-check, but it's not working. That knot in my gut is in my throat once more.

"Why did you come here?" he repeats.

"I wouldn't have come back at all if Glenn hadn't practically begged me to," I shoot back.

"You selfish bastard!" he yells, "Go the hell back to Calgary and don't bother comin' back! I only have one son and he's a real man!"

Dad turns from me and walks away. I watch him go in silence. He rounds a corner and disappears behind some houses on his way back to his home. The home I grew up in…the home where I'm no longer welcome.

I'm alone on the street, my hands clenched in anger. I look at the surrounding houses just in time to see a number of small parts in the curtains of living room windows pull shut quickly. I'm on public display again…a humiliated faggot once more.

That does it! I've had enough of him putting me down! I've had enough of this humiliation! Right now I hate his guts! No more! I'm going to teach the old bastard a lesson if it's the last fuckin' thing I ever do!

I go after him rounding the same corner he took only moments before. There he is. With each breath I take the anger within me grows. With each step I take toward him the more I focus on only him. My pace quickens. Nothing else matters to me accept my angry determination.

Then both of my feet fly out from under me as I slip and fall backward on the icy sidewalk. I kneel up from the ground only to see that he keeps walking. He doesn't look back. I watch him. The anger still coursing through me leaves me motionless like a hand keeping me still on the icy concrete. The Manitoba cold stings my eyes as my angry frustration causes them to well. One tear, another, a third.

No! Stop this Jim, I think to myself, no crying.

I stop and wipe the tears away. I slowly get up to silently watch him walk further away from me. I'm still focused on him. My heart rate still rapid, and my breathing still quick. Something changes in me. I realize that nothing is going to change between Dad and me, and now that David is gone, my life will never be the same again. I watch Dad's figure grow smaller with each step he takes, and with him, my sense of everything I was. My anger melts to resignation, but with that grows a firm resolve.

"Alright Dad," I say under my breath, "I'm going the hell back to Calgary. I've got a life to live there, and I'm going to live it whether you like it or not.

With newfound determination, I walk back to Glenn's place.

∞

I haven't felt myself all day. I don't feel sick, just out of sorts. This is just as well because even though this is the Easter weekend, I wasn't planning on going anywhere or doing anything. In fact, it's just about midnight on Thursday night and I'm in bed, which is unusual for me at the beginning of a long weekend. I'm usually out with Sparky who's gone out to the club **for the evening,** so he probably won't be back until 2:30 or 3 AM. In the meantime, I'm trying to get to sleep but it's difficult because my mind is racing with all of the changes in my life that have happened since Christmas.

I haven't heard from Dad since then. Glenn has phoned me a few times, and according to him the two of them are having some intense arguments about me. Dad continues to deny me, still claiming he only has one son. Glenn is defending me to the point that he's threatened my father with not seeing his grandkids anymore if he doesn't change his opinions about me. That has only made my father dig in his heels.

I've discouraged Glenn from doing that, "Don't bring the kids into it Glenn. This is between Dad and me."

"No it isn't, it has to do with the family, and I'm not going to stand by and watch him treat my own brother, his son, this way."

"It's not fair to the kids to be used just to make a point to Dad."

"And Dad is being fair to you? He has to learn that we are all the family we have left. He either accepts us all as one family, or he accepts none of us, period!"

"Look, I can't worry about how Dad feels about my life anymore. I've got to live it."

"And I appreciate that, Jimmy, but you're part of this family and for him to try to deny you that is wrong; it's just plain wrong, and I'm not going to let it happen."

They're both equally as stubborn, and I don't see how this is going to change anything. But I've decided to let them go for it because if it wasn't me they'd be arguing about, it would be something else.

I roll over in bed and my thoughts turn to Bert. He's finally living in Calgary, having moved from Edmonton a couple of weekends ago. He's staying with his sister and brother-in-law in the southeast part of the city, and is looking for an apartment so he can have his own space. But in the meantime, he's settling in with his new position at work. It's the same job he had in Edmonton, so this is a lateral move work-wise, but of course he has to get used to his new surroundings. We've been on a few apartment-hunting expeditions together, and one stands out in my mind.

We had been to see this place right downtown and Bert liked it. As we finished viewing the place the manager was called

93

away for a few minutes. We agreed to meet her back outside her office on the main floor. Since we were only on the second floor, we decided to take the staircase down rather than wait for the elevator.

On our way down the stairwell, we had to maneuver around a drunken middle-aged woman on the landing. She was leaning against the wall and could barely stand. She had her shirt off with her boobs hanging out. We both quietly walked by her and, as we were nearing the bottom of the stairs, she started yelling at us.

"GET LOST!" she shrieked as it echoed throughout the stairwell.

We both laughed.

"You're nothin'!" she continued.

"Oh shush," Bert giggled.

"You're fuckin' nothin'!" she continued yelling.

When we saw the manager in the lobby, she questioned us as to what that noise was coming from the stairwell. We told her what had happened and she rolled her eyes and mumbled, "Not again."

She went down the hall to the door leading to the stairwell, and opened it. Bert asked her if she needed any help, and she assured us that she did not as she's had to handle this before. Then she turned her attention to the woman in the stairwell saying,

"Barbra, what have I told you about this?"

The woman suddenly stopped yelling. The manager went into the stairwell and the door closed behind her. Bert and I left the building laughing about it, and he decided not to take the place.

"I don't want neighbours like that," he said.

I roll over onto my back and put my hands behind my head; my thoughts turn to David. It's only been four months since he's died and words cannot describe how much I miss him. I can see his face clearly in my mind. I remember last summer when he took me in while the rest of the world seemed content to throw me aside, especially after the tribunal. Emotionally, the first couple of weeks were hell for me. I was still feeling hurt and betrayed, but David turned out to be a real friend and treated me like a person—a person with feelings. He listened to me when I needed to vent, he held me when I needed to be close to someone, and he was patient with me while I was getting myself together.

94

I remember him as a strong, caring and well-loved man. I recall his funeral when the church was so packed that people had to stand along the walls during the service because there was no more room to sit. His employees loved him, and organized a huge reception at a nearby community center after the service.

I chuckle to myself as I remember that constant horny gleam in his eyes and the sex parties he used to have at his place. For him, sex was not only recreational; it was a religion. At first, I did not want to join in. My emotional state, being what it was, I just wasn't into it. But he was insistent and would not let up on me, telling me that it would be good for me to stay and get into it.

"There's nothing like a good debauch," he would say,"to cure what ails you."

I'm glad I did stay. I met some great guys I would not have otherwise met; guys who usually did not go to the club, or to the steams. These were guys that he knew through his business associations, and I'll never know how he was ever able to talk them out of their clothes and into sex parties for that matter. Many of them were closeted for business reasons, and some were married with kids. But David had that kind of charm.

I'm startled back to reality. I thought I heard something. I listen intently for a few seconds. Nothing. Oh well, I roll over to try to sleep...there it is again...it sounds like somebody knocking on the front door. I'll bet it's Sparky who's forgotten his keys again. I get out of bed and put my housecoat on.

"That dizzy fuckin' queen," I mumble as I turn on the hallway light; go through the living room, turn on the front porch light and push aside the blind that covers the front door window.

My jaw drops as I see Mickey standing on the front doorstep with his old hockey bag resting beside him. I unlock the door and open it.

"What are you doing here?" I smile.

"I told you I'd be out to see you some time," he grins.

"That's right, you did," I answer, "I guess that I didn't really expect that you would actually show up like this."

"I knew I was chancin' it, comin' out here to see you without tellin' you first," he says, "but I wanted to get the hell out of Lefler and surprise ya."

"Well mission accomplished," I say, "come on in."

Mickey comes in and puts his hockey bag on the vestibule floor.

"Here, I'll take your jacket," I say closing the door behind him.

He doffs his coat and hands it to me. Then he removes his boots.

"It's a damn good thing for you that I decided to stick around town for this Easter weekend, or else you would have come out here for nothing," I say as I hang his jacket in the hall closet. I turn and face him. We stand silently smiling at each other for a couple of moments.

"It's good to see you, Mickey."

"It's good to see you too."

We stand close to each other, motionless.

"Well," I say putting my hands on both of his arms, "C'mon in."

He follows me into the living room and I turn on a lamp.

"I'm sorry for getting' you up," he apologizes.

"That's okay, I couldn't sleep anyway. Do you want something to drink?"

"I'll have a pop if you have got it."

"We've got Coke."

"Perfect."

I go into the kitchen and grab a can of Coke from the fridge.

"So how are things in Lefler these past few months?" I yell from one room to the other.

"Same old," he answers as he comes into the kitchen, "nothin' changes in that place, and I don't wanna stay there no more."

"I remember you saying that at Christmas," I say as I hand him the can.

"Oh, thanks," he says. "Well, it's true. Seeing you then got me thinkin' that way."

"So you're thinking that you want to move to the city?"

"Yeah, somethin' like that, maybe even this city," he grins, "all I know is that I've been in Lefler for too long. And besides, movin' here's done you a world of good."

"Hmmm," I say incredulously, "given what's happened to me over this last little while I don't know about that."

"But would you move back to Lefler?"

"No."

"Well, there you go."

"Ok, you've got a point there," I chuckle, "let's go sit down."

We go back into the living room and sit on the couch together.

"Nice place you got here," he says taking a swig from his can of pop and quickly looking around the living room.

"Thanks. So did you take a taxi from the airport?"

"No, I drove out," he says putting his Coke on the coffee table.

"What? You mean the Ford Fiasco actually made it this far?"

"No problem there," he smiles. "Come and see," he says as he gets up, goes to the living room window, pushes back the curtain and points. I look outside to see a brand new black 1980 Ford pickup parked in front of the house.

"Ain't she a beaut?" he exclaims.

"Yeah! When did you get that?"

"Back in January," he smiles. "This truck lot in Brandon was having a sale of last year's models, so I figured now was just as good a time as ever to get a new one."

"So," I say, "after having bought it, you decided to take the new truck for a road trip and you just happen to end up here?"

"Well, I went to see Flo' last night, and was tellin' her how I wanted to come out to see you."

"Oh yeah," I say knowing what kind of response that might elicit from her, "and what did she say?"

"She said, 'Quit talkin' about it, go home, pack some things, and get the Jesus out there to see Jimmy before I gives ya a good swift hoof up the backside!' So here I am."

"Well," I say running my hand up his arm, "I'm glad you're here."

He smiles at me and says, "Me too."

In the silence, a delicious sexual tension rises between us. We pull each other closer.

"Ya know," he says quietly, "I've been thinkin' about you a lot,"

"Yeah?"

He nods his head.

"I…I've been thinkin' about what happened back on Christmas Day, ya know, what you said to me in the truck."

"Oh yeah? What did I say to you?"

"Remember you asked me if I could ever kiss a guy like I could spend the rest of my life with him?"

I nod my head and he leans forward and presses his lips to mine. I put my arms around him he wraps his arms around me. Then he breaks our kiss and says, "I just did."

"Well, I approve."

"I'm glad you do."

"C'mon," I whisper gently taking his hand, "let's go to bed."

He quietly follows me into the bedroom.

∞

The airport is busy. I scan the waiting crowd at the Arrivals looking for any glimpse of Glenn. I can't believe this is happening. Mickey leaves to drive back to Lefler the day before yesterday, and I get a call from home about what's happened yesterday morning. Had the call come sooner, I could have driven back with Mickey. But here it is Wednesday morning and I'm at the Winnipeg airport worried sick. All I can think about is Dad. Why didn't things at Christmas turn out differently? We almost were father and son again. If only I had tried harder to understand his point of view. I see Glenn. He waves when he sees me. I walk quickly over to him and we hug.

"How is he, Glenn?"

"I don't know if he's gonna make it or not, Jimmy," he sighs, "the doctor says in his present state he could have another stroke anytime, and that could be fatal.

My body droops. I have a sinking feeling of helplessness. My father could die at any moment and there's not a damn thing I can do about it.

"If he gets through this," Glenn continues, "the doctor says he'll need special care for the rest of his life."

"That'll be tough for him to deal with," I say as I shake my head sadly.

"It'll be tough for us all to deal with, Jimmy. You know what he's like."

"Is he conscious?"

"Yeah."

"Can he speak?"

"Barely, out of the right side of his mouth. The left side of his body is paralyzed."

"When was he brought here to Winnipeg?"

"The ambulance pretty much brought him here right away."

"Who found him?"

"Me," he answers. "By coincidence I had to go over to get something from his place. I knocked a couple of times and, when he didn't answer, I let myself in. That's when I found him on the bedroom floor. He couldn't move and could barely speak. I phoned the ambulance."

Silence.

"How long had he been laying there Glenn?"

"The doctor says he was probably there about six hours."

We're silent for a few moments. I don't know what to say or do.

Then Glenn says, "You'd better get your luggage, and we can get going."

I go over to wait at the baggage carousel, and I'm in deep thought. I barely notice all of the excited people that surround me as they crane their necks looking for their suitcases. More than ever, at this moment I just want to be with Dad.

I see one of my pieces of luggage go by on the carousel. I take it off and immediately I see the other one. I take them both and rejoin Glenn. We quietly go out to Glenn's car, put my bags in his trunk and we drive out of the airport parking lot. We head into the city.

"I've rented a hotel room for a few days," Glenn says not taking his eyes from the road. "It'll be too far to make the trek every day to Lefler and back. We'll drop your stuff off there and then go see Dad in the hospital."

"Are Marny and the kids here too?"

"They'll join us on the weekend."

Glenn is withdrawn as we eventually come into the downtown area and pull in front of the hotel. We retrieve my luggage from the trunk of the car and go up to the room. I set my luggage on the floor.

Without warning Glenn puts his arms around me and his eyes well, "Jimmy," he sobs as he holds me close; "I really need you right now. We can't lose him, not Dad."

For the first time since we were kids I see my brother weeping. The two of us hold each other closely and cry.

∞

I sit beside the bed with my hand resting on his arm and silently watch him while he's sleeping. I feel like I've been here all day though it's only been a couple of hours since we arrived at the hospital. Glenn stands at the end of the bed quietly staring at him. His eyes are still red from our earlier cry back at the hotel, and mine still feel heavy and sore.

An oxygen mask covers Dad's mouth and nose and two clear plastic tubes run from underneath the bed sheets. One of them runs from an intravenous bottle on a stand beside the bed, and the other tube is connected to the top of a large glass bottle on the floor partially filled with urine.

I watch Dad and remember Christmas. I remember the words exchanged between the two of us. I remember how hurt and angry I felt. Then I think about Christmases from when Glenn and I were kids. Christmas was always Dad's favourite time of year. He'd take time off work and decorate the outside of our house with numerous strings of blinking lights, and a few floodlights just for effect. Ours was always one of the brightest lit in Lefler that time of year. Then I remember a number of Christmases when he packed us in the car and we'd go to our grandparents' place in Thunder Bay.

That sparks memories of other trips we took as a family. I think of the time he surprised us all when we went to Expo 67 in Montreal. None of us suspected he had planned this trip, paid for everything, and arranged for a hotel room for the family. I remember how excited we all were when he told us, he had a twinkle in his eyes and a broad smile on his face. His greatest pleasure in life was seeing us smile.

Then I remember how Glenn and I tried to be strong for Dad when Mom died. It was Dad, however, who was strong for us. But I recall the nights when I'd be lying in bed listening to Dad crying in his bedroom as he repeated Mom's name.

I focus on him once more, his closed eyes, the constant beep...beep...beep of the heart monitor, the sound of his breathing through the oxygen mask, and I'm frightened. Is this where our road ends Dad?

"Why don't you take a break?" says Glenn as he comes over and puts his hand on my shoulder.

"No, Glenn, I'm okay."

"Have a break, Jimmy. It'll do you good to go for a coffee or something. I'll look after things here."

I do feel tired as I nod my head in agreement. "I'll be in the cafeteria," I say quietly. "Come and get me if there is any change."

Glenn smiles, "You'll be the first to know."

I leave the room and walk down the corridor. Just as I approach the nurses' station, I see him. It's Mickey. He's standing with his hands in his jeans pockets, his denim jacket opened to reveal a black t-shirt with the words: A Half-Breed Ain't Half Bad emblazoned on it. And as always that damn black Ford cap on his head. He looks lost when he spots me and a sympathetic grin draws across his face.

"Wow, that was a fast trip from Calgary," I say.

"I gun-booted it across Saskatchewan and just got in last night. I had to come when I heard what happened," he says. "How's your Dad?"

"We don't know yet Mickey."

He bows his head in sadness and his eyes sweep the floor.

"Thanks for being here, Mickey, but why didn't you just come down to the room?"

"I only arrived a couple of minutes ago and I guess I was psyching myself up to go down there."

"Psyching yourself up?"

"I don't like hospitals and I'm bad in these kinds of situations, Jimbo. I never know what to say or do."

"Showing up is all you have to do, Mickey," I assure him, "and I'm glad you did." We smile at each other momentarily. "I'm going for a coffee in the cafeteria, come join me."

∞

I quietly stare into the almost-empty white coffee mug I hold between my hands. A small white plate sits to my side with half a date bran muffin lazily leaning to one side. Mickey sits across from me.

"Thanks again for being here Mickey, it means a lot to me."

"That's what buddies are for."

I smile and nod my head.

"So, what's the news from Lefler," I ask.

"Same as usual," Mickey says. "Although I got back to find out that Flo' had to put her cat down while I was in Calgary."

"Bennie?"

"Yeah. She was pretty torn up about it."

"It seems like she's had Bennie forever."

"Damn near sixteen years."

"How's Flo' now?"

"Gettin' on with it. Besides she still has George. But he keeps lookin' for Bennie wonderin' where she's gone. Flo' sends her love to you and Glenn, by the way and she hopes your dad will be fine."

"Tell Flo' that I appreciate that, Mickey," I smile.

We're momentarily quiet.

"You know," Mickey says solemnly, "after my father died it was your dad who included me in with a lot of your family plans."

"Yes, I remember."

"Remember that time he took me along with you guys to Expo in Montreal? I'll never forget that."

"I was thinking about that earlier," I chuckle, "that was a fun trip wasn't it?"

Mickey smiles at me again, "That's the trip we became really good buddies."

I smile. We're silent once more.

"Mickey?"

"What?"

"What's my problem?"

"What do you mean?"

"I've been thinking about something my friend Bert said to me a couple of weeks ago. He asked me what happened to all of the training I did at Royal Military College."

Mickey looks confused. "What about it," he asks.

I lean forward to him and say, "All that training taught me how to strategize, it taught me how to think on my feet, how to treat people in my command, and how to control my emotions so I can better handle crisis situations. But guess what?"

"What?"

"Those things don't always work in the real world, especially when it involves somebody close to you. Emotions just get in the way and all that training means nothing."

Silence.

"When Dad and I had our big blow-up on Christmas Day I told myself, no more crying. But try as I might, Mickey, it's hard for me to control my emotions these days."

I pause for a moment. I can see by the look on his face that Mickey doesn't know what to say.

"Mickey."

"Yeah."

"Do you believe in karma?"

He has a blank look on his face, "Who the hell is that?"

I laugh.

"What's so funny?"

"You," I chuckle.

Embarrassed, he looks down to the table and then he looks over to me.

"Jimbo."

"Yeah?"

He struggles to say something to me.

"Well, like, I know this probably ain't the best time to say this…but, like, are you gonna be stickin' around for very long?"

"As long as I can. Why?"

"Well, like, while I was drivin' here this mornin', I got to thinkin'…Like, when you're ready to go back to Calgary…"

"Yeah?"

"Can I drive ya back?"

"To Calgary?"

He nods his head.

"Mickey. Why you would…"

"It's no problem. Really," he quickly adds.

"Why are you bringing this up now?"

"Truth is Jimbo…I…I wanna go back to Calgary with you."

"Look Mickey, I'm not even thinking about Calgary right now. I've got Dad lying upstairs and I may lose him. There's a lot going on right now."

"I know this ain't the best time to bring it up…"

"This could have waited."

We're both silent.

"Sorry," Mickey apologizes, "I, I didn't mean to…"

"No, no, I'm sorry, Mickey. I didn't mean to use that tone of voice with you. All I can tell you for now is that, when it comes time for me to go back to Calgary, of course we can go together."

We're silent once more.

Then I look at my watch and say, "We should be getting back up to his room."

He nods his head, and we get up from the table and leave the cafeteria.

∞

We return to my father's room to find Glenn sitting on a chair at Dad's side, he glances at us as we enter and smiles. He motions me over.

"Dad," he says, "guess who's here to see you?"

I go over and stand beside the bed.

"No, over here," Glenn motions to me getting up from the place where he sits.

"He can't see on that side," he says as I come around the bed and take Glenn's place in the chair.

"Hi Dad," I smile not knowing what to expect.

104

My father smiles a half-smile and reaches for me. I take his hand and he says something. His speech is so garbled I don't understand him.

"I'm sorry Dad, I didn't catch that," I say.

He attempts to say it again.

"Sorry Dad," I repeat, "I don't understand."

He snatches his hand from mine. He lays his head back on his pillow, closes his eyes and breathes a heavy sigh. I feel Glenn's hand on my shoulder. I look up at Glenn and we both look back at my father in silence.

"He was getting pretty frustrated when I was trying to talk with him before you guys came back," he says quietly.

We're silent again.

"The doctor says that he will probably regain some of his abilities," Glenn continues, "but we'll have to wait and see what those will be."

I look over to Mickey, and he looks back to me. There's concern in his eyes but I also see tenderness as he looks at me.

"So he might be like this for the rest of his life," Mickey asks moving closer to the bed.

Glenn shrugs, "It's really hard to say, Mickey…"

Then Dad starts snoring.

Glenn looks at him sadly for a moment then says, "He drifts off to sleep an awful lot too. Let's go out to the hall where we can talk without disturbing him."

As we file into the hall a middle-aged woman is on her way into his room. She is wearing a white smock and has a pleasant smile on her face.

"Oh," says Glenn, "Doctor Weyburn, this is my brother Jimmy and a close family friend, Cliff." We all shake hands and exchange our greetings. "Dr. Weyburn is looking after Dad while he's here," Glenn continues.

"If you just excuse me a few moments, I'm going to check on your father right now," she says. "Then I'll come back and talk to you.

"He's dozed off again," Glenn warns.

"In his present state," she says, "he'll do that a lot. Why don't you guys go down to the lounge? I'll be down to join you shortly."

She enters the room and we silently walk down to the lounge at the end of the hall. It's a big room with huge windows; which bring in lots of daylight. The afternoon sun streams in brightening the room even more. Children's toys are scattered in front of a toy box in one corner of the room. While in another, a colossal television is playing a soap opera. Mickey and I sit on a couch together and Glenn takes a seat on a brown leather chair facing us.

There's a galley-type kitchen across from us were a couple of young high-school aged girls in striped aprons are replenishing the fridge with juice, cream and milk and refilling the coffee urn, while setting out assorted packaged cookies and sweets.

"Do you guys want a coffee," Glenn asks.

"No thanks," I answer.

"Sure," says Mickey. The girls tidy up the counter area and are leaving as Glenn and Mickey go over to the coffee urn.

I silently survey the room. A young man and woman are sitting on a couch on the far side of the room talking with an old woman who is dressed in a housecoat, and attached to a pole and drip. They talk quietly.

A well-dressed, middle-aged man stands looking out of one of the windows with his hands in his pants pocket. He has a worried look on his face. Just then Dr. Weyburn enters the lounge. She comes over to where I sit, pulls a chair in front of the couch and smiles at me.

"Your father's still asleep," she says, "and right now that's a good sign."

"How do things look doctor?"

"I'll be honest with you," she says, "There's a good chance that your father could have another stroke."

I breathe a heavy sigh as Glenn and Mickey return to where we're sitting.

"We're keeping a close eye on him, but he can't swallow, so he can't have any solid food or drink any liquids orally."

"Dad's a stubborn man, he's going to want his food," Glenn says settling on a chair beside the doctor.

"And he'll probably have a tantrum if he can't get it," I add.

The Doctor shakes her head and says, "If he attempts to eat or drink anything there's a good possibility that he'll choke. You probably noticed the little pink swabs by the side of his bed?"

106

Glenn and I nod.

"Whenever your father is thirsty, dip one of those swabs in a cup of water and wet his lips only, don't let him suck on it. Patients tend to want to suck on them."

"He might choke on that too?" Glenn asks.

Dr. Weyburn nods her head.

"But how's he gonna get food?" Mickey asks.

"We'll probably use a feeding tube so he can get his nourishment," Dr. Weyburn responds."

"If he does have another stroke," I ask, "would it be fatal?"

"It could very well be fatal, Jim."

Glenn and I look at each other in silence again.

∞

As I write this, it's been a couple of days since I've been in Winnipeg. Marny and the kids will be here in a couple of days, but Mickey I are leaving for Calgary first thing tomorrow morning. I hate to leave Glenn and Marny alone to deal with this, but I have to go back.

Glenn and I have been spending all of our time over at the hospital, taking time off only for going back to the hotel to sleep or time off for something to eat. We still can't understand Dad when he tries to speak, so his frustration level is to the point where he constantly curses at the nurses when they are trying to help him. It's a funny thing, when he tries to speak, we can't understand him, but when he curses it's very clear what he's saying. But it's frustrating for Glenn and me too, because it seems he saves his all-out swearing and his tantrums for when we're trying to help. I try to be very understanding of what he must be going through, but it is very difficult. The only one he seems to behave for is Dr. Weyburn.

When he's not expressing his frustration he's still dozing off a lot. Then other times when he's awake, he's hungry and quite vocal about it. This morning he got so frustrated that he ripped out his intravenous in his quest for real food. He doesn't want to accept the fact that for now, he cannot take anything orally. He wants his ground chuck and potatoes and he wants it now. I've been doing a lot of thinking of these past couple of days, and I've come to a conclusion...

(Later that day)

Glenn and I sit in a restaurant not far from the hospital. Dad dozed off again so we decided this was a good time to go for some lunch. Glenn slowly eats what's in front of him, and I pick at my food, having barely touched it. The staff has a local radio station playing in the background. The song Bette Davis Eyes by Kim Carnes is just finishing as the announcer tells everyone to stay tuned for the news headlines coming right up after the commercial.

"You're quiet," Glenn says to me.

I shrug my shoulders, "What's there to say?"

"That's true," Glenn sighs.

"Glenn, have we already lost Dad?"

"What do you mean?"

"Is this going to be his permanent state of being, or will he somehow recover?"

"And now here's what's making the news this hour," a voice says on the radio playing over the restaurant's speaker system. "Solidarity is allowed to broadcast weekly programming and statements on Polish TV and radio..."

"I wish I knew the answer to that," Glenn answers. "In any case, Dad is going to need help for the rest of his life depending on how much he recovers, if he does at all."

"...The U.S. Navy accepts responsibility for last week's collision of a nuclear sub with a Japanese freighter," the voice continues on the radio, "The Reagan administration agrees to pay damages to families of slain Japanese crew members. Meanwhile Cuban-American veterans commemorate the Bay of Pigs at ceremonies held in Miami, Florida."

We're silent while the radio continues in the background...

"Soviet President Leonid Brezhnev calls for non-military use of space following the successful flight of U.S. orbiter Columbia. And a funeral service for boxing great Joe Louis was held at Caesar's Palace, Las Vegas today; Muhammad Ali, Frank Sinatra, Sammy Davis, Jr. and Jesse Jackson were among those present. For details on these and other stories stay tuned at the top of the hour to Winnipeg's best rock!"

"I guess this means we'll have to put Dad in a home or something," I say.

Glenn adds, "Dr. Weyburn did tell me that these days they are allowing some patients to go home and be looked after by their families. But that requires a lot of changes to the household."

We're silent once more while Phil Collins sings I Missed Again on the radio.

"Glenn?"

"Yeah?"

"I've been thinking a lot over these last couple of days, and I've come to a decision."

"Yeah? About what?"

"I'm moving back to Manitoba."

Glenn looks like he can't decide whether to be ecstatic or concerned about what I'm saying.

"Ah...look, Jimmy, you just can't up and leave Calgary, what would you do for work? You know the employment situation is not good around Lefler. You're living in the best place in the country right now as far as jobs go."

"I know that Glenn, and I'll find something to do here. Besides, I can't lay the entire responsibility for Dad's care on you and Marny."

Glenn rests his elbow on the table and cups his hand around his chin like he's thinking about what I'm saying.

"Jimmy, I appreciate that, and it would sure be good to know that you would be there for us if we need you. But you should think more about this one. That's one hell of a move you're talking about, and we still don't know what's going to happen with Dad. He might not be able to come back home."

He continues to eat.

"In any case Glenn, I want to be here. I can't help but remember what you've said to me on the phone."

"What did I say?"

"You told me that we're the only family we've got left. We're in this together."

Glenn smiles. "Yeah, I remember saying that, but like I said, think about this a bit more before you decide to make a move."

We're silent. Phil Collins is still singing, "Did I miss again? Oh, I missed again, Oh-ho."

The walls of the hallway are sterile cinder block white as I enter the Calgary Remand Centre. I approach a glass-enclosed booth, and I'm asked for identification by the older looking guard sitting inside.

"What's your business here?"

"I'm visiting someone."

The guard glowers at me with his spectacles sitting precariously off the end of his nose.

"Yeah," he gruffly asks. "And who are you visiting?"

"Bert Gilhius."

"You related to Gilhius?"

"No."

"Are you bringing anything into the Remand Centre?"

"No."

He looks at me again, "You're sure?"

"Yes," I say as I slide my birth certificate and social insurance card under the glass to him. He picks them up and inspects them.

"Do you have any picture ID?"

"Just my old Armed Forces ID."

"How old is it?"

"About a year."

"Let me see it."

I reach into my wallet and pull out a plasticized card with my photo, name, rank, birthplace and date, religion and serial number on it. I hand it to him and he examines it. "Lieutenant huh?"

"Yes."

A smirk cuts across his mouth as he reaches to a small wall rack at his side to get a card for me. "I was a Sergeant for many years."

"When did you retire?"

"A couple of years ago."

"Who were you with?"

"Royal Canadian Horse Artillery…Petawawa. Here you go, Lieutenant," he says handing me a yellow card with a black V on it.

I take the card and say, "It's been a while since I've been called that."

I sign in and the guard lets me move on. "Carry on, Sergeant," I half-grin to him as we're leaving. He half-grins and gives me a mock salute and says, "I'll send a guard to bring Gilhius down for you."

"Thanks," I say as I move on.

In front of me, two guards are standing by a metal detector. One of them directs me to empty my pockets into the little baskets sitting on the small table in front of the machine. I do so and walk through the detector and it beeps.

One of the guards says, "Stand over there and put your arms out to either side of you.

I do what I'm told. The guard passes a wand over me. It beeps as it is moved over my watch. I take off my watch as instructed and the wand is passed over me again. It doesn't beep this time so the guard says, "Okay you put these back in your pocket."

I put everything back into my pockets and put my watch back on.

"He'll take you to the Visitors Area," the guard says pointing to a younger guard standing nearby. I follow him up a short hallway to a large, austere, florescent-lit area. Four guards with walkie-talkies watch from behind a counter at the one end of the open space facing a couple of glass-enclosed small rooms.

I noticed a young man and an older woman sitting in one of them, their voices are slightly muffled but I can still hear them. The young man is speaking quietly to the older woman as she sobs. I can't quite make out what he is saying to her but I can hear clearly as the woman cries out, "NNOOOOO!!!"

"Look Mom you've gotta listen to me…," the young man scolds, then he speaks quietly again.

"You can wait in there," the young guard says pointing to the other room. There's nothing but a table and three chairs inside of it.

I go in and sit behind the table silently surveying the room. The white painted, cinder block walls and the glare of the fluorescent light from the ceiling makes it look twice as stark and sterile as it is. The guards-on-duty closest to me watch as if everybody is suspect of something in here.

Just then a guard escorts Bert into the room. A smile draws across Bert's face when he sees it's me. He sits across the small table from me.

"It's so nice to see a friendly face," he says.

"Bert what the hell happened?"

"I don't know one minute I'm talking to this good-looking guy I met at the bar, the next thing I know I've got handcuffs on me and I'm brought here in a ghost car."

"Start from the beginning," I say.

Bert sighs, "I went to The Parkside the other night, I was only going to have a couple of drinks then go home." He's momentarily silent.

"So what happened?"

"I'm there for a few minutes when I see this good-looking guy smiling at me. I smiled back at him and waved him over to the table."

"And then what?"

"After we talked for about, I don't know, twenty minutes to half an hour, he invited me across the street to the park to smoke a joint with him." Bert pauses a moment. "I can't believe this is happening to me," he sighs.

"So you went out to smoke a joint and what happened then?"

"We're smoking a jay, when this guy shows up out of nowhere. He says hi to us and starts talking to Lyle."

"Lyle?"

"The guy I met in the bar. Anyway, this guy is talking to Lyle like he knows him, so I figure they're friends. I've got the joint and I pass it to this guy. Next thing I know he has my hands behind my back and is slapping a pair of cuffs on me. Then this third guy appears out of nowhere and I'm being told I'm under arrest for trafficking..."

"Trafficking? How can they arrest you for that? You weren't selling the stuff."

"Unfortunately," Bert sighs, "I've found out that under Canadian law the mere act of passing a jay to another person is considered trafficking. FUCK! It wasn't even my joint!"

"Did you tell them that?"

"Yeah, but they wouldn't believe me."

"Did they arrest Lyle too?"

"He fucked off as soon as he saw what was happening. These two cops didn't even go after him."

"So obviously these guys were plainclothes policemen."

"Yeah, and I don't think it helps that Lyle and I were two guys in a known gay cruising area."

"Do you think that will work against you?"

"I don't know, it could."

"Have you talked to a lawyer?"

"Yeah."

"What does he have to say?"

"It doesn't look good because not only was I was caught with the joint in my hand, but I was passing it to a police officer."

I'm momentarily silent. "What kind of a sentence might you be facing?"

"Six to eighteen months. I suppose that depends on how conservative the judge is."

"When's your trial date?"

"It hasn't been set yet. Fuck, Jim, I don't want to go to jail! I don't deserve this!"

Hearing the confusion in his voice and looking into his frightened eyes make it more difficult for me to tell him what I have to. "Bert," I say hesitantly.

"Yeah," he answers weakly.

"I've got something to tell you that you're not going to want to hear."

That startles him, "What is it?"

I'm hesitant again. "I'm moving back to Manitoba."

"What? When?"

"The day after tomorrow."

Bert sits back in the chair, folds his arms across his chest. His face drops and he bows his head like a man who has lost his last hope.

"My father's going into a care home. He's finished his initial recovery in the hospital. I should be there for him...and for my brother. I can't let Glenn do this by himself, especially if he's making the regular trip from Lefler to Winnipeg."

Bert sadly nods his head in agreement.

"I understand," he says, "I understand you wanting to be closer to your dad, and rightly so, you should."

I'm silent.

Bert sits forward and rests his elbows on the table with his hands folded in front of his mouth. A tear streams down his cheek.

"I've been thinking a lot about this over the last few months while I've been flying back and forth to Manitoba," I continue to explain, "and I think this is the best thing I should do for now."

Bert silently nods his head in agreement.

"Bert I'll always be fond of you. I'll always have great memories of what we've had, and I'd still like to be friends."

We're both silent.

"So," Bert sighs, "you're moving back to Lefler."

"No. Winnipeg. Glenn found a really great care home there. I can be close to my father, and Glenn and his family can stay with me whenever they are in town visiting him."

Bert stares silently down at the table. This moment of silence seems like forever.

"I'm going to miss the hell out of you Jim. It's too bad you're leaving, we could have had something really good together."

Then he takes a deep breath and says, "What does it matter though? I'm probably going off to jail for the next little while, and even if you stayed here, I probably wouldn't be seeing much of you for God-knows-how-long anyway."

We're silent again.

Then he says, "I think it's good that you're going back to help your family in their time of need." Then he says, "I really hope your father will be okay, somehow, and I really hope that someday you can come back to Calgary."

I smile at him and nod my head.

One of the guards knocks then opens the door and says, "Five minutes to count Gilhuis!" Then he shuts the door and goes back behind the counter.

"Count?" I ask, "What's that?"

Bert looks at me sadly and says, "That means you have to go. They stick us back in our cells just to make sure we're all still here," he says with a sigh. "They do this to us about three or four times a day."

We're momentarily silent again.

"Bert, I won't forget you."

"Jim, I sure as hell will never forget you. Promise that you'll write to me?"

I smile sadly and tell him I will. I slowly get up from the table. I look into Bert's eyes wanting to say something, anything that won't sound trite or superficial. But what do I say at a moment like this? I want to kiss him, to hug him, but I don't dare, not in here.

As if reading my thoughts Bert says, "You don't have to say anything. Just go. You have a life to live."

I bow my head and leave the room. I open the door I look back to Bert. He has a sad but stoic look in his eyes.

"Goodbye, Jim."

My voice cracks as I say, "Goodbye, Bert." I turn and walk through the door.

I feel overwhelming sadness. It's strange where time brings everybody. I think of my life and twists and turns it's taken over this past year and a half. I think of Bert, my father, Glenn, Bryn and Marcel, the military and the tribunal. I think of Mickey who has made a special trip out from Manitoba and is at my place packing some boxes for me. I think of how every change in my life seems to be more dramatic and comes at me more quickly. Somehow though, I seem to muddle through those changes and manage to carry on.

I don't know what these next years are going to bring, but I can tell you this much, I'll conquer every single one of them. This I promise myself.

∞

I wake up and look at the surroundings. I'm not sure what time it is, but outside I can hear the occasional muffled roar of transport trucks as they head down the highway to parts unknown. It was pretty late when we left Calgary yesterday, so we've spent the night at a motel outside of Swift Current.

Mickey sleeps beside me; his rhythmic breathing and occasional snort make me chuckle to myself. Mickey and I are going to move in together when we get to Winnipeg. Once we find a place, he's going back to Lefler to pack up some of his stuff and get his place ready to sell.

We've let Glenn and Marny know about our plans. Marny's happy and Glenn's ecstatic by the fact I'll be closer to home. Their kids, Mikey and Tiffany are excited their Uncle Jim is coming back to Manitoba to live, and Glenn told me on the phone yesterday that Dad's looking forward to having me back in Manitoba. I'm happy the gap between Dad and I seems to finally be closing.

Dad doesn't know about Mickey and me, but I suppose he'll figure it out soon enough. And I'll find out if my returning to Manitoba is a mistake or not. But my gut instinct tells me this is exactly what I need at this point in my life. I need to be around the people I grew up with, the people who know me like nobody else in the world.

The rude, yellow light shining from outside of our motel door floods through the crack in the curtains making a strip of a light across the otherwise darkened ceiling. I look over to the window to see pale daylight blue peeking through the crack in the curtain beckoning me to take a look outside. I hear the muffled thunder of another truck down the highway outside. I get out of bed stark naked, go over to the window and kneel on a black Naugahyde chair underneath it. I rest one elbow on the back of the chair and push aside the curtain a bit with my other hand to look out on the awakening prairie world. Cliff's new Ford sleeps out front of our room with my stuff in the back covered and tied down with a blue tarp. I see other vehicles sleeping quietly along the length of the motel.

The entire sky is cloudless and pale blue mixes with the various shades of gold that cover the rolling hills of southwestern Saskatchewan. I see glints of the rising sunlight sparkling off the windshields of passing vehicles. In the distance I can see a lone communications tower flashing its strobe lights against the oncoming day.

Beyond this parking lot is the highway. It's relatively quiet save for the few who've decided they're getting an early start on things and already glide along its blacktop. On the other side of the highway a truck stop is serving early morning breakfast to waking customers. Another transport truck, a light show on eighteen wheels roars past.

Soon it will be time to get up and get back on the road. I watch as clouds of crows wing their way from east to west as the day comes alive. I rest my chin on my hands as I drink this whole scene in.

Over six years ago I left Lefler because I wanted something more than it could offer me. I went to Royal Military College, did a couple of tours of duty overseas and up north, met a whole lot of great people and had a lot of great sex. I reflect on how my life is about to come full circle.

I further reflect on all of the people I've known in the last six years. I think of Marcel and Bryn. I know the tribunal was my fault, and I know those in charge sent Bryn to Halifax, and I still can't help but feel a little bitter at the whole scenario. But what's done is done and I can't change the past. That episode will remain my biggest regret.

My thoughts turn to David, and how I still miss him. I'll always love him. He was one of the few people who would have anything to do with me after the tribunal. He was my angel when I really needed one.

I chuckle as I think of my crazy roommate Sparky. He has promised me he will make my life miserable by keeping in touch with me. I know we will keep in touch, because I have this crazy feeling that someday I will be taking Mickey back to Calgary to live. Sparky is one guy I never want to lose touch with. As well, I think of our neighbour André and Mrs. Kwiatkowski. I'm going to miss his constant praise of Lech Welesa, and his stories of growing up in Poland during the war. He has sent along six bottles of his fantastic homemade wine with me to deliver to Glenn with a message, and that is for the two of us to keep in touch with him.

And then I think of Bert. He told me that he loved me and wanted to spend his life with me. I suppose I could have loved him, eventually. He was a great companion, and a very caring man. I'm certainly fond of him, but I didn't love him. I felt so helpless when I visited him in the Remand Centre. What could I have possibly done to help him out? I hope one day I do see him again, but I have to concern myself with what is happening with my life right now. I told him I will write, and I will. We'll see what the future has in store.

I'm startled by Mickey's sudden, "Hey babe," as he touches my butt. "Sorry," he whispers, "didn't mean to scare ya."

117

"It's okay," I answer. Mickey puts his arm around me as I make some room for him on the chair. He crouches beside me with one leg on the floor.

"Ain't that a neat picture," he says pointing to the scene before us. I put my arm around him, smile and nod my head in agreement. He rests his head on my shoulder and I rest my head against his. We silently look out on the new day.

"I'm glad you're comin' back," Mickey says turning to me.

"Me too," I answer as I pull him closer to me.

"Babe?"

"What?"

"I've never lived in a city before, what do you think we'll do in Winnipeg?"

"I'm sure that we'll figure something out."

"Think your dad will be pissed off when he finds out about us?"

"It's hard to say Mickey. I like to think he won't be, but you never know."

"Oh," says Mickey sounding disappointed and looking back out the window.

"I guess by tonight we'll be there," I say.

"That's right," Mickey smiles.

Silence.

"Babe?"

"Yeah?"

"Are we really ready for this?"

"Ready for what?"

"Us, together."

"You having second thoughts Mickey?"

"No, but there's people that aren't gonna like it."

"I've never known that to stop you from doing anything before."

He smiles and nods his head. "Well…I guess it won't be like we'll be holdin' hands in public or nothin'," he says.

I chuckle and draw him closer to me.

"Who'd have thought when we were kids that we'd end up together," Mickey smiles.

"Who'd have thought," I smile back.

He kisses my cheek and moves away from the window. He turns on a lamp beside the bed. Then he turns on the small radio on the nightstand and starts dialling through the stations. He stops when he hears The Eagles singing Take It To The Limit.

"Ahh that's it," Mickey says as he turns down the volume to barely audible and crawls back beneath the sheets.

"C'mon," he says to me, "it's still pretty early. Let's lie down a little longer before we have to get back on the road." He turns out the light.

I move away from the window and join him in bed.

"Hey," Mickey smiles, "remember this song?"

"Yeah, takes me back home," I say as I crawl under the sheets beside him.

He puts his arms around me and says, "And home to Manitoba is where we're goin'."

I smile and snuggle closer to him. I close my eyes and feel the warmth of his body against mine and the gentleness of his arm around me. I can hear him breathing and I can feel another smile draw across my mouth.

Yes, life is good after all I think as The Eagles continue to play.

PART FOUR

MAY 1983 – BERT GILHIUS

Is this what it feels like when you wake up after sleeping for what seems like twenty years? It's been four months since I've finished my prison sentence, and it still feels like the time I've spent inside has been some kind of bad dream.

When I went into prison in September 1981, Calgary was a boomtown where there were good jobs to be had everywhere. Now here it is May 1983, and as I walk around town I see apartment buildings that are almost empty, For Sale signs on the front lawns of houses and I'm hearing too many stories of people leaving to get jobs in Toronto. What happened? This drastic change occurred and I feel like I was asleep. To top it off, it's been another frustrating morning at the Canada Manpower Centre because I'm limited in the jobs I can apply for due to the criminal record I now possess.

In spite of all that, it's late spring, the sun is shining and I feel okay. After being confined for eighteen months, I appreciate what a great feeling it is just to walk down a city side street and enjoy the sun whenever I want to.

It's around 11 AM as I walk back to my sister's place through the streets of Calgary's South East side. This neighbourhood has seen better days. It was one of the first suburbs in town. Turn-of-the-century cottage-style wooden homes line the well-treed streets. And for every home that has been renovated over the past few years, there are two that have been left to the ravages of time. Drunks, prostitutes, people on fixed income, transients, even a group of outlaw bikers have all called this part of town home at one time or another. Now it seems that everyone is just eager to sell and move on.

As I approach the corner of 10th Street and 17th Avenue S.E. I can hear the sounds of a circular saw and hammering somewhere nearby. These days that can only mean that somebody is fixing a house to sell it. A two-storey brick building housing a corner store with a small apartment on the second floor stands across from me. From this corner I look east and have a clear view of Calgary's industrial area next door to us. Like being on the upswing of a teeter-totter, the trees and lawns of the neighbourhood slope down a gentle incline to the swirling dust of industry. So we call decrepit transient hotels, Stockyards, miles of train track, belching transport trucks, shunting trains, busy thoroughfares, and a landscape of electrical towers our neighbours.

A fellow rides by on a ten-speed. He smiles and says hello to me. I stop and watch him as he disappears around a corner. Goddamn he reminds me of Jim. Jim! I forgot all about him. What a revelation that is, considering how hard I fell for him. I did receive a couple of letters from him since he moved to Winnipeg, and everything seemed to be going okay. I did answer both of them from jail, but then I didn't receive any more. I don't know why the letters suddenly stopped and maybe I never will. It's too bad; because Jim was one guy I would have done just about anything for had we gotten together.

I walk across the street to my sister's place, the house I've called home since I've been out of the slam. The boulevard tree standing outside the house is starting to bloom.

I ascend the three steps to the veranda and unlock the door. I enter the silence of the house. I'm the only one at home again since Patty and Keith are at work. I take off my shoes and head into the living room. Puddles their cat meows at me as I pass him, I bend down and give him a few short affectionate strokes on the top of his head.

"Hey Puddles," I say to him as he purrs. "How's your day been so far?" I go to the phone to see if any messages were left for me. A small piece of paper is lying beside it. Hopefully this is a job interview.

It says Bert, call Warren and a phone number is scribbled across it. I immediately smile, this is the best news I've had in four months. He said he'd phone me when his sentence was through.

Warren Givens, I met him not long after I began my sentence, and from the beginning he showed me how to survive in prison. We became good buddies during my time inside, in fact he was one of my few buddies. In the course of our sentences we discovered that we're both gay, well he says he's bi. But as far as I'm concerned, he likes sucking cock and getting fucked too much to be straight.

I remember when Givens, (I'm used to calling him by his last name because that's how everyone referred to each other inside), was in a good mood he would talk to me with a mock-Mexican accent, and it would always be sexual.

"I like eet when de pedros poke me wid der pepitas," he would smile and say. I would always laugh, almost spilling my coffee; (I always had a coffee cup in my hand in those days). Coffee and cigarettes were the only "pleasures" allowed us, and since I don't smoke you could say I've become a caffeine addict.

I remember that whenever a new guy would come on to the unit and Givens thought he was sexy, he would whisper to me in that Mexican accent, "He make my poosy sing." From that point on, whenever the guy would be around Givens would look at me, raise his eyebrows and hum so only I could hear it. I chuckle as I'm reminded of those times.

Givens grew up on the streets of Edmonton where he begged, stole and hustled to survive. He was a small-time pot dealer that managed to land himself a two-year stretch. The two of us kept to ourselves and to the handful of guys we learned to trust, because, contrary to popular belief, the inmates don't like faggots, so of course our hanging out together generated talk among the other inmates. Some of the other guys called all of us The Gaylords, and a couple of times we were threatened with violence, but nothing ever came of it. The guards would usually appear at the first sign of trouble or I would hold Givens back if he was being provoked. They especially liked prodding Givens because they knew he would react to it. But all of us knew we would lose the few privileges we had if we got involved in a scrap, and since nobody wanted that, we minded our business and the other inmates generally minded theirs.

Yeah, Givens and I became fuck buddies too. On several occasions we'd blow each other in the shower when we were sure we were alone, or when we figured it was safe.

I can feel a broad smile on my face as I pick up the receiver and dial the number on the slip of paper. The phone rings twice on the other end.

"Hello."

I recognize his voice right away.

"Does your poosy still sing?"

A laugh from the other end, "Hey Gil!"

(Gil is what I was called while I was inside, it's short for my surname Gilhius.)

"How the hell are ya?"

"Great, now. When did you get out?"

"The other day, I wanted a day to get settled in before I got hold of you. So how's life been on the outside for you man?"

"I'm still having trouble adjusting. I can't believe how Calgary has changed since we've been inside."

"Yeah," Givens agrees, "What's with all these For Sale Signs I've been seeing all over the place?"

"That's exactly what I'm talking about."

"Why the hell is everyone leaving town?"

"No jobs here anymore," I answer.

Givens is momentarily silent, and then says, "Who'd have thought, eh? Say listen, you got any plans tomorrow?"

"Not other than my daily dose of frustration down at Canada Manpower, why?"

"Let's hook up for lunch and some beers."

"I don't know, I've got to watch my money these days…"

"Ah c'mon Gil, we've got some catchin' up to do."

"Ah, why not," I laugh, "where do you want to meet?"

"You know this town better than me man, you got any ideas?"

"You know where Toronto Dominion Square is?"

"Yeah, I think it's right downtown."

"There's a restaurant on the third floor, I forget the name of it, but you can't miss it because they've got the front set up like a patio with umbrellas."

"You're shittin' me."

"Uh…no…why?"

"Sounds pretty faggy."

"Faggy–yeah right, and who's the one who sleeps with his ass in the air?"

He laughs, "Fuck you, Gil."

"Fuck who?"

"Okay, I'll find it. What time do you wanna meet there?"

"11:00 sound okay?"

"I'll be there."

"I'm looking forward to this, Givens."

"Me too, Gil; it's been awhile. I'll see you tomorrow."

"Till then bro'." I hang up the phone and I suddenly feel like my life is about to take an exciting turn.

∞

Thomas Dolby exclaims, "She Blinded Me With Science!" over the restaurant's sound system as I get in the small cue forming at the entrance. I can see Givens with a beer bottle in front of him, an ashtray with a half-burned cigarette to one side of it, and a couple of menus strewn across the table. I watch him as he's concentrating on peeling the label off the bottle.

"Shit," he says as the label tears. Startled by his own outburst he quickly looks around at the tables immediately surrounding him to see if he attracted attention. That's when he spots me in the line and waves. I wave back.

"Table for one Sir," the pleasant young hostess asks.

"Oh," I say diverted by her question. "I'm going to join a buddy of mine inside. That's him over there," I say pointing him out.

"Go right on in then Sir," she smiles.

"Thank you," I say as I go over to the table in the smoking section where he sits.

"Looks like you're off to a good start," I say pointing to his half-empty bottle of beer.

"Gil! How are you, man?" He jumps up and shakes my hand.

"Doin' good," I say as I take a seat at the table.

"Feels kind of strange being back among real people again," he says.

"Yeah, I was watching you from the line."

"I'm not used to being in big open rooms like this, Gil," he says sitting down once more.

"Well, I haven't been to many restaurants since I've been out for that very same reason," I say, "but I am getting used to it again. It's just taken longer than I thought it could."

"And it feels weird wearing real clothes again," Givens says. "Luckily I've got some money waitin' for me." He gives me a sly smile and winks.

I remember him talking about the money he made while he was dealing and how he has a place where he's stashed some of it so he could use it in an emergency.

"Don't tell me," I say, "the less I know the better."

"I wouldn't do that to ya, Gil," he says.

"So are you staying with your buddies up in northeast Calgary like you said you were going to?" I ask him changing the subject.

"Oh yeah, I'm sleeping on their couch, listening to their little kids as they tear the living room apart every morning."

"So you're not getting much sleep these days?"

"Nope. But I don't mind. Ya know, Gil, I kind of like the sound of little kids playing now. I realized how much I missed little things like that. Hearing the kids playing in the morning makes me feel like I'm alive. It beats the hell out of the sound of keys janglin' at 7AM."

"That is too true, my friend," I agree.

"Can I get you something to drink?" the pleasant young waitress asks.

"Oh sure," I answer startled by her seemingly sudden appearance, "I'll have a coffee."

"Sure. And how is your beer, Sir?" she asks Givens.

He nods, "Sure, I'll have another."

"A Canadian? Certainly, Sir," she smiles and walks away.

Givens smiles at me and says, "Looks like you 'n me are startin' our lives all over again."

I think about that for a moment, "Good point, Givens, damn good point."

He beams a proud smile. Having been told that he's stupid most of his life, it's a bit of an ego boost for him when somebody affirms that he has made a good observation.

"So," he says, "you're havin' a tough time findin' work these days?"

"Yeah," I sigh, "it's bad enough that I have a record but what makes things worse is that the economy here has turned to shit. Just my luck."

The waitress returns and tells us our drinks will be along in a few moments.

"May I take your orders now, or do you need a couple of more minutes?" she smiles.

"Oh, I haven't even looked at the menu yet," I say.

"That's ok," she says, "I'll be back in a couple of minutes."

"Oh no, I'll decide right now," I answer quickly perusing the menu. I decide on the lunch special. Givens says he'll have the same thing. She takes the menus and leaves.

"So Givens," I say, "I guess the question we have to ask ourselves is, 'what do we do now?'"

He nods his head silently like he's thinking about it. But he doesn't answer. He's busy being distracted by the people at the surrounding tables.

"You know," I continue, "when I first started my bit in the slam, I thought that eighteen months was a long time and I was just going to serve the time and get out. I knew there would be changes that I would have to deal with…"

"…Yeah," Givens says still looking around the restaurant, "I remember us talking about that."

"But you know something Givens?"

"What," he responds turning his attention back to me.

"I never counted on the extent of the changes I would face back on the street. It's like everything has changed, and I still don't know how to deal with that."

"Maybe it's a good thing that you and me are out here together then," Givens says. "If you're havin' a tough time dealin' with it, then it makes me wonder how I'm gonna deal with it, man."

"I guess we can help each other out then," I suggest.

"That's what I'm thinkin' Gil. No one else knows what you 'n' me have been through except you 'n' me."

"Another good point my friend," I answer.

Givens smiles proudly once more.

"Trouble is," I continue, "where do we even begin?"

"I wish I knew man," Givens says as he takes his half-burnt cigarette from the side of the ashtray and relights it.

The waitress returns and puts our drinks in front of us, while another song plays over the stereo system and Givens pats his hands on the tabletop in time with the music saying, "I've heard this song a couple of times and I really like it, you know who this is?"

"Yeah, it's The Pretenders. My sister has this 45."

"...I thought I recognized the voice," he says, "What's the name of the song?"

"My City Was Gone," I answer, "and that's how I'm feelin'."

Givens shakes his head and says, "You know what, man?"

"What."

"Let's worry about finding work and starting all over again and all of that shit tomorrow. Today, let's you and me celebrate old buddies getting' together."

I knew my life was about to take an exciting turn, "Givens," I say smiling, "you never cease to amaze me." I take my coffee mug and raise it to him, "to buddies. He raises his beer bottle to me, "To buddies," he repeats. We clink coffee mug-to-beer bottle together and take a drink.

∞

The first thing I'm aware of is the music playing a little too loudly for my liking. Boy George is singing, "But you and me you know we've got nothing but time. And time won't give me time," as I slowly open my eyes. Where the hell am I? I look around me, then down at the floor to see clothes lying in a heap beside the bed. Oh right, the events of yesterday afternoon and evening are slowly returning to me. I'm lying naked on a narrow bed in the local bathhouse, and Givens snores bundled under a sheet beside me.

I feel groggy. I don't feel sick or head-achy, but my body feels like it's been wrung like an old rag and I feel like I've got hairballs in my throat.

I lay here trying to block out the music, and recount the events that led us here. I remember meeting Givens yesterday, having lunch and then a couple of beer with him before we left the restaurant. Then we decided to go for a walk around downtown to see the changes that Calgary has undergone while we've been inside. Of course Givens, having only been to Calgary a couple of times before, this was his first real close look at downtown.

At one point I suggested that we go a new gay club in town called Trax. I had been there a couple of times, and didn't stay too long either time. I didn't feel comfortable being there on my own among strangers. But I thought that going for Happy Hour might be good, and he liked the idea too. We spent the majority of the time at the pool table in the back corner of the club, and little by little the both of us got drunk.

I remember seeing a lot of good-looking guys there, and getting into light conversations with a few of them. At some point, a lot of what went on became nothing more than a blur. But I do remember Givens coming up to me, looking right into my face and saying,

"You know something man?"

"What?"

"I've haven't been fucked since you left the joint."

"I can't believe that you of all people couldn't get sex inside," I answered.

"I'm serious man," he continued, "I didn't fuckin' trust anybody after you left."

"What about Barker, McCracken and Cardinal? Couldn't you have given them the occasional blow job or something?"

"Yeah, but none of them would throw a good fuck into me, not like you Gil."

Then he laid a kiss on me like he never has in the time I've known him. Well, we agreed what else are good buds for but to help each other out. Since neither of us could take each other back to the places we're staying, we ended up here.

I try to sit up but my body falls back to the uncomfortable mattress in this narrow bed. Givens stirs and mumbles something about "yeah so fuckin' what?" I rub my eyes, and attempt to sit up again. This time I do it.

"What the fuck's goin' on?" Givens groans.

"It's just me man," I answer, "I'm gonna go take a shower."

"Yeah, ok," he says as he rousts himself up. He squints as he looks around him, and then says, "hand me my shirt will ya, Gil?"

I pick his shirt from the heap of clothes on the floor and hand it to him. He rifles around it looking for the front pocket and retrieves his pack of smokes. "I'll have one of these and then I'll come and join ya," he says hoarsely.

"See you in a bit then," I say as I pick a white towel off the floor, wrap it around my waist and open the door. "Don't forget the key to the room," I remind Givens."

"Yeah, sure man I'll bring it," he answers.

I go out to the hall shutting the door behind me. I feel a little unsteady as I walk toward the shower room. The hallway is devoid of people, no signs of life at all, making the music playing take on a slight echo effect. Many of the rooms have the doors wide open and are empty. One of the guys on-duty is busy cleaning out one of the rooms as I pass. He scrubs as he tries to remove the stench of drunken sex from the night before and replace it with the equally foul smell of pine-scented industrial cleaner. Once at the showers I remove my towel, hang it on a hook along the wall and then make sure the water's temperature is comfortable enough for me to stand under and let it run over me. My muscles feel like they're beginning to melt as the water pours over me making my entire body feel fluid.

"Aahhhhh," I sigh. I close my eyes enjoying this sensation when I hear somebody enter the room and another shower is turned on.

"That was a quick smoke," I say.

"Sorry?" comes the answer from a stranger's voice.

I open my eyes to see a handsome bearded man looking at me with a grin on his face and a sparkle in his eyes.

"Oh sorry," I say, "I was expecting my buddy."

"That's okay," he says checking the shower temperature with his hand.

We both stand under our showers in silence. I keep one eye on him, and I notice that he's continually glancing over to me.

"Do you know what time it is?" I ask.

"It's about 9:30," he says.

We're silent again. I don't usually go for men with beards, but I can't help but look at this guy.

"Mmmmm," he sighs as he immerses himself under the torrent of hot water.

"Rough night?" I ask.

"Just got a little drunk with the friend that I'm staying with, that's all," he answers, "and decided to come here to check things out."

I may not feel my best right now, but I don't want to let this guy go off without knowing a little more about him either.

"Much luck?" I ask smiling.

"Good enough," he smiles back.

We're silent as we stand under our showers enjoying the sensation of the water on our bodies, and the intimation that we're both interested in sex with each other.

"You say you're staying with a friend, so you're not from Calgary?" I ask.

"No," he answers, "I've been living in Toronto for the past few years. My friend has been living here for about three years, so I came out to visit her and to finally see this town. You a Calgarian?"

"I guess you could say I am. I've been away for a while and I've only been back here for four months."

He starts soaping himself up, I follow suit. The two of us continually exchange glances and smiles.

"Staying in town long?" I ask.

"A few days," he answers. "I want to see this city and it's been a while since I've seen my friend. So I want to spend some time with her as well."

We're silent as he rinses off. We smile as we give each other a prolonged look into each other's eyes.

"So your buddy," he says, "are you and he an item?"

"We're good friends and fuck buddies. Over the last couple of years we've helped each other out a lot, and we've gotten close because of it, but no, we're not an item. My name's Bert, by the way, Bert Gilhius," I say extending my hand to him.

"Neil Logan," he responds extending his hand. We shake, but then he slowly runs his hand up my arm. I'm happy to let this go wherever it leads. He's getting a tasty looking hard-on, and I guess I'm not feeling as bad as I thought I was because I'm feeling my cock swell.

This delicious little spell is broken by Givens who comes shuffling into the shower room seemingly unaware of Neil and me. He walks right by us, hair dishevelled, eyes half closed and belches as he turns one of the showers on. Neil and I look at each other and smile as if to say, we'll continue this later.

I go back under the shower I was running, look over to Givens and say, "Well, it lives."

"Fuck off," he replies.

Neil looks at him, then over to me. He raises his eyebrows to me and nods his head towards Givens as if to confirm this is your buddy?

I nod my head yes to him.

He looks back at Givens who has his back to us while turning on his shower. Then Neil looks back at me, smiles and nods his head approvingly.

Givens gets under the shower, "AHHH," he yells as he bolts out of the stream of water.

"Too hot," I ask.

"Yeah," he says as he turns to face us, and is taken aback that there are actually three of us in the showers together.

"Neil," I say, "This is Warren." I turn to Givens and say, "This is Neil."

Givens looks at Neil's cock in its semi-erect state and says, "good to meet ya."

"You gonna survive?" I ask.

"Oh yeah," he answers while looking back at me.

Neil looks at me and smiles appreciating the admiration that Givens is showing him. He finishes his shower, turns it off and reaches for his towel.

"You're not going already are you?' I smile.

"I should find a phone and let my friend know I'll be back at her place soon, and besides I really need to get some food into me, You guys know a good breakfast place around here?" he asks while he towels himself off.

"That's a great fuckin' idea," Givens says looking at me.

"I could sure use a coffee," I add. "There's one not far from here," I say, "mind if we join you?"

He stops momentarily, "Sure," he says, "I'd like the company. Why don't you guys meet me by the front door in a few minutes?"

"Sure," I say.

"Yeah, that's a great idea," Givens agrees.

"Okay," says Neil, "I'll meet you guys out front then."

Neil leaves the showers to go get dressed and Givens looks at me, smiles and says in his mock-Mexican accent, "He make my poosy sing."

∞

The restaurant looks full, but luckily we manage to get seated in a booth almost right away. Our coffees sit steaming on the table in front of us and we're waiting for our orders to arrive. With a lot of the small talk out of the way, Neil is telling us about his plans for the next little while.

"After I visit here, I'm driving out to Vancouver to spend the summer, and who knows, if I like it, maybe I'll just stay there."

"Jeez, that must be nice," Givens says.

"I'm looking forward to it," Neil answers.

"Let me guess," I say, "you're going to lay on Wreck Beach all summer."

"Something like that," he grins. "I've always wanted to spend a summer doing nothing except what I want to do. And although I've never been, I've heard Vancouver is the spot to do just that."

"I've been there a few times and it is a pretty spot," I say, "Not much work there these days, but if you want a summer of leisure that is the place to do it."

"I've been told it's the San Francisco of Canada," Neil says.

"I agree with that," I answer. "The gay life in Vancouver is fantastic. The entire West End is one big Gay Ghetto. You just walk down the street and you get heavily cruised. If you wanted to you could party at a different club every night and sex is really easy to get in that town."

"I'm there," smirks Givens.

"You got friends there?" I ask Neil.

"No, I'll probably stay at the "Y"".

The waiter arrives with our breakfast orders and places them in front of us. "Enjoy," he smiles and leaves.

"Are you gonna do any exploring while you're here?" Givens asks as he picks a strip of bacon off his plate and eats it.

"I'd like to do more," Neil answers as he cuts into one of his pancakes. "I've already seen the Calgary Tower, the Stampede grounds and I've taken a ride on that C-Train you guys have."

"That C-Train's kind of neat lookin' ain't it," says Givens.

"Yeah, it is," Neil agrees. Then he turns looks out the window.

"Hey Gil," Givens says, "What's say we show Neil around while he's here?"

"Yeah, we could do that," I answer turning back to Neil. But I see he's staring out the window and noticeably lost in thought.

"Earth to Neil," I say.

He snaps out of his state and smiles at Givens and me.

"Anything the matter?" I ask.

"Well, to tell you the truth," he begins, "there was another reason I wanted to see this city."

"And what was that?" Givens asks as he picks up another slice of bacon with his fingers and devours half of it in one mouthful.

"I was supposed to move here to Calgary a few years ago with another friend of mine. Who am I kidding, we were potential lovers but it didn't work out. We were driving out and got most of the way here, and I ended up moving back to Toronto. Part of the reason I came here was because I was curious that there would be some weird chance I might see him again."

"What happened that you got almost here then went back to Toronto," Givens asks.

"It's a long story, and I don't want to go into it. Let's just say that we had made all kinds of plans for when we got out here. Then he suddenly decided he wasn't gay after all."

134

"That's fuckin' weird," Givens says.

"He got scared then?" I ask.

"Yeah he did," says Neil. "I remember saying to him are you telling yourself or me that you're not gay, or something like that. He didn't like that and we had a huge argument about it. I went back to Ontario and he carried on to Calgary."

"Did you guys have jobs lined up here?" Givens asks.

"He did," says Neil, "he was an officer in the military. I was working in Camp Borden in Ontario at the time I met him."

I shake my head and sigh under my breath, "An officer in the military, wouldn't you bloody well know."

Neil gives me a puzzled look.

"Sorry," I say to him, "There was a guy that I fell in love with who used to be in the military. He got discharged and then he and I met and started seeing each other. I wanted a relationship with him, but he said he wasn't ready. He went to live in Manitoba because his dad got ill, and I haven't seen or heard from him in a while now."

"You mean Jim?" Givens asks,

"Yeah, Jim," I repeat. "I really fell hard for him."

"Well Bert," says Neil.

"Please," I say, "call me Gil. My friends call me Gil these days and I've gotten used to it."

"Ok, Gil," Neil says, "I guess there's one thing that you and I have learned from our experiences with military men."

"And what's that?"

"Stay the hell away from soldiers," Givens interjects.

Neil and I look at each other and chuckle.

"I couldn't have said it better," Neil says. "Say look," he continues, "I don't know what your time is like right now but I wouldn't mind hangin' out with you guys for the time I'm in town. Cheryl's busy working during the day so…

"…Gil and me got lots of time right now," Givens jumps in.

"Really?" Neil asks.

"Givens," I interject.

"Oh yeah," he continues, "The two of us ain't workin', so we can spend time showin' you around."

"Well I like to spend some time every week lookin' for work," I quickly add.

"That's understandable," Neil says.

"C'mon Gil," Givens says, "You can afford the time for the next couple of days."

I look at Neil who is smiling at me. I can't resist those eyes of his.

"Sure," I say, "It might be a good distraction for me."

A broad smile draws across Neil's face.

"That's more like it, Gil," says Givens.

"So when do you figure you'll be off to Vancouver?" asks the ever-inquisitive Givens.

"Don't know," Neil answers, "probably in a few days."

"So you're not sticking around for Stampede then?" I ask.

"When does that start?" Neil asks taking another sip of coffee.

"I think it starts sometime the end of June this year," I answer.

"Nah, I want to be soaking up the sin in Vancouver by that time," he smiles.

"Jeez I wish I was going' with ya man," says Givens. "Maybe I'll pretend I'm a hitchhiker and hitch a ride with you to Vancouver."

"I wish I had that luxury," I say, "but I've got to think about my life and what I'm going to do to get it back on track."

"What do you mean?" Neil asks.

I look at him and realize what I've said. "Well I might as well tell you, Remember when we were in the shower this morning I told you that I had been away from Calgary for a while and I'd only been back for four months?"

Neil says, "Yeah I remember something like that."

"The truth of the matter is that I got out of prison about four months ago…"

"…and so did I," Givens adds, "just a few days ago."

Neil's eyes grow wide,

"Yeah," I continue, "Givens and I knew each other inside. That's where we met and became buds."

"It's almost like we're married now," Givens smiles.

"Really?" Neil asks, "What were you guys in for?"

"I had a small racket going up in Edmonton," Givens says not caring who's listening. "You know, selling pot, none of the hard

136

stuff, too much bullshit with that. But I had my steady customers and I kept them happy."

"So what happened?" Neil asks.

"The cops got wind of it, raided my place and found my stash. I got two years less a day."

"How about you Gil?" Neil asks turning to me.

"Gil got set up," Givens jumps in.

Neil looks confused, "How so?"

"It's a long story Neil," I say, "I didn't exactly get set up, but I was arrested and charged with trafficking an illegal substance."

"So were you selling illegal substances?" he asks.

"The only thing I was guilty of was passing a joint I was smoking to an undercover cop."

"Oops," Neil says.

"Yep," I answer, "I got eighteen months for that one little mistake."

Neil is silent while he considers what we've just told him. "Now I know the reason you're finding things frustrating," he says.

I smile and nod my head. "It's almost like coming out again."

"I guess it would be," Neil smiles.

"Yeah," says Givens, "it's like you've got this secret that you don't want people to know, but you're going to have to tell them at some time."

That observation sparks a discussion of life in prison, with Neil asking questions and Givens and I answering. Givens doesn't appear to be bothered, but I feel conspicuous as we're talking. It's like I can feel everybody at the surrounding tables listening to the things we're saying. But the more we talk, the more interested Neil seems to be in us, or maybe specifically, me, (I hope).

∞

Neil's car pulls up to Patty and Keith's place while the tape machine is playing After the Fire's Der Kommissar. I've always liked the beat of this song and Neil is tapping his hands on the steering wheel in time to the music. We've just dropped Givens off and since I've been out all night, I want to go and have a nap.

"So you've got my number?" I ask Neil.

"I sure do," Neil smiles.

"Please use it."

"I sure will." He hesitates then asks, "What are you guys up to tomorrow?"

"Other than spending some time looking for work in the morning, nothing. I don't know what Givens has on his plate. Why?"

"I wouldn't mind going for a long drive somewhere. Would you guys be into coming with me?"

"Sure, I'd like that," I say. "Do you want me to call Givens?"

"Sure. I want to get an early start so do you think you could give up looking for work for one day?"

I hesitate a little bit, but I look into his eyes and say, "Yeah. Why not?"

That delicious spell that enveloped us earlier in the showers wraps itself around us again. He leans over and we kiss.

"What's a good time for me to arrive," he asks.

"How about 8 o'clock?"

"Okay, see you then."

I get out of the car, and walk toward the house. Neil gives me a couple of short honks on his car horn as he pulls out to the road and travels back up the street.

∞

What a great day! The sun is shining and warm, not a cloud in the sky in fact it's t-shirt weather. And I'm surprised as the small park by this river is deserted except for us. Just the river roaring and the birds singing is all I can hear. Neil picked Givens and I up this morning and we've driven west of the city to a spot just out of Bragg Creek. I remember Jim and I came out here once, and I'm surprised I remembered how to get here after all this time. I'm back from taking a small hike through some local trails. Neil is taking photos of almost everything in sight, and Givens is sitting quietly at a picnic table butting out what's left of a cigarette I sit down beside him as he stares out over the river.

He takes a deep breath and says, "This is great. It's nice to be out here."

"Yeah," I say, "I guess I've needed to come out to a place like this just to stop for a little while."

"Look at the water in that river, Gil. Look at how clear it is. I've never seen water so clear."

"Oh c'mon Givens. You're telling me you've never been to Jasper or into the Rockies at all?"

"Well yeah I have, but I was too busy getting' stoned with my buddies to notice anything else."

I laugh and say, "Well I guess spending some time in the slam has made us both appreciate these things a little more."

"You've got that right, Gil. Say, I'll bet that water's great to swim in. Wanna go for a dip?"

"Well, it's still only spring, the water will still be freezing."

"C'mon man," he says as he takes off his shoes and socks, "don't be a wimp. We never got to do this inside" He pulls his t-shirt over his head, undoes his belt buckle and pulls off his pants.

"I don't know Givens, I…"

"…Last one in is a sissy!" He yells and runs naked into the water diving under the surface.

In an instant he bolts back on shore yelling, "JEEEEEZZZZIIIIIZ! THE WATER'S FUCKIN' COOOOLD!"

Givens runs out of the water yelling like a madman while Neil laughs, snapping pictures of him.

"This ain't fuckin' funny, man," Givens protests, "I'm fuckin' freezin'!"

"Are you kidding," Neil continues to laugh, "That was great! I couldn't have asked for a better model, Givens."

"You're pricks with ears," Givens spits in disgust standing on the shore shivering, "ya hear that? Pricks with ears! The both of youz!"

Neil, still laughing, goes to his car and gets a blanket out of the trunk. He comes back and throws it to Givens who immediately wraps himself in it, then comes over and hunches beside me at the picnic table getting warmed up.

"You have to admit, Givens," I say, "it did look pretty funny."

He scowls at me then turns away.

"Ah c'mon, Givens," I say, "we're just havin' fun with you."

"Fuck you guys! Have it with someone else!"

I know exactly what will make his mood better.

"Why should I have it with someone else," I smile as I start to poke and tickle him.

"Fuck off, Gil," he responds.

"Oh no you don't," I say as I continue to tickle him, "I know you like this."

"Fuck you," he says with a smirk.

I reach under the blanket and tickle his side.

"Fuck off, Gil," he giggles and squirms to avoid my prodding.

Neil is on to this and he tickles Givens as well.

By now the blanket has fallen off of Givens, and he's naked as he giggles and squirms still trying to be pissed off at us.

That's when I break his laughter by kissing his lips. He stops giggling immediately and puts his arms around my shoulder. Our kiss deepens. We stop, look into each other's eyes, then Givens moves forward to kiss me again. I can feel my cock swelling. Neil joins in immediately and kisses Givens as soon as I'm done. I can see Givens already has a boner as he gently runs his hand along Neil's cheek and strokes it almost lovingly.

Neil and I then kiss each other, break our kiss and look back at Givens who undoes my belt, unfastens my pants.

"So are you guys gonna take off your clothes or what," Givens asks.

I look at Neil, he looks at me, then he stands and takes his clothes off while Givens and I kiss. Neil looks at me, smiles and says, "I hear Givens really likes bending over."

"Yeah, I can take on both you fuckers," Givens replies.

"You bragging?" Neil grins back at him.

"Try me," Givens dares Neil.

∞

The three of us are quiet as we drive back to Calgary. The only sound is Men at Work playing the song Overkill on Neil's cassette player.

"You guys want to stop for a burger before we get back home," asks Givens from the backseat, "Gettin' fucked makes me hungry."

Neil and I laugh out loud as I turn back to look at Givens. He looks like he's just realized how that sounded and grins at me.

"Sure," answers Neil still laughing, "we can stop at the next McDonald's or something."

I look at Neil and say, "I've had a good day, thanks for suggesting this."

"De nada," he smiles. Then he glances over to me with a smile on his face and says, "You know, my friend Cheryl and I were talking just this morning about when I'd be leaving for the coast."

"And what have you decided?" I ask.

"June first."

"That's this Friday," Givens says.

"Yeah it is," Neil says, "so can I ask you guys something?"

"Sure," answers Givens.

"What are you guys planning to do for the next little while?"

"What do you mean?" Givens asks.

"I mean for the next couple of weeks…"

"Well you know I want to get back on my feet work-wise," I answer.

"And I just want to get a life again," Givens continues.

"Why do you ask?" I query.

"I know this may be asking a lot of you two, but I'd sure like it if you came out to Vancouver with me. We could take turns driving, and if we all share the expenses then it wouldn't be very much for any of us."

"YEAH!" Givens shouts. "That would be a hoot!"

"It sounds tempting, Neil," I say, "but I don't know…"

"Ah c'mon, Gil," Givens says, "the three of us on the road together. Imagine it! Vancouver! English Bay…"

"Wreck Beach," Neil adds.

"The Pacific Ocean," Givens states.

"It would be fun," Neil says.

"I'm sure it would," I respond imagining all of the misadventures that Givens could possibly get us into. I look over to Neil and say, "I'll need a couple of days to think about this. My finances are a little limited right now."

"Hey, Gil," Givens says tapping me on the shoulder, "remember I've got a good stash of cash."

"I don't want to know about it Givens," I remind him.

"And you don't have to know, buddy," Givens responds, "consider it my treat."

"Like I said," Neil continues, "it can only be for a couple of weeks if that's the way you want to play it." He's silent for a moment and then he starts to chuckle.

"What's so funny?" I ask.

"It's really strange," Neil says, "remember yesterday at breakfast I was telling you two about the guy that I was driving to Calgary with a few years back?"

"Yeah," Givens and I respond in unison.

"He and I had almost this identical conversation before I left my parents place in 1979."

"No shit," Givens says.

"Yeah, I was in the same sort of situation as you guys, in between jobs and not sure what the hell I was going to do. He talked me into driving out to Calgary with him."

"But you said that didn't work out for you," I remind him.

"Actually," he says, "when I think about it, it did work out in the long run."

"How so?" Givens asks.

"After he and I parted company, I stayed with my friends in Winnipeg for a couple of weeks, and it was then that I made up my mind to move to Toronto, and I'm glad I did. Things didn't turn out the way I had originally planned when I started that trip, and I lost what I thought was a friend; but I gained a whole new life. So looking back, it was a good thing I made that trip. Maybe the same might happen with you guys if you come out to the coast with me. Maybe you'll find new lives for yourselves."

"Well," I say, "you make it sound tempting..."

"I'm sold," says Givens, "count me in."

"You know," says Neil turning to me, "we would have a great time together."

"If this afternoon is any indication," I answer, "I'm sure we would,"

"It's because of our time this afternoon that I'm suggesting this to you guys," Neil says. "We seemed to get along well yesterday," Neil begins, "and I thought by us spending time today doing a little travelling might give me a good indication of how we'd get along while travelling together."

"And?" I ask.

"So that's why I'm asking you guys along," he answers.

"You in then, Gil?" Givens asks.

"I'm still not sure, Givens."

"C'mon, Gil," Givens says, "you told me yourself how you're going nowhere, and you've got a record now so it's even harder to get a job. I hate to say this, Gil, but how long have you been out of the slam now? Four Months? And are you any further ahead?"

I heave a sigh, "you're right, Givens. You're right."

"And the work situation here in Cowtown ain't like it was when we went inside, man," Givens adds reminding me of the blatantly obvious.

"Givens," I say.

"Yeah."

"You have a wicked way of making your case."

"What do you mean?"

I smile and say, "I mean, you're right. Let's go to Vancouver."

"EEE-HAW! That's the stuff man," Givens exclaims as he pats my shoulder.

"But only for a couple of weeks," I caution. "That's probably all I have the money for."

"I'll look after you," Givens says with a broad smile, "just like I did when you first were put in the slam."

I don't know whether to smile or shudder.

"You guys think you can be ready by this Friday then," Neil smiles.

"I'm ready to go now," Givens says.

"Yeah, I can be ready for that time," I say. "Besides, I think my sister and brother-in-law would like to have their home back to themselves."

"Man, we're going to have us a good time," Givens says.

∞

We agreed that we would get an early start this morning, so I was ready and packed when Neil came by to pick me up at 6:30. Now here we sit in the parking lot of a low rental development in Calgary's northeast waiting for Givens, who has left it until this morning to do his laundry. When I went to the door to get him, he told me he would only be a few more minutes—that was half an hour ago.

Neil looks at me and smirks, "Whose idea was it to bring Givens anyway?"

I smile and point back at him.

"I was afraid of that," he says.

"I should have known this would happen," I say. "Sometimes he gets distracted and forgets everything else."

"Well," Neil says, "as long as we can make it to Kamloops by tonight."

"That shouldn't be any problem," I say.

"I've made arrangements for us to stay at a hotel there," he adds.

Just then the door to the place swings open, and out he comes with a huge red hockey bag. Neil and I chuckle at him as he approaches the car. The size and girth of that bag he carries makes him walk at a weird angle. He notices us chuckling, so he smiles and gives us the finger. He trudges around to the trunk of Neil's car.

Neil gets out and says, "There's no room left in the trunk, put your bag on the seat beside you."

"Okay," Givens answers. He opens the back door and clumsily puts the bag on the seat, closes the door and gets in the other side of the car.

"Sorry about this guys," Givens says as he slides into the back seat.

"Not a problem," Neil says as he gets into the car, turns on the ignition and we're on our way.

"Do you know how to get out of town?" he asks Neil.

"Yeah," Neil answers, "I was studying my city map last night."

We travel north a few blocks to 16th Avenue N.E. then we turn left and drive along 16th Avenue to the point on the western city limits where it meets the Trans-Canada Highway. We are past the city limits in only minutes. Even though the weather is beautiful, there is a cool breeze blowing from The Rockies this morning. I can see their purple silhouettes as they rise in the western horizon. God they look especially beautiful today.

144

Now that we're on the road, I can feel freedom like I haven't felt it in a very long time. I find it difficult to put this feeling into words. The mundane, everyday things seem to take on a lustre like I've never seen before. It's as if Maxfield Parrish himself has painted the landscape before us. On either side of the car, as far as my line of sight takes me, the land rolls like waves on a beach as we travel through the foothills. The sky is a clear, silver/blue, and the morning sun turns the highway into a brightly lit magnet drawing us toward the Rockies on the horizon. I feel like I'm flying. This moment just feels so good.

"Ah shit," Givens says from the back seat.

"What's the matter?" I ask.

"I forgot my camera."

"Too late," Neil smiles, "we're not turning back.

Givens is silent for a moment; he shrugs his shoulders and stretches back in his seat.

I quietly watch the passing scenery. Neil fast-forwards the cassette in his stereo, and presses play Givens brightens up, sits forward and yells, "Yeah! Crank it up! I like this song!"

Neil turns up the volume, and Givens sings off-key.

"Fuck I can't wait to get to Vancouver man," Givens says excitedly. "it's gonna be a hell of a party."

"Yeah," I answer, "this should be interesting."

∞

I've driven through the Rockies many times before. But today, everything is so different. We've passed the town of Golden British Columbia a little while ago and everything is in late spring/early summer resplendence. The trees are showing their full green foliage and the animals are finally showing themselves after the winter's absence.

The melting snow from the mountains takes the form of small waterfalls frequently along this stretch of highway.

"Those waterfalls are really fuckin' beautiful," says Givens from the backseat. "I've always wanted to have sex under a waterfall that would be trip!"

"I could pull over beside any of these," says Neil with a smirk, "and we could take turns at you."

145

"No it would have to be a butch waterfall," Givens responds.

"A butch waterfall," Neil smiles and repeats.

I turn to Givens and ask, "What's a butch waterfall?"

"You know, one that's big and roaring with lots of mist and you can hear it for miles. Not like these wimpy things along the side of the road."

"I thought you just said they were beautiful," Neil says.

"Yeah but they're still wimpy."

Neil and I look at each other, smile and shake our heads.

We drive a little further up the highway and we come upon a small line of cars parked by the side of the highway. Some of the folks are outside of their vehicles madly snapping photos of something off to the side of the road. Neil pulls the car over to the side and Givens exclaims, "FUCK! LOOK AT THAT!" He points over to a black bear up on a small rise to the side of the highway, sitting upright leaning against a tree staring groggily into space. It occasionally looks around to the small crowd of humans gathered in front of him.

Neil grabs his camera and stands just outside of the car door to snap a few photos of his own. I can't take my eyes of the bear yawning and staring to the sky. Freedom, I love this trip already.

∞

We arrived in Kamloops late this afternoon and checked into our room at a hotel near the southwestern outskirts of town off the Trans-Canada Highway, so it will be easy for us to get on the road early tomorrow morning.

We went for a swim at the hotel pool, got cleaned up, and then found ourselves in bed for another round of sex. So we got cleaned up again, went for dinner; and now we're having a beer at the hotel pub before we call it a day. We're sitting at a table near where a group of five guys are having a game of pool. They're drinking and a little on the loud side, just the type of guys that Givens tends to thrive around. Neil's found a video game and is over playing a couple of rounds.

Meanwhile, Givens and I sit at the table and we're drawn to the television monitors that are suspended from the ceiling throughout the pub. That new TV network, Much Music, is flashing colourful images at a hypnotically high speed. I find it fascinating— a whole station that plays nothing but rock videos. I've heard of MTV out of the United States, I guess this is the Canadian equivalent. We're watching a slapstick comedy of a video by a group called Madness, as they're singing, "Our house, in the middle of our street."

One of the band members is dressed as the archetypal British housewife, replete with hair kerchief, flowered housedress, apron and slippers. It reminds me of a musical Monty Python act.

"This kind of takes me back to the rec hall when we were in the slam," Givens says to me.

"How so?"

"The loud music and the loud guys around the pool table," he answers.

"You're right about that," I say, "I remember how loud that rec hall could get sometimes."

"Especially with that music," Givens adds.

"Yeah," I agree, "if I never hear Merle Haggard or AC/DC again it'll be too soon."

"Hey," Givens says, "nothin' wrong with ol' Merle or AC/DC."

"I didn't say there was. I just heard them too much in the rec hall, that's all."

Looking back to the TV monitors Givens says, "These rock video things are quite somethin'."

I nod my head, and the two of us laugh at the antics of the band on the TV screen.

"It would be really cool to be in somethin' like that," Givens continues.

"You want to be a video star?"

"Yeah."

"Maybe you'll get your chance in Vancouver," I smile at him.

"Yeah, right," he says sarcastically, "someone will see me in a restaurant and yell, 'GET ME THAT GUY! I WANNA MAKE HIM A STAR!' Like that's gonna happen."

He and I have a good snigger over it. That's when we hear the guys at the pool table laugh out loud. Givens glances over to them. He appears to be momentarily studying them.

"Hey," he says, "I think those guys at the pool table are laughing at us."

I turn to look then say, "I think you're right Givens, I think they are laughing at us."

"What the fuck's their problem," Givens says annoyed at this.

That's when Neil rejoins us at the table.

"Well," he says, "what have I been missing guys?"

"We're being laughed at," Givens says.

"What?"

"We think the guys at the pool table over there are laughing at us," I say. "We aren't too sure what to think about that."

Neil looks over their direction and sees they're looking at us and laughing.

I'm getting a little nervous because Givens' defences are up which usually leads to trouble. And it has me wondering if they've clued in that we're queer. Are they going to come over and start something with us? I hope there's no trouble tonight.

"What's their problem?" Neil asks.

"I don't fuckin' know," Givens snorts, "but if they don't fuckin' stop it I'll go over there and find the fuck out."

"Givens calm down," I warn.

"I won't calm down man. I don't like bein' made a fool."

The group of guys laugh again and I notice Givens has his right hand clenched into a tight fist. I don't like where this whole scene is heading.

I'm about to suggest we drink up and leave when one of the guys points his pool cue to us and says, "Hey guys it looks like we've got us some graduates from RCMP Headquarters here."

The others laugh. They continue to play and another of them says, "Yeah they must be here on their first posting."

We all look at each other.

The tension slowly leaves and a smile draws across Givens' face.

"Did you hear that?" He says, "They think that we're Mountie Cadets or something."

"Must be our haircuts," Neil says sarcastically.

"How long you guys posted here," one of the guys yells to us.

An entirely different mood comes over Givens. That smile is still on his face, and his eyes brighten. It's obvious to me that he's feeling flattered by this and he plays along with it.

"Not too long," he yells back, "It's just a temp posting."

"We could use a few more cops around here these days," says one of the bigger guys in the group as he lines up a shot on the pool table, "The lumber yard I work at has been vandalized a couple of times in the last month. It takes forever for the Mounties to get out there to investigate," He hits the cue ball and it misses its intended target.

We're silent. Then he turns to us and says, "But in the meantime, we can't do any business because the cops don't want any of the evidence touched. So we have to remain closed until they get there. We're losin' money."

"Is the lumber yard out of town?" Neil asks.

"Yeah, out around Rayleigh," he answers. "You guys know where that is?"

"Heard of it," Givens says.

"Hopefully you'll get to know it more," he says.

"Oh yeah," Givens replies, "we will."

I lean over to him and say, "Watch that, Givens. Don't get us in too deep here."

"I'm just havin' fun with them, man."

"Yeah, well just make sure that fun doesn't get us into trouble. There's five of them and only three of us. I'd hate to think of what they might do if they find out we're not what we're pretending to be right now."

"Ah relax, I'm in control now."

That's what I'm afraid of, I think.

"Well, I'm going to go back to the room after this beer," Neil says. "Remember that we want to be on the road early tomorrow."

"I'm with you," I say.

"You guys wanna shoot a round," the big guy among them shouts to us.

"Yeah," Givens says without hesitation.

"No, gotta get started early tomorrow," I say. Then I turn my attention to Givens, "when you're finished come back up to the room, okay?"

"Ah, c'mon guys, we're on holidays, remember?"

"No," Neil says, "Like I said, I want to get on the road early tomorrow."

"So remember what I said," I say to Givens like a father would to a son, "come up to the room after you finish that game, okay?"

"All right," he reluctantly agrees. We take our leave.

We walk out of the pub.

"Do you think Givens will be okay in there?" Neil asks.

"I hope so," I say. "Unfortunately though, anything can happen with Givens."

"Should we be worried then?"

"Neil, I wish I knew what to think right now."

∞

The phone ringing in our room jolts me out of a sound sleep. I look at the clock radio beside the bed, 4:10 AM. I turn on the small lamp and notice that Givens is not back yet. I awkwardly reach for the phone.

"Hello?"

"Hey Gil."

"Givens? It's four o'clock in the morning, where the hell are you?"

"I'm downtown man."

"What the hell are you doing downtown?"

"After I played pool with those guys, I met these other guys down at the pub. Hey listen, I scored this wild shit we can take with us to Vancouver."

"Givens are you nuts?"

"No man just stoned."

Then he covers the phone receiver, and I can hear him talking to some other guys.

"Givens. Givens, are you still there?"

"Yeah man, I'm here."

"Look, come on back to the…"

150

"Hey, Mario," Givens says talking away from the phone, "you'd be interested in this. It says on this notice that they got this program for people addicted to drugs."

"Whaddya mean 'people addicted to drugs?'" I can hear another voice ask in the background.

"Right here it says they got this program for people addicted to drugs."

"Whaddya mean 'people addicted to drugs,'" the other voice repeats.

"Hey man I'm just kiddin with ya,"

"Whaddya mean 'people addicted to drugs?'"

"Look man, I said I was just jokin' with ya."

Then it sounds like Givens puts his hand over the receiver and I hear the muffled sound of people talking and the tone of the conversation is beginning to sound intense.

"Givens," I say, "quit fuckin' around and get back here."

Givens addresses me on the phone, "I'm talkin' to a hard case here Gil."

"Givens get the hell back here before you…"

"HEY! FUCK YOU!" Givens shouts. I pull the receiver back from my ear at the sound of the phone on his end crashing against the side of the phone booth. I can hear a commotion on the other side of the phone…then I hear Givens' voice in the background yelling, "Fuckin' hit me will ya!"

"Oh shit," I mumble. "Givens, are you still there? Givens!"

"What the fuck's going on?" Neil demands.

"Givens is downtown somewhere with a group of guys," I say taking the receiver away from my ear. "And right now it sounds like he's in a fight with one of them."

"SHIT! That's all we need," Neil mumbles.

"Givens are you there?" I yell back into the receiver. All I can hear is the continuing commotion in the background.

"FUCK!" I say exasperated. I hang up the receiver, get out of bed and get dressed.

"Where are you going?" Neil asks.

"I don't know how much good this is going to do, but I'm going to go to the front desk and ask if they can call the police."

"Do you know where Givens is?"

151

"All he said was he's downtown. I'll see if the cops can do anything to get him and bring him back here," I say as I take the room key and open the door.

"I'll be back in a few minutes," I say as I walk out of the room.

∞

Three-quarters of an hour later there's the sound of a key in the door, and in walks Givens, his eyes are red, his hair and clothes are dishevelled, his shirt is partially ripped, and there's a cut on his upper lip. He has a sheepish look on his face.

"There you are," I say. "Did the cops bring you here?"

He nods his head. "You guys are pissed off at me aren't you," he says.

"Yeah, you could say that," I answer, (Givens never likes it if he thinks I'm pissed off at him).

"Gil, I'm sorry," he says sorrowfully. "I fucked up."

"Givens we don't need episodes like this," I snort. "We just got out of the fuckin' slam we don't need the cops giving us unwanted attention again."

"I'm sorry Gil," he says humbly.

Just then Neil steps out of the bathroom, "Well, look who's finally shown up," he says.

Givens frowns at that comment.

"Look guys, I'm sorry. What can I say," Givens sighs defensively, "Last night started out fun, but, but…"

"You were in a fight," I interject.

He nods his head, "With Mario and his two buddies," Givens answers, "but he started it! He fuckin' hit me first!"

"It doesn't matter who started it," I scold. "I don't know about you Givens but I sure as hell don't want to be in police custody again."

The three of us are silent, and Givens does something I've only seen him do one other time, he quivers and gets emotional. I look at him and my big brotherly instincts toward him kick in. Feeling moved by his near-tearful state, I put my arms around him and draw him closer to me.

"It's okay buddy," I whisper to him.

"They started beatin' on me Gil," his voice quivering, "then one of them yells, 'the fuckin' cops!' They spit on me, got in their car and fucked off. Next thing I know the cops are pullin' up in front of me and they ask me if my name is Warren Givens."

His voice cracks some more as I hold him closer to me.

"So I say to them, 'who the fuck wants to know?'"

I pull back from him and look at him. "Tell me you didn't say that Givens."

"I didn't know how they knew my name, man. I was thinkin' they were gonna send me back to the slam for some reason."

I roll my eyes and sigh.

"So what happened then?"

"So they say to me, 'your buddies back at the hotel want to know. They sent us out here to get you.' I was scared, Gil, I was fuckin' scared. These guys were gonna beat the crap out of me and I didn't know where the hell I was. I wouldn't have known how to get back here."

Neil comes over and puts his hand on Givens' shoulder.

"Do you want to go to the hospital," Neil asks.

Givens shakes his head no. "I'll be okay," he says.

I smile at him, "I guess your pride is wounded more than anything."

He chuckles as if I've guessed it right.

"Hey look," I say to him, "why don't you have a shower, then we can get something to eat, get on the road, and when we get to Vancouver we'll have some real fun."

He smiles, takes his clothes off and heads to the bathroom. Neil looks at me and says, "Are you sure we shouldn't take him to emergency just so they can check him out?"

"No, he's a pretty strong little shit. If he says he'll be okay then he will be," I answer. "Knowing Givens, he's probably more upset at the thought of me being upset with him, than any hits he may have taken."

"Well," Neil says, "I'll go make up the back seat of the car, so he can get some sleep while we drive down to Vancouver."

∞

We got on the road about 9:30 this morning with Givens sleeping in the back seat and me riding shotgun. It's now about 1:30 or 2 in the afternoon and we've reached Hope, BC where we've decided to stop for lunch. We've found a run-down truck stop just outside of Hope. In fact, as we step inside the place, Neil jokes, "They should name this place, Just Outside of Hope."

I snigger as I look around…this place has seen better days. The paint, which I'm sure used to be white has become an aged, nicotine-stained yellow. Strips of flypaper hang from various points of the ceiling, each with a variant amount of dead flies. Yellowed and moisture-stained photos of old trucks from the 1930's to the '50's hang along the walls, and, Kenny Rogers and Dolly Parton sing Islands in the Stream from the jukebox. A big, rickety electric fan installed right into the wall clatters and hums as it tries desperately to circulate the stale air in here.

We get one of the only two other tables left, get settled and the waitress appears almost instantly. She's an older woman who seems to know everybody in the place on a first-name basis. She lays the menus on the table in front of Givens, and takes our drink orders while Givens distributes the menus to us.

"By my calculations," Neil says, "we should be in Vancouver in a couple of hours."

That's when the waitress returns to give us our drinks and take our orders. We all decide on the meatloaf special that's hand-written on a small piece of paper and clipped to the top of the menu.

"That was easy," she smiles as she heads toward the kitchen. In an instant she's back and says, "Sorry boys, we're all out of meatloaf."

"Ah c'mon," Givens grins, "I was looking forward to that."

We all consult the menus again. Givens decides on a burger and fries while Neil and I order the hot roast beef sandwiches. The waitress goes back to the kitchen and in another instant returns saying, "Sorry boys, only one roast beef sandwich left."

We all laugh.

"Not our lucky day today," I say.

"Okay give the roast beef to him, "Neil says pointing at me, "I'll go with a burger and fries too."

154

The waitress returns to the kitchen. We continue to talk about the plans we have for when we get to Vancouver when a couple of big guys come into the restaurant and sit at the booth adjacent to us. They both sport oil-stained truckers caps, dirty t-shirts, and blue jeans replete with dirt and oil stains. One has a beard like the guys from the rock band ZZ Top, while the other has a moustache and hasn't shaven all week. They don't look at the menu as the waitress approaches their table.

"What'll it be today boys," she asks.

They order two plates of spaghetti and meatballs; she takes the order and leaves. We listen to them talking about things going on in the locale as the waitress returns to them saying,

"Sorry boys, only three meatballs left."

They decide to stick with the order anyway, and after she leaves one of them looks to the other and says, "You'll probably get two of them because she always liked you better."

The three of us silently look at each other and grin.

∞

It's about 4:30 in the afternoon when I reach behind me to the back seat and shake Givens whose been napping again,

"Hey, sleeping beauty, we're here."

"What?" he answers groggily, "Vancouver? We're here?"

"We've just entered the city now," Neil answers.

Givens yawns.

"Did you sleep okay?" asks Neil.

"Uh-huh," Givens responds.

I turn forward as we drive and notice a large brown wooden sign off to my right saying simply, Rupert Park. Then I notice the scenery beyond. The mountains to the north of the city are still snow-capped.

"Look over there Givens," I say pointing to them as they rise dark green and white. The sky above them is cloudless and brilliant light blue. "There are some great looking mountains."

"Wow," Givens says quietly, "This is going to be great. Turn on some music, man."

Neil reaches down and flips on the cassette player:

"Sweet Dreams are made of these,   Who   am   I   to disagree...."

"Crank it up man," Givens says excitedly."

Neil does and says, "Gil, there's a street map in the glove compartment, could you take it out please. You guys have to help me out here."

I take out the map and unravel it. Givens moves forward and looks over my shoulder tapping his hands on the back of the passenger seat in time with the music; Neil's doing the same thing on the steering wheel.

"Okay," says Neil, "We've got to find our way down to Burrard Street."

"Where are we now?" Givens asks.

"Well," I say pointing to a spot on the map, "it looks like we're about right here,"

"Why do we want Burrard Street?" Givens asks.

"That's where the YMCA is," Neil answers. "It's between Nelson and Barclay streets."

Givens glances over the map, points and says, "Okay, we keep following this street we're on all the way down to here. What's the name of that street Gil?"

I squint my eyes and turn the map a little sideways. "It looks like it says Main Street."

So, following Givens instructions we find our way down to Main Street, turn north to the corner of Main and Hastings Streets. We look at the sights around us. Pieces of garbage are blown along the street by the tailwind of passing vehicles; people dressed in filthy, tattered clothes push shopping carts along the sidewalks, while others lay in doorways and in gutters oblivious to their surroundings. An old, shabbily dressed man with a long grey beard standing kitty-corner from us shouts at everybody and nobody at the same time.

On the corner across from him an ambulance, its lights still flashing, is stationary while the Paramedics tend to somebody passed-out on the sidewalk.

The light turns green and we turn west down Hastings Street to Burrard. Then we turn south and get to the "Y". We don't see any parking spots near the building, so Givens, while still looking at the map, suggests we drive up to Davie Street and turn west. We do so and find a parking spot just before we get to Denman Street.

"You're good at this Givens," Neil says. "You're a good navigator."

"Yeah," I add, "We'll have you up at the front next time."

Givens beams proudly.

Neil parks the car and the three of us get out and walk down to the corner of Nelson and Denman. I feel like we've landed in the middle of Paradise. Everywhere I look I see hot men of every description: clean shaven gym bunnies in matching shorts and t-shirts, dark-haired mustachioed clones in plaid shirts and 501's, we've even seen a couple of guys holding hands walking down the street.

"Fuck," says Givens pointing them out, "you never see that in Alberta."

"True," I say, "you'd get the crap beaten out of you before you get to the next corner."

"Where are they all coming from?" Neil says as if in a daze. "I've never seen so many good looking guys in one spot."

"Let's do some exploring then," Givens suggests.

"Sounds good to me," I say. "Which direction do you wanna go?"

"English Bay is near here," Neil says, "I wouldn't mind seeing that."

"It's this way," Givens says pointing south.

We walk from Nelson and Denman toward English Bay. The three of us must look a sight, our heads moving side to side in unison as we gawk at all of the exceedingly handsome men passing us. Each one of them looks to me like they could be a centrefold out of a porn rag.

We cross Davie and Denman Streets.

"Look at that," says Neil pointing to a small park at the intersection, "Palm trees in the middle of a Canadian city."

"Think they're real?" Givens asks.

"This is Vancouver," Neil responds, "I wouldn't doubt they are."

"I don't know about you guys," I say, "but I could sure use a coffee."

"Gotta feed your addiction," Neil smirks.

"Let's go walk along the beach first," Givens says.

I suppose I can hold off for a while longer. We arrive at English Bay Beach and walk through the sea of, mostly male bodies, some prostrate and others supine, wearing nothing but Speedos, sunglasses and suntan oil. Some share their beach blankets with blaring portable cassette recorders or radios. It's then that I notice there's a snack stand at the beach. I approach it like it's a beacon shining above all else and order myself a coffee to go. Neil and Givens come with me, order cold sodas, and we continue our walk along English Bay.

I look across the water to a park. The sky over the park is full of colour as numerous kites lazily sway back and forth in the breeze brushing the sky like acrylic paint on canvass. This whole scene is idyllic.

Givens produces a joint from seemingly out of nowhere and sparks it.

"What are you doing?" I scold, "Do you want to get us in trouble? Where did you get that thing?"

"I rolled it in Kamloops, remember? I scored this shit before we left. Hey, haven't you noticed? We've been walking by guys on their beach blankets doing the same thing and nobody's bothering them." Then he passes the jay to me and says, "Want a hit?"

"Givens," I sigh, "what the hell am I going to do with you?"

"What's say we go and get checked in at the 'Y,'" Neil intervenes. "Then we can really relax and have a good time."

The three of us are silent, Givens has another toke, I look at Neil, and then at Givens like a disapproving older brother and snort, "that's probably a good idea."

∞

I gaze out of the window of the room I'm sharing with Givens here at the YMCA. Neil has a room on his own. The early evening crowd of people, shoppers and gawkers are moving steadily up and down the sidewalks to destinations unknown.

Neil and Givens have been down the hall in the showers for the last little while, and I've taken this time to be on my own. The only sound I can hear is the traffic from Burrard Street. Across the street I look onto an excellent example of a 1950's Moderne style of office building. The guys at the front desk told us it's the headquarters for BC Hydro. It's handsome with its chrome trim and greenish coloured glass exterior.

But right now, I'm thinking about my life and where it's going to go from this point. Should I stay here for only a week or two then go back to Calgary? Should I get a job, any job, work for a while then upgrade some skills at college? Should I see how things go here and maybe move here permanently? I have to admit, from what I've seen of Vancouver in past trips, makes me think that I could get used to living here. But I guess the time I spend here will determine that.

That's when the door to our room flings open and Givens comes in with a big shit-eating grin on his face.

He looks at me and his eyes are sparkling.

"You look like you just got fucked," I say to him.

He laughs.

"Too bad you weren't with Neil and me," he says. "There were these other two guys there...."

"Don't tell me," I say, "you let them all take turns at you."

"No, the one guy fucked me while I blew Neil and the other guy."

"Givens," I smile, "you are a first class pig."

He chuckles and gives me the thumbs-up.

I shake my head and smile.

"Well maybe I should go in for a quick shower," I say.

"If you hurry the other two guys might still be there," Givens says, "they're horny bastards."

"Yeah right, I'll be back in a few minutes," I laugh as I grab a towel and my shaving gear and head down the hall to the showers.

∞

It's half an hour later, and I'm getting dressed after my shower when there's a knock on the door.

"Hey guys," says Neil.

"Yeah," I answer.

"Wanna go for a beer?"

I open the door and there's Neil looking like he's ready for a night on the town.

"Where do you have in mind," I ask.

"I hear The Castle Pub is the place to be this time of day. I thought we could have a couple of pints there, go somewhere to eat, then go the Shaggy Horse later."

I look at Givens and say, "Does that sound like a plan to you?"

"Fuck, yeah," he shouts.

"We're in," I say.

"Ready to go now?"

"Lead on," I answer.

The three of us walk out of the "Y" building and on to Burrard Street. As we get to the first corner a fire truck trundles down the side street heading east. It has a full contingent of firemen on board, but they don't seem to be in a hurry to go anywhere.

"Yeah, fire studs," Givens says as he smiles and waves at the guys.

A couple of them wave back but the rest look at him stone-faced.

We continue to walk north and for a block and around the corner from Burrard to Robson Street. Once again my head feels like it's on a swivel as I look back and forth and back at the crowds of people out for the oncoming Saturday night. It's been a long while since I've seen downtown sidewalks packed with people at this time of day. I had become used to Calgary and Edmonton where they roll up the downtown sidewalks at 6pm. Then the time I spent in jail makes this whole scene seem almost foreign.

My first impression is the majority of the folks out on the street are gay men. This would fall in line with Vancouver's reputation of being San Francisco North. T-shirts, tank tops, cut-offs, 501's, black leather, and even a touch of drag here and there, the whole West End seems to be on the street to enjoy this balmy June night. We walk east along Robson Street, past the old courthouse and Eaton's Department Store to Granville Street.

If I thought Robson Street was busy, it seems the whole damn city is out on Granville Street right now. I look to my left and my right to a sea of people strolling along the sidewalks, buskers singing or playing guitar, meanwhile kitty-corner from us, a group of Bible Thumpers are out to convert the wicked, and small-time artisans are selling their wares on tables with large patio umbrellas shading them from the evening sun.

Even though I've been to this city before, it's like I'm seeing it for the first time. It's amazing what time away from civilization will do to a person.

We cross Robson, then Granville, and walk half a block north to a small entrance with only a pair of glass doors. Instantly we are transported into another world. Ahead of us we see what looks like an impenetrable gathering of people. We hear the din of the crowd and the sound of recorded music being played just above it. We walk down a short but wide corridor with small groups of people gathered around the chairs and small pub tables on either side of us.

As we reach the crowd the three of us stand in awe of the place. I'm struck at the large open area that is the main part of the pub. Right away I can see men with their arms around other men, men kissing and hugging other men.

The place is tacky Tudor style with faded white walls and highlighted with dark wood. I'm impressed with the fact there's even a place like this that exists at all. We don't have this type of thing in Calgary. Well, that's not entirely true, there is the King's Arms Pub at The Palliser Hotel but that isn't considered a gay establishment. In fact they've been trying to oust the gay customers there for a couple of years. So the management there has been closing it every evening at 7PM. At least that's the popular rumour. It's great being able to have a long time establishment like this to go in the afternoon and have a drink with other gay guys, which is what impresses me.

As we slowly penetrate the crowd inching toward the bar to order a beer I look closely at the surroundings. The first thing I notice is a bunch of old timers have perched themselves on the half dozen or so stools that line the bar. Meanwhile in the opposite corner of the room I can hear, but barely see a jukebox on which The Fixx is singing One Things Leads to Another.

I make eye contact with a tall rugged looking middle-aged man. He has a stocky build, salt and pepper hair, blue eyes, a bushy moustache, and a pleasant smile.

"How are you?" he smiles.

"Good," I reply.

"This must be your first time here," he observes.

"I've made it that obvious have I?"

"Yeah, the way you're looking around the room, and the fact I've never seen you here before tells me that. Where are you from?"

"Calgary, well, Edmonton originally. My buddies and me are here for a couple of weeks."

"Calgary," he says, "I haven't been there for a couple of years but nice people in that city."

"Thanks," I say. We're silent for a moment. My eyes follow a black cone-shaped air vent in the middle of the ceiling that comes down and hovers over a raised gas powered fireplace in which a small, friendly flame is burning. Then through the crowd of patrons I notice a narrow countertop surrounds it, and chairs encircle its entire width.

"This is quite the spot," I say to this man. "I like the fireplace in the centre of the room, nice touch."

"Yeah," he says, "wanna hear a little trivia?"

"Fire away," I smile.

"This is one of the oldest gay places in Vancouver."

"No shit," Givens says jumping into the conversation.

"It's true," he continues, "According to urban legend during World War Two American sailors on shore leave were warned to stay away because of the gay guys who frequented here."

"So this place is more infamous than famous," Neil adds.

"You could say that," the guy laughs. "By-the-way, I'm Michael."

"I'm Bert, but my friends call me Gil."

"Good to meet you Bert, or Gil," he smiles as we shake hands.

Then I introduce him to Givens and Neil.

"I'm here to meet my other half and some friends," Michael says. He then does a double take toward a raised area at the back of the pub.

"In fact, there they are now." He waves. We look that direction to see a small group of guys wave back.

"Why don't you guys come and join us?"

"Bonus," says Givens excitedly giving the thumbs-up.

"Sure," agrees Neil.

The four of us eventually make our way to the bar and order a beer.

"He's a fuckin' hunk," Givens says quietly to me indicating Michael.

"Yes, he is," I agree.

After we've got our beer we snail our way to the upper space that Michael calls Welfare Flats.

"Why is it called that," I ask.

"Because on Welfare Wednesdays, that part of the pub is full of guys who venture out only when they get their welfare cheque. For some reason that's the part of the pub to which they gravitate."

"So is that why you guys go up here?" Neil smiles.

Michael laughs, "It's not Wednesday."

We arrive at the table where three guys sit and Michael introduces us as being from Calgary.

"I'm actually visiting from Toronto," says Neil.

"Oh, Toronto," one of them smiles, "I'm Dean," he says extending his hand to Neil.

"What was your name again?" asks a tall good-looking dark-haired guy with a moustache.

"My friends call me Gil."

"I'm Robert," he says as we shake hands, "and this is Alex," he says pointing to the third person.

We exchange salutations, then comes the effort of looking for extra chairs to put around the table…none are available. So we make do with standing for the time being.

"Are you guys staying in town long?" Michael asks me.

"Probably a couple of weeks. If I like it here, maybe I'll stay permanently."

"So you're looking for a change of pace, are you?" Michael asks taking a sip of his beer.

"Yeah, you could say that. Everybody's leaving Calgary these days."

"I hear the boom has gone bust there," Michael says.

"But the job market here is so-so right now," Robert adds. "People are migrating to Toronto if they want a job. They come here if they want to party."

I laugh. "Well, for now I'm in the latter category. If I decide I'm going to stay here, then I'll look for work in earnest."

We're momentarily interrupted as a small table-full of guys somewhere on the other side of the room break into a drunken version of Happy Birthday to You. The entire pub breaks into applause when they are through singing.

"So how long have you lived in Calgary?" Michel asks me

"I originally moved there in late 1980, then I went away for a while and went back a couple of months ago."

"The last time I went back to Calgary was in late 1980," Michael says. "I was staying at the hotel at the airport when I met this fellow named Jim on the bus going out to the airport. He said he was meeting his brother who was flying in from Manitoba. Since he had some time to kill he came up to my room..."

"Hold it, you say his name was Jim?" I ask.

"Yeah."

"And he was waiting for his brother from Manitoba?"

"That's right."

"When did you say this happened again?"

"I'm pretty sure it was around September1980."

"Jim's last name didn't happen to be Whitelaw did it?"

Michael thinks for a little bit. "You know, now that I think about it that does sound familiar. When he gave me his phone number I seem to remember that was the surname he wrote on the piece of paper he gave me. Do you know him?"

"He and I were seeing each other at the time," I grin.

"Oh, sorry," Michael says, "I hope I didn't overstep a boundary."

"That's okay," I chuckle. "So you're the R.C.M.P. officer he met there."

"Busted," Michael smiles.

"I have to tell you that you were the subject of some lustful conversation when Jim's roommate and I found out that you and him played at the airport hotel."

"Really?" he smiles.

"Don't say things like that," Robert says to me, "he'll be impossible to live with."

All the while I'm talking with Robert and Michael, Givens and Neil have struck up conversations with Alex and Dean. Their conversations have been blending into the background until I hear Givens say, "Okay, you want to go and blow one then?"

164

I turn to see Givens leave the table clenching something in his hand and Alex looks like he's going to follow him.

"Are you two coming," he asks Dean and Neil. They're content to stay put. Givens comes over and says,

"Alex and me are going to the back alley to blow a joint, wanna come with us?"

"Is that all you're going to blow?"

"Fuck you Gil," he smiles, "ya comin' or not?"

"No thanks you guys go ahead."

"How about those two?'

"I don't think so Givens," Michael says, "you and Alex go ahead."

Alex and Givens leave and I watch them disappear out of the alley entrance to the pub.

"I notice the alley entrance gets a lot of use here," I say to Michael.

"Yeah, people use that entrance to go across the alley to the Ambassador Pub or go down the alley a few steps to smoke a joint and have sex in the back stairwell of the hotel."

"Do all the cops know that?" I smile to Michael.

"We've known it for **years," Robert smiles back at me.**

"We only act on things like that if we receive a complaint," Michael adds.

"Yeah, we've got better things in the city to attend to," Robert smiles.

Are you a Mountie too?" Neil asks Robert.

"No I'm a city cop," he answers.

"Well I'm blown away," I say. "I've never known a gay cop before and now I meet two of them, and they're lovers to boot."

They laugh while I look out over the crowd. I see nothing but men squeezed together all talking trying to be heard above the din of the rest of the mass gathered here. The waiters maneuver through by carrying the trays on their shoulders and snaking their way back and forth.

"So how long have you guys been together?" Neil asks Michael and Robert.

"About three years," Robert answers.

"It must be hard on you guys sometimes."

"It can be," Robert answers, "It's no secret that police forces don't like gays in their ranks. So when we come here for a drink with our friends we're taking a risk that we'll be seen by somebody we work with..."

"...Or worse yet, somebody that we've dealt with on the street," Michael adds.

"On the other hand it can be good as well," Robert continues. "Because anytime we've had a bad day, we know we can talk about it, and the other one will understand exactly what the other is going through."

"Almost like free therapy sessions," I quip.

"You could say that," Michael smiles. "But getting back to Jim, how is he?"

"He moved back to Manitoba with his new lover in 1981."

"It's too bad, I would have liked to have seen him again. I remember he was fascinated with my Red Surge."

"Yes," I add, "he always did like uniforms. Sometimes I think that was the reason he joined the military in the first place."

"Robert and I wanted him to come out to the coast to visit us..."

"Yeah," Robert smiles, "we could have both shown him our uniforms."

"I'll bet," I grin.

"Are all you guys originally from here?" Neil asks.

"I am," Roberts says.

"I'm from Kelowna," says Dean.

"I moved here from Montreal," Michael says.

Alex and Givens join us once more. Their eyes look like little red slits and they sport big stupid grins.

"That was fast," I say to Givens.

"We only had a couple of tokes each," he answers. "This is wicked shit and should be smoked a little at a time..."

"And fuck and am I ever glad we did," says Alex. The look on his face says it all, he's flying. "Shhhhit," he continues, "This stuff is wicked Givens, where the hell did you score this?"

"Kamloops," he smiles and answers.

Michael and Robert only look at each other, shake their heads, smile, and Robert says, "I'm glad we're not on duty right now."

"I imagine that's a tough spot to be in," Neil says to Robert, "knowing some of your friends toke."

"Yep," Robert smiles pointing at Alex and Givens, "if the circumstances were different I'd have to haul the two of you to the whoscow."

The two of them sit there with those same stupid grins plastered to their faces. It's at that moment where there is a let-up in all conversations around us just long enough to hear a guy two tables down from us loudly and drunkenly say, "...I bring my own fuckin' lube when I go to the tubs."

Everyone laughs.

∞

Fresgo's Inn on Davie Street is the place suggested for something to eat before a night at the Shaggy Horse. It's cafeteria style, it's cheap, and there's barely an empty booth or table in the place. It doesn't serve the best food in the world, but the Mushroom burger isn't bad. Piled high with mushrooms, and served on a platter with a mountain of fries it's too much for me to finish. Givens has the Mushroom Burger just like me, and the biggest piece of cheesecake I've ever seen. I swear it's a quarter of the whole cake.

"Have you got room for that," I ask him in amazement.

"Oh yeah," he answers as he shovels the first portions of it in his mouth. "I've got the munchies from smokin' that shit. Besides, this is a lot better than the shit they fed us inside."

I'm struck cold by that remark. I look at Michael and Robert to see if they caught on to what Givens just said. Michael is looking at me with raised eyebrows.

"Inside?" he asks.

I don't know whether to acknowledge that or not.

By then Givens has clued into what he has just let slip. But unlike my embarrassment, he lets it be known in his own blunt way...

"Yeah, me and Gil did some time together in the slam. That's where we became buds."

I'm dying a thousand times over.

"Givens," I say, "I don't think they want to hear about that."

Michael and Robert look at each other, smile and then look back to us.

"You guys were in jail?" Alex asks.

"Yeah," Givens answers straight away.

"Were you doing federal time?" Robert asks me.

Then once more, I'm explaining what had transpired two years ago and how frustrating it has been for me to get my life back on track.

"What I find especially frustrating," I say, "is the fact that this is a chapter of my life that I want to put behind me, but I continually find myself explaining to people about it. I wish I could just forget about it."

"Eventually you will," Michael says. "But until then you're going to be explaining this over and over for the next few years anyway. I hate to tell you that but it's true."

"Yeah," adds Robert, "I sympathize that you got caught in the circumstances you did, but you were the one charged and that's that. Have you applied for a Pardon?"

"To be honest," I say, "it never even entered my mind."

"Well," Michael says, "maybe we can help you get the ball rolling with that."

"Really? You guys would help me get a Pardon?"

"If your story checks out," Michael says, "there is no reason why you shouldn't be pardoned. And we know the places that will help get you started."

"Hey! Way to go Gil," Givens exclaims.

I look over to Neil who smiles and winks at me. I can feel a smile draw across my face. This is the first time I have felt like people really give a shit about me since I've been out.

"Guys," I say, "I really don't know what to say. How can I thank you for this?"

"Don't get too ahead of yourself," Michael cautions, "It hasn't happened yet. But I think you have a good case."

∞

The Shaggy Horse is on Richards near Robson Street. It's a non-descript, white building with black double-doors that stands across from a large parking lot. There are small square signs on either side of the entrance with the Shaggy's logo emblazoned on it. I notice their cartoon-like logo of a sitting horse sporting a western hat bears a strong resemblance to a penis with testicles.

We walk into the place, through a wide but darkened hallway past large display cases on either wall exhibiting various community and sports trophies, photos of baseball teams, medals and sashes from local leather title holders. We arrive at a coat check to our left. A late, middle-aged and well-dressed drag queen is behind the coat check and greets us. She has big, plastic-rimmed glasses, black curly hair, a white blouse and black skirt. I find it refreshing that she's not got any of the outlandishness that drag queens usually have, such as the exaggerated hair or outrageous eyelashes and make-up.

"How are my two favourite policemen?" she smiles as we approach the counter.

"Fine," Robert answers, "How's Shirley tonight?"

"I'm doing well. It's still pretty quiet around here, and I don't expect it will be busy at all tonight."

"Shirley," Michael says, "I want to introduce you to some fellows in from Calgary."

The three of us are introduced to her.

"Welcome to Vancouver boys," she smiles. "I hope you have a really good time while you're here."

We exchange pleasantries and then Robert asks, "Is Walter coming to get you later?"

"Just the same as usual," Shirley says, "he'll probably arrive a bit early as usual and have a beer with the boys before we leave. I suppose you boys aren't going to hang around to see him."

"You know us Shirley," Michael says.

"Yes I do," she says, "always in bed early you two."

"That's us," Robert says.

"Well the bunch of you have a good time tonight. Nice to meet you Calgary boys."

"Good to meet you too," Givens says as the seven of us leave the coat check and walk into a great open space.

"That get-up isn't bad," Givens says to Michael.

"What do you mean?"

"The drag queen we just talked to, he could probably pass for a real woman."

Michael laughs.

"Hey Robert," he says, "Givens thinks Shirley is a drag queen."

Robert laughs.

"He could probably pass for a real woman," Michael says, "because she is a real woman."

Givens' mouth drops open, "really?"

"Yep," says Michael, "She's worked here for years and patrons just love her."

She looks upon the regulars as "her boys," and often her husband Walter will come in to have one beer with the patrons before taking her home when her shift is over.

We sit at a table to the back of the room. We find the necessary amount of stools from other tables and settle in.

We get seated and a waiter dressed as a cowboy with a big, thick moustache comes over and takes our order. I notice his name badge – Frank.

He smiles at Michael and Robert and says, "You guys always come here early in the evening. The action doesn't get started until around 10:30."

"Well," says Robert, "I guess we just don't like big crowds that much."

Frank smiles and says, "So does that means that you guys aren't going to stick around until after my shift so you can arrest me and take me back to your place?"

Michael laughs, "You'll have to do something to make us arrest you Frank."

Frank smiles and says, "Let me think of something devious then."

He takes our orders and goes back to the bar.

"Robert smiles at us and says, "Frank's been trying to go home with us for quite a while."

"Why don't ya take him?" Givens says. "He's fuckin' good lookin'."

"Hey Bill!" yells one of the bartenders across to a group of three men huddled around a nearby table.

"What?" answers one of the three.

"This is the sound your ass makes!" the bartender replies as the wand in his hand punctures a keg of beer. As the keg emits a loud and high-pitched squeal the few of us that are in the place laugh. Givens laughs so hard he almost falls off his stool, which makes us laugh harder.

"I fuckin' love the people in this town," Givens proclaims struggling to regain his balance and giggling, "they're fuckin' great!"

Then he gets up and goes to the washroom nearby.

Michael and Robert glance at each other and smile. Michael looks toward the washroom and back at Robert and makes a small signal toward the washroom. Robert smiles at him then nods. Michael disappears into the washroom. Robert turns back and smiles. He sees me looking at him with a knowing grin.

"Very smooth," I grin, "So the two of you like Givens do you?"

"We've been admiring him since we all met," smiles Robert

"He's a great looking guy," Neil says.

"Cops tend to like bad boys," Robert says.

"If you guys take him home it will be the highlight of his whole trip."

"That's what we figured."

"Yes, the ironic thing about Givens is he might be an ex-con, but he has one hell of cop fetish."

"Yeah," Robert says, "we had his number right away."

Michael and Givens come back from the washroom, Givens with a big grin on his face.

"Officer Kearney," says Michael, "I'm placing this man under arrest."

"What are the charges Sergeant Bader?"

"Failing to show a peace officer my cock when ordered," grins Givens.

We all laugh.

"I recommend we take him back to our place and place him in detention until such time he learns a good lesson," Robert says.

"I would further recommend corporal punishment," Michael adds.

"I think that's a good recommendation Sergeant Bader," Robert replies.

Givens cannot contain his excitement.

"Hey Gil," he yells, "I'm gonna get fucked by a couple of cops!

"Bitch," yells Frank the waiter as he passes nearby.

We laugh.

∞

The three of us descend a path in the woods that are on the southwestern edge of the University of British Columbia campus. The path twists and turns like steep switchbacks that alternate between bare pathway and terraced wooden sections that act as a staircase.

Finally, we reach the bottom, we pause to get our bearings, and look out over the water. A haze hovers between the ocean and sky making the mountains in the distance seem all the more far away.

I'm a bit taken aback by the sight of a young naked guy running by us piggybacking a small naked boy who is laughing along with the man carrying him. Two shapely young women walk nearby wearing sunglasses, brightly coloured sarongs around their waists. I can't help but look at their bare breasts as they walk by. They remind me of characters in a Gaugin painting. An older couple snail along the beach hand-in-hand right behind them.

We walk toward a crowd of people while the sand beneath my feet is beginning to get a little too hot for my liking. I hear the sound of Bob Marley being played loudly from a tent-like structure. The smell of curry wafts from inside the tent as two young men sporting dreadlocks cook from hibachis and sing along to the tune.

"Isn't this something," I say as I look out over a sea of naked people. Some share blankets in groups of four to six while others are paired off on separate blankets. I see what looks like the occasional family, with mom, dad and a couple of kids all naked.

"Welcome to Wreck beach," Neil smiles at me.

"This is fuckin' fantastic," Givens says with his eyes nearly popping out of his head.

"Beer! I got beer over here!" A young man yells in a heavy French accent. He carries a red cooler with Canadian Tire logo embossed on the side. He wears only a pair of sandals and a money pouch around his waist.

"Thai stick! BC Bud!" yells another half-naked young man as he wanders through the crowd.

"Oh, I gotta get me some of that," Givens says.

"What happened to the stuff you scored in Kamloops?" Neil asks.

"I smoked it," Givens smirks as he dashes over to the vendor.

"In the meantime I suppose we should find a place and get settled," I say.

Neil agrees and we wander through the crowd to an open spot close to the water. We take our towels out from the backpack that Neil has brought along and unroll them on the sand. Then we take off our clothes and get settled. Neil takes out a copy of The Body Politic, opens it and begins reading.

I keep my eye on Givens who, by this time has finished his drug transaction and is scanning the crowd trying to spot us. I stand up and wave at him. He comes toward us with a big grin on his face.

"Fuck man," he says as he arrives, "this is gonna be a great day!"

"Beer! I got beer over here," the young French guy yells as he wanders closer to us.

Givens waves him over.

"What kind of beer do you have?"

"I got Bud, Canadian, Labatt's Blue, High Test..."

"Three Canadians."

"Ah, just like you guys," the young guy smiles as he opens the cooler and takes out three beer cans.

"What part of Québec are you from?" Neil asks.

"Trois Rivieres, I come out here every summer and do this."

"So you don't live here permanently?" I ask.

"No," he answers. "I have never seen you guys here before, you visiting?"

"Yeah," I say, "we're here from Calgary,"

"And I'm visiting from Toronto," Neil adds.

"That's okay," he smiles at Neil, "you are forgiven."

"Thanks," Neil grins.

"What's your name?" Givens asks him.

"Luc," he smiles.

Givens introduces all of us then says, "So Luc, is it true what I hear?"

"I don't know, what do you hear?"

"That there's the main beach and then there's a side that the gay guys go?"

"Ah oui," he answers as he points over to an area where a bunch of people are having a game of volleyball. "See where they are having the volleyball game over there?"

"Yeah."

"Go past there and keep following that direction, you will see a path going into the woods. Keep following that path for about five minutes and you will get to the place. But before you get there, you will notice some naked men in the bushes looking for sex…"

"You guys wanna go?" Givens asks excitedly.

Luc and Neil laugh, I roll my eyes and smile.

"Givens you're a fuckin' slut."

"Hey, we're on vacation, man. I'll never see these people again."

"You are looking for a blow job are you?" Luc asks through his laughter.

"To hell," answers Givens, "I wanna give someone a blow job."

Luc laughs out loud. "Well my friend, you will find a lot of business in there."

Givens can hardly contain himself, "C'mon guys, let's go."

"I'm fine sitting right here," I say to him.

"Me too," Neil says hoisting his copy of the paper.

"So I just keep following that path through the woods?" Givens asks Luc.

"Oui, just keep going for a few minutes and you will see the men."

"You guys gonna be here a while?" he asks Neil and me.

"Don't worry," I say, "we won't leave without you"

"Great," Givens says as he hands Luc some money for all of our beer, puts on his shoes and gets up to leave.

"I don't know how long I'm gonna be," he says, "But wait for me."

"We're not going to sit here all afternoon Givens," Neil says. "The car will be leaving at about four o'clock. So if you're going to be leaving with someone else, at least let us know."

"I will man," Givens says excitedly. Then he quickly walks off to the bushes.

"Hey," yells Luc after Givens, "your change!"

"Keep it," Givens yells back to him.

Luc arches his eyebrows as he watches Givens then he looks back to us smiling, "you guys mind if I sit here for a while?" he asks.

"Sure," I say. "Our friend gets a little excited sometimes," I add almost apologizing.

"I can tell," Luc answers, "he like a lots of sex?"

"You could say that," Neil smiles, "he's also known to take off and do something totally different at a moment's notice. That's why I gave him that four o'clock warning."

"Ah," Luc says as he sits on the sand beside us, "have you guys been in town long?"

"Just a few days," I answer.

"So why don't you live here permanently Luc?" Neil asks. "Vancouver seems like it's such a nice place."

"I have something going in Montréal every winter," he smiles. "I play with a band and we do the bar scene every winter."

'Can't you get gigs in the summer," I ask.

"I can make more money doing this every summer, than if I was back in Montréal."

"Don't the other band members get kind of pissed off that you're not around?" Neil asks.

Luc laughs, "They are all out here doing the same thing that I am doing. This is how we get the money to get new equipment and buy studio time. Hey, while you guys are here you should do some exploring."

"I think Givens has beat us to it," Neil grins pointing to where the gay section of the beach is.

"No," Luc smiles, "I mean you should take a walk over that way," he says as he points in the opposite direction. "There's an old gun tower from the Second World War."

"That sounds interesting," I say. Then I turn to Neil, "we should check that out before we leave."

Neil nods his head in agreement. Luc and I engage in chit-chat for a little while longer.

Then he says, "Well, I am going to sell more beer. It was nice to meet you guys, hope to see you back here soon and have a good time in Vancouver."

"Thanks Luc," Neil and I say in unison.

He smiles, winks, picks up his cooler and continues on his way. I watch him as he gets stopped by another group of people only a little way down from us.

"He's kind of cute," I say to Neil.

"Yeah he is," Neil says as he goes back to reading The Body Politic.

I look around at the activity on the beach, and once more I get lost in the freedom I'm feeling. I think of how confined I was in prison, how regulated my life was, how being outside in the yard was a privilege granted to us only a couple of times a day, sort of like recess in school. How we were told what to do and when to do it. Now I'm sitting here buck-ass naked on a beach with hundreds of other buck-ass naked people. I close my eyes and take in a deep breath of the saline air that gently blows across the water. I take another swallow of the cold beer in my hand. Now this is living.

Just then a tall thin man with a balding head, glasses and a wisp of a beard appears carrying a small, quivering Yorkie with a blue bow tied on its head.

"Chablis," he yells, "Chablis!"

He approaches us and says, "Have either of you seen a small Yorkie run this way?"

We both shake our heads no.

"He got away from you did he?" Neil asks.

"Yes she did," he says sadly, "I put them both down for a moment to do something and when I turned to get them Chablis had taken off. Someone close-by said they had seen her run this way."

"Does she look like the one you're holding?" I ask.

"Exactly like this one, except she has a pink bow on her head."

"What's this dog's name?" Neil enquires pointing at the Yorkie in his arms.

"Frottage."

Neil and I look at each other.

"I'm afraid we haven't seen Chablis at all," I tell him.

"But if we do spot her," Neil says, "we get her and bring her back to you."

"I appreciate that," the man says, "I'm worried about her. She's not used to being on her own."

"We'll keep an eye out for her," I promise.

"Thanks," he says, "I'm right over there by the breakwater," he points.

Then he carries on down the beach yelling, "Chablis!"

Neil looks at me, "Chablis?"

I look back at him, "Frottage?"

"Maybe that's a typical Saturday night for him," Neil giggles.

We both have a good chuckle.

∞

After we got back from Wreck Beach yesterday afternoon we got cleaned up, went for dinner, a couple of beer at The Castle, then we went to John Barley's, which is the leather bar in Vancouver. It's down in an area that nobody likes to go after dark, the Downtown Eastside. All the buildings are turn-of-the-century, and in several stages of decay, burnt out or boarded up. We have to enter the bar from the alley, people call it Blood Alley—which I say is misnomer because it's the smell of urine that hits us like a wall as we enter. We approach the bar and a line of motorcycles comes into our sight.

"That must be where it is," Givens says excitedly.

"I would say so," Neil agrees.

"I fuckin' love Vancouver," Givens shouts.

"Fuck you," answers a gruff voice from out of nowhere. We look around and see a drunk with a bottle huddled beside a dumpster.

"Fuckin' faggots!" He yells in his gruff, almost hoarse-like voice.

The three of us laugh and move on.

"Get the fuck back here, ya fuckin' faggots!" he continues yelling as we walk away from him, "I'll beat the fuck out of all of youz cock suckers!" He's frozen to his spot while he yells.

"Poor bastard doesn't even know which way is up," Neil smirks. I nod in agreement.

It's 10 PM as we go up a flight of stairs and stand in a small line. We enter the door, get our hands stamped and we go inside. The crowd! Leather men, cowboys, a couple of guys dressed in construction drag, and even some tall guy dressed in white leather, (maybe Naugahyde), with matching vest, hat and chaps with gold studs trimming all of them. "Fuck," says Givens as he looks around, "this is just what I need."

The three of us survey the crowd. Once again, there's nothing like this in Calgary, or Edmonton for that matter. I don't know where all of these guys have been hiding but I don't think I've ever been in a bar full of such sexy looking men! And it seems that each guy that walks by us is sexier than the last. If I were to imagine a place called Heaven, this might be it.

"Where did Givens go?" Neil asks.

I'm pulled back to Earth and quickly look around us to see if I can spot him, I don't see him anywhere. I hope this doesn't turn into another Givens adventure.

Just then a guy selling tickets approaches us to buy some. I'm thinking they're for a fifty-fifty draw but as it turns out they're for a Tacky Tourist Cruise, all proceeds to go to finance SEARCH, the local gay and lesbian organization.

"Well that sounds like fun," Neil says.

"Why don't I buy two for us," Neil says.

"Okay, I'll get one for Givens then."

"You sure Givens will be interested in going?" Neil asks.

"Don't worry about that," I answer, "if it means booze, partying and the possibility of sex he'll be interested."

"Should we get a pair for Robert and Michael," Neil asks.

"Yeah, let's," I answer, "That'll be fun if they come along."

Meanwhile Givens shows up with two guys he has in tow, Ray and Paul. Givens quickly introduces us, takes the ticket I bought him, thanks me for it then tells me he'll pay me later. Then Ray, Paul and Givens disappear back into the crowd.

When it's time to leave, Givens wants to continue hanging out with them while so Neil and I head back to the "Y".

∞

It's late afternoon as we drive to the dock where the Tacky Tourist Cruise is to begin. We park the car, the five of us get out and approach a brightly clothed crowd of tackily dressed people waiting at an open gate beside a party boat called Britannia Two.

In a last-minute effort to get into the spirit of the cruise, Neil, Givens and I went to a local thrift store to get tacky tourist type clothing this morning. Neil managed to get a really loud Hawaiian shirt with a pair of green pants, Givens got an orange shirt, hot pink tie and yellow pants. He reminds me of the New Wavers from a couple of years back. I've settled on a checkered sports jacket with striped pants, and a multicoloured Trilby. Robert and Michael are both wearing matching short pants and t-shirts that say I'm With Stupid with arrows that point at each other when they stand side-by-side. They also sport propeller hats on their heads.

As we walk closer to the waiting crowd I smile and shake my head at what I see. The entrance of the deck where we are going to board the boat is decorated with plastic palm trees and multicoloured Tiki lanterns are strung along either side of the gangplank to the boat. Two large speakers stand on guard at the entrance of the dock with fiddle music and a square dance caller that I'm sure people blocks away can hear. As we get closer to the crowd I can see all of the men dancing are all wearing matching Hawaiian shirts, and half of them are wearing brightly coloured crinolines, while the other half are wearing shorts. Neil already has his camera out and gets some of the action on film.

It would probably take pages to describe some of the characters that I see here.

Two large middle-aged men are adorned in floral dresses with large matching flowery hats. They both have stickers on their left breasts saying Hello My Name is…with one saying Anna Lee and the other saying Ora Lee. They call themselves the Do-All Sisters.

Over to my left I see another guy in a moustache dressed in a muumuu, sandals, a straw hat and cats-eyed sunglasses. He's got a pillow stuffed under his muumuu to make him look pregnant. There's a small sign pinned to his hat; which says Muumuu Mama. The fellow beside him is dressed in a zebra-patterned mini skirt with a glittery turban on his head and white go-go boots.

Just ahead of me are three guys dressed in matching, one piece, yellow sequined bathing suits with white bathing caps, goggles and sandals. Neil is presently getting them to pose for him; which they gladly do. The music ends, a roar of approval goes up from the crowd and the dancers take their bows and disperse. An announcement over the P.A. signals the arrival of three drag queens that lip-sync and choreograph Aquarius/Let the Sun Shine In by the Fifth Dimension. They step and twirl to the shouts and encouragement of the crowd, until the final strains of the song fade away.

Just then a taxi races up to the gate, honking its horn furiously. Everybody in the crowd turns to watch it as it skids to a halt just where the plastic palms guard the gangplank. As if on cue, a guy in a full beard and in full drag, jumps out of the car, turns to everyone, screams, "I'm late!" Then runs up the gangplank toward the boat with a tourist map unfurling behind him.

"Everybody!" yells the fellow in the turban, "Follow that woman!"

The theme from the 1970's TV series Love Boat swirls up from the speakers. Several of us laugh and start heading to the gangplank.

"This is gonna be fun," Givens says to me as we walk.

A van pulls into the parking lot and several more tacky tourists emerge. We give the guy at the boat's entrance our tickets and go inside. I see staff preparing a smorgasbord for when we set sail, and I can hear some dance music coming from the upper deck. No doubt it's the DJ getting warmed up for the dance after the meal.

Since we're one of the first on board we really don't know whether to grab a table down here or go upstairs to see what's going on. Michael points toward the staircase to the upper deck, so that's where we go. There are small tables and chairs

180

situated around the perimeter of the huge dance floor in the middle of things. The DJ has Blue Monday by New Order playing over the speakers and Givens starts to dance by himself. I've never seen him do that before.

"Havin' a good time already Givens?" asks Michael.

"I haven't felt this fuckin' good in a long time," he almost laughs as he continues to move back and forth waving his arms in the air and shaking his ass. It's good to see him so happy and carefree that he feels like dancing.

We take a table by a window while Neil and Michael go up to the bar and order drinks for everyone. Givens can't seem to sit still.

"Who wants to dance?" he asks looking back and forth between Robert and I.

"That's just the effect of the toke you had before you came on board," smiles Robert.

A big grin draws across Givens' face and he says, "Okay smart-ass, come and dance with me."

Roberts shrugs his shoulders and they both move to the middle of the vastness of the empty dance floor. I glance over to the bar and see Neil tap Michael on the shoulder and point at Givens and Robert. Michael laughs and points at Robert. Robert sticks his tongue out at Michael. Givens is the far more animated of the two as he continues to shake his ass, crouch low to the ground, jump up, twirl and wave his arms in the air. Robert dances a little more stiffly, moving his feet side-to-side, and not much else.

Then as Givens is doing one of his twirls, one of his outstretched hands hits poor Robert in the nuts. Which brings an abrupt end to their dancing, as far as Robert is concerned. I can see Givens apologizing to Robert and Robert giving all kinds of assurances that he's okay as they walk back to the table. That's when Michael and Neil come back from the bar with beer for everyone, and my usual coffee.

Givens does a double take toward the doorway to the room. "Be back in a sec'," he says as he disappears. Neil and I look at each other. "I wonder what that's about," Neil says.

"I don't know," I respond, "but I have a feeling we'll find out soon enough."

∞

As the cruise is ending and the evening is still young, the four of us decide to go to the Shaggy Horse for a couple of beers. We haven't seen Givens since he disappeared into the crowd earlier this evening and I've wondered what he's gotten up to. I'm about halfway through my last beer when in walks Givens with those same guys, Ray and Paul from John Barley's the other night. He points us out to them and brings them over to meet us. Givens' eyes are like two little red slits he's really stoned.

The three of them join us at the table and I notice an exchange of looks between Robert and Paul. Nothing is said but I have a weird feeling about this. Paul says something to Ray in his ear. Ray glances at Robert and quickly averts his eyes. I wonder what that's about.

"You guys originally from Vancouver?" asks Neil.

"Nope," says Paul and again, says something in Ray's ear. I notice both Michael and Robert quietly looking at Paul and Ray. They say nothing but they have serious looks in their eyes, and I'm starting to get concerned for Givens. After sitting with us and talking for just a couple of minutes, Paul taps Givens on the shoulder and motions for him to go with them. The three of them leave abruptly and without a word.

Robert leans forward to me and says, "I recognize that Paul fellow and he's bad news. I'd look out for Givens if I were you guys."

"I hope he's careful around them," Neil says.

"In Givens' present state," adds Michael, "I'm not sure he knows what planet he's on."

∞

When we got up this morning and Givens told us that he was going to be spending the day at Wreck beach with Ray and Paul, and Neil told him, "Givens be careful, I know you like them, but Robert's warned us about those guys."

"Hey man, they're good guys and besides I can look after myself."

"If you say so Givens, I just…"

"Don't worry, I'll see you guys back here later this afternoon."

And with that he flung his newly acquired backpack over his shoulder and left.

We took him at his word and since then, Neil and I have spent the afternoon exploring various sites around Vancouver. We eventually found our way to Little Sister's Bookstore and explored the merchandise in there for about an hour. Now we're back at the "Y" because I want a bit of an afternoon snooze before Givens gets back from the beach and makes all kinds of noise. We enter the lobby and the fellow behind the desk summons me over to him.

"Mr. Gilhius there's a message here for you," he says. "The guy said it was urgent."

I look at the piece of paper that he's handed me, Please give me a call at work…URGENT, Michael Bader, and a phone number.

"What gives?" Neil asks.

"It's Michael, he wants me to call him at work."

"Oh shit," Neil says, "I have a bad feeling about this."

"Suddenly I do too," I say as I go over to the public phone. I dial the number, it rings twice and Michael answers.

"Sergeant Bader."

"Hi Michael, it's Gil returning your call."

"Gil, I'm glad you called back. Just a moment," then I hear the sound of a door closing in the background. "I wanted you to know as soon as I could," he tells me in a lowered voice, "Givens has just been taken into custody."

"What? What happened?"

"Two of our plainclothes officers were making the rounds down on Wreck Beach this afternoon and Givens was found selling marijuana with two other individuals. They were arrested as they were returning from the beach at the top of the main trail."

"Ahhh fuck!"

"But that's not the worst of it," Michael continues.

"There's more?"

"What's going on?" Neil asks.

"Givens tried to escape once our officers had him under arrest."

"GOD-DAMMIT!" I yell in anger, startling Neil and the few people who are in the lobby with us.

"What's happening?" Neil asks again.

I repeat to him what I've just been told. Neil shakes his head and says, "That stupid little shit."

"Did he have any dope on him Michael?"

I hear paper shuffling on his end of the phone, "according to the report each one of them were carrying a number of small plastic bags with varying amounts of cannabis for sale, and large amounts of cash was found on each of them."

I sigh.

"Please don't be offended by this Gil," Michael says, "but I have to ask."

"Ask away."

"Were you aware that Givens was doing this?"

"No I wasn't Michael."

"I hate to tell you this but now you have to be really careful because you have a record, and because you're a close associate of his, the department may be looking at you too."

I'm stunned. That never occurred to me. Fear strikes me. I can suddenly hear those iron gates slamming behind me once more.

"Are you still there Gil?"

"Yeah. When was he brought in?"

"About an hour ago. Our department has checked his history and we know that he has just finished spending time in the Alberta corrections system for the same offence. So Gil,"

"Yeah?"

"Would you take some advice from a police sergeant?"

"Yeah I would."

"Are you really serious about getting your life back on track?"

"Yeah I am Michael."

"Then I'd suggest you move on with your life and forget about Givens."

"I, I can't do that, he's my buddy..."

"Gil, listen to me. I know I'm treading on soft ground here, but believe me; he will eventually drag you down with him. I've seen this type of thing happen in the past too many times.

Fact: he was caught with the goods on him. Fact: he tried to escape police custody. And Fact: he has not denied that he was selling drugs. It doesn't look good for him. The chances are good he's going back to jail. I don't want you being under our microscope only for being buddies with him. Do you understand?"

"Yeah. Where is he being held?"

"They took him and the other two over to the Vancouver Remand Centre on East Cordova Street."

"I'd like to bring his stuff to him then, Michael."

"That's not a good idea Gil. In fact, I would advise you to steer clear of anything having to do with Givens immediately."

"What do you mean?"

"I mean just that. In fact I would say move your stuff into Neil's room right away, then when things settle down check into a local motel. Do that this evening if you can."

"What about Givens' stuff?"

"Leave it right there. You just make sure your stuff is not there."

"But Givens might say something to the authorities about me bunking with him."

"He may, but you have a head's up. You have my home number?"

"Yes."

"Just do as I say right now, and call me tonight. We haven't had this conversation, understand?"

"I understand."

I slowly hang up the phone. I don't know whether to feel sad or pissed off. I look over to Neil who has anger in his eyes.

"So Givens is in deep shit," he says sternly.

"He's in police custody. He was caught selling drugs on Wreck Beach and then he tried to escape police custody."

I can feel Neil's silent anger. "Look Gil, when I invited you guys along on this vacation, it was with the idea of the three of us having fun together, not brushing up against the law."

I'm suddenly aware that everyone else in the lobby is still fully focused on the two of us as we talk.

"Neil, can we continue this conversation upstairs please?" I quietly ask.

Neil looks around the lobby and walks up the stairs with me following him. I unlock the door to my room and we go inside.

"I'm sorry about this Neil. I…"

"It's not your fault Gil, it's Givens who keeps flirting with trouble and now it's landed him in deep shit, again. Remember what happened in Kamloops? I guess we should have seen this coming back then."

"Believe me Neil I never thought that something like this would happen."

I tell Neil about Michael's instructions for me to clear my things out of the room.

"There's a man who has seen this type of thing before and knows what he's talking about."

Then he looks around the room. "Where's your stuff," he asks.

I point to the chest of drawers and say, "the top two drawers."

"C'mon," Neil says, "let's get your stuff over to my room now. You don't deserve any of this shit, Gil. And to be honest with you, I don't know what to do with Givens anymore. I know you guys were like lovers in jail and you've become close friends. You probably feel really indebted to him, but look at what this is doing to you. The longer you're around him, the more you have to pull him away from trouble. It seems to me you'll always have to be the one who cleans up his messes. Is this what you want from a friendship? It sounds like too much work to me."

"It's not that he doesn't care Neil, he just doesn't think about what he's doing."

"Quit making excuses for him, Gil. He doesn't think about the consequences of his actions period! This is now affecting the two of us, and I for one resent it. Look at what's happening right now! You've been advised to move your stuff into my room right away so you don't get incriminated along with that stupid shit. What kind of a friend does that?"

I look around me and my eyes stop at the bed that Givens has been sleeping in. I shake my head.

∞

I know this goes against everything that Michael and Neil have said to me over the last few hours, but I feel the need to at least return his stuff to him and say goodbye. I don't know why I have a strong feeling to do this but something inside keeps urging me on. Maybe it's like Neil said, I feel some kind of indebtedness to Givens, or maybe, in spite of everything, I just love the guy.

I remember how I felt when Jim came to see me while I was in the Calgary Remand Center. His visit was like a beacon when I felt myself slipping into a dark oblivion. So here I am, Givens' hockey bag packed with his stuff, and scared shitless to enter the place.

The Remand Centre looks like a modern fortress with its red brick walls and narrow barred windows. Its terraced roof rises above me as I stand on the sidewalk staring up at it. I look at the main entrance's double glass doors as if they are the gates of Hell. I'm afraid.

I'm feeling all sorts of emotions right now and say a prayer that I will suddenly wake up and find this whole thing will have been a bad dream, but I know it's not. Damn you, Givens! Why have I put up with all this shit from you? I almost wish I'd stayed in Calgary and let Givens come out here on his own. Then I advance to the main entrance and with each step I want to give him a good piece of my mind and tell him to take his lumps.

"Can I help you?" a voice from behind me asks.

I turn to look directly into the eyes of a uniformed police officer. My blood freezes.

"I—uh—I'm going inside to visit a friend of mine, and bring him his things," I manage to say.

"This is your first time in Remand then?" he asks.

"No, I mean—yes! I mean…I'm just really nervous about the trip inside, that's all."

The cop chuckles, "I could tell the way you've been hesitating the last few minutes I've been observing you. If you like, I'll escort you inside."

I nod. What can I say? As we walk through the front doors I feel like it's me being taken into custody, again.

On our way inside I explain to the uniform about my leaving town tomorrow and that the stuff in the bag belongs to my buddy. I've brought it here because I didn't know what else to do with it.

"That's okay," he says. "We'll do our routine search of all of it then keep it for him when he gets out."

As the sunny light of day quickly segues to the harsh incandescent lights of the cinderblock hallway, I am escorted up to a counter where two more uniforms sit.

"This gentleman is here to visit a buddy of his," says the cop who brought me in here.

The two behind the counter look at the bag I'm carrying.

"So what's with this?" one of them asks, pointing at it.

"It's his buddy's stuff," the officer who escorted me in answers.

"We've been on vacation here together," I further explain. "I'm going to be leaving tomorrow so I figured I'd bring it here for him."

One of the uniforms behind the counter takes it, unzips it, and begins rifling through it.

"What's the offender's name?" asks the other one.

"Uh, Givens, Warren Givens."

He scans a chart in front of him.

"Oh yeah," he says, "he was one of the three brought up from Wreck Beach yesterday," he says to two other guards in the room.

"Ah yes, Mouthpiece," one of them laughs.

"Yeah, Mouthpiece," repeats another.

"Please empty your pockets and put the contents in here," one of them says as he places a shallow plastic tray in front of me. I comply.

"Picture ID please," he says, I take some out of my wallet and show him.

"Sign in here," he says as he places a clipboard and a pen in front of me. I sign in.

He looks at my ID, then looks at me. Then he takes my ID and the clipboard to a small group of uniforms at the back of the room. They all look at the ID then at me. One of them sifts through an open file on the desk in front of him.

Oh Fuck, I think.

They look at the file then talk amongst themselves, then look back at me.

188

Jesus Christ, I think.

One of the uniforms returns to the counter and says, "Mr. Gilhius, come through here please." A door suddenly opens to my left and a uniform points down a small hallway.

"Why?"

"Just follow these three officers," the uniform instructs.

I'm escorted to a small empty room with a solitary chair in the middle. I'm asked to sit. I do, facing the three uniforms that escorted me here. One of them, a stocky man with red hair directs one of the other officers to close the door. A young officer with glasses does so. The third officer is tall and thin and stares at me sternly.

"According to our information," Red begins, "you have done some jail time with Mr. Givens in Alberta. Is that true?"

"Yes sir."

"The two of you were charged with trafficking marijuana in Alberta?"

"Yes sir."

"And you claim that you and he are on vacation here in Vancouver. Is that correct?"

"Yes, sir."

"Now Mr. Givens is being charged with that same offence here in BC and suddenly you show up with his possessions saying you're leaving town tomorrow. What are we supposed to make of that?"

"Just as it appears, sir," I answer.

"How long have you been on vacation here, Mr. Gilhius?" Red asks.

"Only a few days, sir."

"And yet your buddy gets arrested and you're going to leave town?"

"I know all this looks really suspicious sir…"

"You're damn right! This does look really suspicious," Red interrupts. "Now—mind telling us what's going on here?"

"There's nothing to tell, sir," I say, staring ahead of me.

"Try us," the thin one challenges. "We've got all afternoon."

I explain everything that's happened from the time I left prison in Alberta until now.

"So you had no idea that Mr. Givens was selling drugs at Wreck Beach yesterday?" Red asks.

"No, sir I did not."

"And who is this fellow that you two came here with?" he asks.

I reluctantly give them Neil's name.

"Check that name," he says to the thin one, who quickly leaves the room.

"So tell us how you knew that Mr. Givens was here?"

I explain to them about the phone call from an RCMP Officer. Red laughs, the young officer smiles.

"Well," says Red, "this is the first time I've heard that one. So who is this officer that has been so free with information to you?"

I hold my tongue because I don't want to get Michael in trouble.

"I don't hear you," he continues. "It's obvious to me you're making this up as you go along. Now, what's really going on here?"

I repeat my story.

"I suggest," Red says, "that you, Mr. Givens, and this Neil Logan came out here to sell drugs, Givens got caught and now the two of you are skipping town so you don't go down with him."

"It's true that I don't want to go down with Givens, but it's not because I was selling any drugs…"

"Bullshit! According to our information, that's what landed you inside last time?"

"It's not bullshit," I answer.

Red leans right into my face and says, "Well, it smells like bullshit to me. And if you don't want to be our guest then I suggest that you tell us the truth. Why is it you want to see Mr. Givens?"

"To bring him his stuff, sir."

Just then the thin one re-enters the room, "We can't find anything on this Neil Logan."

"Okay," says Red, "he's in the clear for now. So that leaves you, Mr. Gilhuis. How do we know you're not trying to smuggle something in to Mr. Givens?"

"Have a look in his bag," I say now feeling scared.

"You know we're doing that as we speak," says Red. "There's only one way to find out."

Oh fuck, I think. I know where this is going because I've been there before.

"You can't strip search me," I protest, "I'm not under arrest."

"The law states that we can conduct a strip search if we have reasonable grounds to believe that a visitor is carrying contraband!" states the thin one matter-of-factly.

"That's right," continues Red, "and we suspect you of bringing something in to one of the offenders and we have a duty to make sure this is not the case."

"I can file a complaint," I say while my hands shake.

Red raises his voice, "You yourself admitted this all looks suspicious! Under these circumstances, who do you think any committee or tribunal is going to believe, three uniforms or an ex-con?"

I realize everything is stacked against me. I shut up, and the silence is deadly.

"Stand up," orders Red.

I slowly stand and the young officer takes the chair from behind me. I can hear my heart beating in my ears and my hands still shake as I face them.

"Remove your shirt," commands Red.

I do so.

"Now shake it out!"

I comply.

"Turn it inside out," I do so, "and toss it over there," he points to a corner of the room.

I throw it to the corner. I feel just like I did when I first went to jail in Alberta, my life isn't mine anymore.

"Now," says Red, "Remove your shoes, bend them in half, hold them by the tip and bang them together, then put them with your shirt."

Done.

"Remove your pants, turn the pocket inside out, shake them out, and then throw them into the pile with you shirt."

My heart pounds and my hands shake as I do so.

"Remove your socks, pull them inside out, shake them out, and add them to the pile of clothing."

I'm naked and the young officer puts a pair of rubber gloves on and goes over to the pile of clothing and begins examining each article.

"Bend your head forward and run your hands through your hair," Red commands.

I do.

"Lift your head and turn it to the right."

I do, then to the left.

"Bend your ear forward."

I comply as Red takes a small flashlight out and shines it behind my ear. The same procedure is repeated for my other ear.

I watch as the thin uniform puts on a pair of rubber gloves. I bring my eyes forward and in spite of my hands quivering I put on as stoic a face as possible.

"Tilt your head back," says Red.

I do so while he shines his flashlight up my nostrils.

"Open your mouth."

I open it.

"Wider."

I stretch my jaw wide.

"Place your tongue on the roof of your mouth." He looks under my tongue.

"Now stick out your tongue." The flashlight is shone into my mouth.

"Now lift your arms above your head."

While I do, the thin uniform closely inspects my armpits.

"Put your hands out in front of you and spread your fingers wide. Now turn your palms up."

The thin uniform inspects my fingers and fingernails. With each new order given to me, I just want to tell them to fuck off and let me go. I feel like I'm being laughed at.

"Lift your penis."

I do so and the underside of my cock is closely inspected.

"Pull back your foreskin."

Anxiety is now growing to anger as I continue to stare ahead of me while they look me over like a side of beef at an abattoir.

"Lift your testicles with one hand, and run your other hand underneath them in a scraping motion."

I comply.

"Now turn around and face the wall."

I do.

"Move closer to the wall. Put your hands on the wall and lift your right foot toward us."

As I lift and lower each foot, the undersides of both my feet and between my toes are all inspected.

"Bend over keeping your hands on the wall...further. Now spread your buttocks and cough." I take my hands from the wall and spread my ass cheeks and cough.

"Now squat and cough."

I do what they ask.

"He's clean sir nothing in his clothes," I hear the young uniform say.

"We haven't done a cavity search," says Red.

"You can't do that!" I protest.

Red moves in close behind me, "You got something to hide Mr. Gilhuis?"

"You can't violate me like that without a damn good reason!"

"Suspicion of smuggling contraband is plenty good reason!" he yells.

"Are you sure this is procedure?" asks the young officer.

"Make yourself useful and ask the front desk for a tube of lubricant," says Red.

The young officer exits the room leaving the door open for the whole world to see me stark naked. I'm humiliated. I hear a noise coming from the hall and turn my head toward the door to see two other uniforms going by in the hall. One is in a Sheriff uniform, and one is a Vancouver Policeman. The Vancouver cop does a double take at me as he goes by. I can't see his face clearly because the brim of his cap hides his eyes, and the Sheriff is blocking most of my view of him. He looks at me momentarily then he continues on his way. I turn quickly back to the wall trying to hide the humiliation I'm feeling.

My whole body shakes in anger. I hate this place, I hate these uniforms and right now I hate Givens most of all.

"Okay, got some," the young uniform says re-entering the room. He hands the tube to the thin, gloved uniform and closes the door.

The cold clamminess of the K-Y on my asshole is followed by the intrusion of the uniform's finger. I wince as I feel a second finger slide into my hole. My body shakes intensely as almost immediately he forcibly probes my ass. I feel a knot of emotion rise from my chest to my throat. Although my eyes are squeezed tightly from the discomfort of being probed, they begin to well. I feel one tear fall, another, still another until my cheeks are wet while these bastards treat me like something hanging from a meat hook.

A knock on the door interrupts the proceedings.

"Yeah," says Red.

"You can let this guy go," says another uniform as he sticks his head into the room.

"Why's that?" Red demands.

"One of our guys has just vouched for him."

There's a silence in the room. The type of disappointed silence that children have when disapproving parents have interrupted their playtime.

"Well, there you go Mr. Gilhius," says Red. The thin uniform takes his fingers from my hole and removes his gloves. "You can get dressed and leave now."

The three of them leave the room and shut the door behind them. I'm left alone, naked, slowly pounding my fist on the wall and crying like a hurt little boy, Goddamn you Givens! Goddamn you!

∞

I sit on the bed listening to the silence. I never did see Givens this afternoon. After the way I was treated at the Remand Centre there was no way I was going to stay there any longer. I spoke with Neil about what happened when I returned Givens stuff. After admonishing me for ignoring good advice he suggested the best thing we do is get back on the road tonight.

"Why wait until tomorrow morning?" he asked. "I want to get on the road again and you don't want to be here anymore. We can drive east for about an hour or so then bunk down in Abbotsford or Chilliwack."

So I packed as soon as the decision was made. Michael did try to warn me something like this might happen, but I didn't listen to him. Why do I sometimes have to learn the hard way, especially when I feel some kind of loyalty to someone who doesn't deserve it?

The Vancouver policeman who vouched for me this afternoon was Robert. It was him who did a double take at me from the hall while I was naked. I don't know what he told the others that got me released, and he wouldn't tell me. But whatever it was, it got me the hell out of there. He'll have my never-ending respect for that. He gave me a ride back here to the 'Y' and apologized for the behaviour of his colleagues all the way back from the Remand Center. He also told me that Givens is well on his way back to jail. I told him I didn't give a shit anymore. Maybe one day I'll find it in my heart to forget about Givens brushing against the law putting Neil and I in the spotlight like that. But mainly I need to forgive myself for being so fucking stupid and getting myself into that situation…and just move on. Robert understood.

Before he let me out of the car he gave me his phone number and address.

"Gil," he said, "I'm serious about helping you obtain a pardon. Let's keep in touch and make this happen." Once again, Robert and Michael have my undying respect and gratitude. My thoughts are interrupted by a knock at the door.

"Gil, you ready?" Neil asks as he opens the door, his luggage in hand and a pack on his back.

"Yeah. I'm ready to go. I've had it with this place."

We gather up my stuff, lock the door, check out of the 'Y', and pack our stuff in Neil's car.

We get in. Neil puts his arm around me and says, "I'm glad you're coming with me."

"I'm glad you asked me to."

"Ready?"

"Yep."

"Well then, let's go."

As Neil turns the ignition the radio comes on and is playing Stand Back by Stevie Nicks.

"Hey Neil?"

"Yeah?"

"I know we said that we'd stay a couple of days back in Calgary, but I'm into staying just long enough to say goodbye to my sister then move on."

"That's okay," he responds. "We could go from there down to Suffield so I can say goodbye to my friend Cheryl."

"Yeah, we can do that," I answer, "I'm looking forward to a new life in Toronto."

Neil smiles, "Welcome to my world."

PART FIVE

JUNE 1983 – WARREN GIVENS

Fuck! Jail! Probably for another couple of years! I look around this cell and it's the smallest I've been in yet, not even enough room to change my fuckin' mind. Nothing to do except sit and wait for my trial to see what's gonna happen from here. Fuck knows where I'm gonna end up when I leave this Remand Center, or how long I'm gonna be wherever I get to.

One of the Screws told me that Gil was in to return the clothes I left at the "Y". Gil told them that he and Neil were leaving town the next day. I hear the Screws gave him a hard time because he was an associate of mine, so he didn't come in to see me.

I'm getting choked up, just what I fuckin' don't need. What the fuck is the matter with me that I can't stay out of trouble? I could be gone from Vancouver by now on my way to God-Knows-Where with Gil and Neil. I miss those guys already, especially Gil. He was like the older brother I never had, great sex too.

I'm sorry that I got the two of them so pissed off at me that they've moved on with their own lives and left me behind. I can't blame them though. I wasn't thinkin' about them when I started selling the shit again; got caught with the money and the goods on me. My fault, and here I am…again.

I sigh and bury my face in my hands. I want to cry but what good would that do, it ain't gonna change a fuckin' thing, and that's why cryin' is always useless. If Gil were here he'd probably say something like, "Think of something good that comes of this."

Okay, so let me think…lately I've been talkin' to one of the guys a lot. His name is Derek and like me he's in here for sellin' shit. We'll work out together whenever I go down to use the gym or sit together in the cafeteria. He's a cute bastard, I've always had a thing for guys with red hair and blue eyes, and I've managed to see him in the shower a couple of times, tasty lookin' man.

So just this morning down in the gym him and me are talkin' about our lives and what's happened that led us here. I was tellin' him about me growing up in northern Alberta and some of the shit I've gone through. I told him about meeting Gil and how I ended up in Vancouver. That's when Derek looks at me and says, "You should write a book about your life."

"Yeah, right. And who the hell would care enough to read it?"

"You never know Givens, write it down and see what happens."

To Be Continued…

Many Thanks To:

- My life partner Steven Foster for all of your love, understanding and putting up with my many whims and shenanigans over the years, and my family for supporting my creative efforts. And hugs to our roommate and good buddy Frank Franze.
- Tony Costantino and Kelly Mahoney for over half a lifetime and two provinces worth of a fantastic, ever-growing friendship!
- To Lloyd Nicholson and (the late) Dr. Gary Gibson of Saltspring Island BC for all your advice. The Victoria BC Crew: Jim Ahlers, John Viellette and (the late) Gary White.
- To the Powell River, BC Crew: Al and Judy, Debby (and my late Uncles Murray & Jim), Colleen and George, Lennie and Stan, Sharon Edwards and last but not least Shane Bodie of Studio 56
- Dr. Stuart Sanders and Linda Nyeste of Calgary for being wonderful and loving friends
- The Members of the Monthly Writing Group: Georgina Daniels, Shiela Smart, Dr. Pega Ren, Stephen Emery, Brian Frazier, Claude Hewitt, Eric Brown, Bennet, Tyler Tone, Ken Tomilson, Steven Kates, and Gerry McCadden for your suggestions and for being there.
- My Peer Editors: Steven Foster, Ed Stringer, Gerald Goldie, Don Durrell of Vancouver and Richard Beamish of Budapest Hungary for your willingness to assist.
- Ron Culver of Winfield BC – you were there when I needed a good buddy back in Calgary – 1979 to present. Thanks for being there all of these years later.
- Frank Dernbach in Offenbach, Germany.
- To Zoe Duff, Ashley Duff and Kelly Duff of Filidh Publishing for your suggestions and support.

- To Kempton Dextor, Anita Miettenun, Margo Bates, Margaret Hume and all of the Vancouver members of the Canadian Authors Association for the same.

- To Fernando Esté for your assistance in getting my work "out there."

- To: Don MacDougall of Brownsburg-Chatham, Québec, André Melnyk and Maja Olson of Vancouver.

- A fantastic buddy and life coach: Darren Royea, Vancouver BC

- The good folks at the Vancouver Métis Community Association for all of your support over the years: especially: J. Paul Stevenson, Tyler Ducharme, June Scudeler, Ken Pruden, Don MacDonald, Laura Baird, Sue Didier, Naomi Linklater, Chad Girardin, Brenda Caplette and Andrew Watson.

- To all of those wonderful people, too numerous to mention here, who have supported my creative efforts along the way.

- To all of the GLBT Community who lived through the "in-between" years, 1979 to 1983, (the end of the heyday of gay liberation and the arrival of the first wave of AIDS). To the warriors we've lost, and to better times ahead.

www.ingramcontent.com/pod-product-compliance
Lightning Source LLC
Chambersburg PA
CBHW020431180626
46812CB00003B/1183